The Rider

THE RIDER

R. D. Amundson

iUniverse, Inc.
Bloomington

THE RIDER

iUniverse books may be ordered through booksellers or by contacting:

iUniverse
1663 Liberty Drive
Bloomington, IN 47403
www.iuniverse.com
1-800-Authors (1-800-288-4677)

ISBN: 978-1-4759-9502-2 (sc)
ISBN: 978-1-4759-9504-6 (hc)
ISBN: 978-1-4759-9503-9 (ebk)

Library of Congress Control Number: 2013911058

Printed in the United States of America

iUniverse rev. date: 06/25/2013

Chapter One

The sky didn't lower; it flat out dropped, not on the ground, but close enough to scrape the crown of the man's hat as he crested Gobbler's Knob. Reined in to a stop, his big buckskin snorted out clouds of steam into the December air.

Bleak . . . dismal . . . empty, he thought as he gazed out at the frozen Kansas landscape, his gun metal gray eyes as hard, as cold, and as deadly as the large bore Colt hanging on his right hip.

A roiling wall of white, stark against the darkening sky, bore down on the plain from the northern horizon coming hard and fast and taking over the sky.

How far away was hard to know for sure, somewhere in the distance. Distance went on forever in this deceitful immeasurable country. Short or long made no difference. Surviving it was all that mattered. Short could take days to reach, long was sometimes reached in a heartbeat, maybe two at the most. You never knew until you got to your destination.

Off in the distance between him and the obliterated horizon, an earthly constellation of golden yellow lights hovered above the billowing wall of snow, offering hope of comfort, if he survived the distance to get to them. But he knew those lights offered no more comfort than did the light of greed in a whore's eye's offer comfort from a warm heart.

Whether housed in a blatant stand-alone hotel, or in the dingy rooms above a rowdy watering hole, every cow town west of the Mississippi offered an ample supply of "ladies of the evening," and he had explored them all.

Lay your money down, leave before sunrise, and he wouldn't have it any other way. Anything more led to pain, the kind you can't see, for at least one person, most likely for both.

And that he knew . . . right well.

A smattering of ice granules stung his face—a light kiss from the north wind—as the blizzard picked up speed.

Not able to gauge the distance between himself and the lights of the town, or between the town and the surging wall of white coming in behind it, he went for the town, figuring he and the oncoming blizzard would hit it at about the same time, dark fall.

But no matter, the oncoming storm could cover the town in a shroud of white before he got there. But he would get there, his horse had been on this cattle trail many times.

The powerful gelding had no quit in him and so far had gotten him through all the storms the country could throw at them.

So far covered about seven years now.

The man pulled his red bandana up over his nose, and then pulled down the wide brim of his hat for protection against the increasing sting of the ice pellets. Loosely wrapping the reins around the saddle horn, he replaced the gloves on his hands, leaned forward and whispered in his mount's ear, "Take us on home Gabriel," then thrust his hands into the slits on the sides of his buffalo robe overcoat. He lightly touched the horse's ribs with his boot heels, urging him into a walk. The buckskin tossed his head, snorted out a cloud of frosty breath, and moved forward at a steady unhurried pace.

Before dropping his chin to his chest, he peered out from under the brim of his hat. The lights had disappeared into the cloud of swirling white as the wind from the north howled in his face like a lost banshee bitch.

He felt at peace. Aloneness and oblivion were his only constant companions and that's the way he wanted it.

The horse's rhythm, the unbroken white of the landscape, the wall of the soon to arrive blizzard, along with the drumming of ice pellets on his hat, combined to have a mesmerizing effect on him and caused his mind to slip uneasily back to a time when he had the ability to feel. But make no mistake, he did not labor under any illusions, he knew that where his heart once was, a cold chunk of granite had lodged in its place, wrapped in a bleak, dismal emptiness, matching the Kansas landscape, wrapped in an emptiness so vast and cold it made a mockery of the Kansas winter.

Oh yes . . . he felt at peace as he hunkered down into his buffalo robe overcoat, letting the rhythm of the horse's body, the spirals of swirling whiteness, and the steady drumming on his hat take him into a dream to a place where he once could feel. He let his mind drift, trying to find that place where he'd slipped off track and could no longer feel anything except the rage that often erupted out of the constant simmering anger within his lava filled heart. The broad stroke, of course, was the Civil War, the goddam Blue against the goddam Gray.

Before dropping his chin to his chest he peered out from under the brim of his hat. No lights were visible.

He felt at peace, oblivion the refuge he sought.

CHAPTER TWO

"Virgil John Jordan," the squat, red-faced man called out. His jowls, framed by white mutton-chop sideburns, jiggled as he spoke. Looking through spectacles Ben Franklin may have worn, he pronounced, "Doctor of Jurisprudence." As Virgil moved to the podium, Dr. Rutherford, the President of the University of Virginia, stepped forward, handed him his diploma with his left hand and shook his right with his own.

A step closer to fulfilling one of his life-long dreams, to protect the rights of all men, he stepped down from the dais to stand in line with the other graduates, another step closer to fulfilling his other life-long dream, to wed the sweetheart of his youth.

Starry eyed, he gazed out over the heartily applauding audience to locate his betrothed. He spotted her without any strain. She was the one on whom the light of heaven fell.

Their eyes met. The rest of the world faded to a translucent blur as time first suspended and then ceased to exist, becoming one of those special moments forever etched in the mind, always there, but over time, harder and harder to reach.

Virgil Jordan was a man of ideals, and "justice for all" was the one he had decided to champion. But the goddam war had killed that ideal by taking away, along with his way of life, his home, his wife, and the six-month-old son he had never had the pleasure of laying his eyes on. Everything he had ever held dear had been beaten, or burned, or pillaged, or raped, or murdered by sadists in Blue Coats, whose acts were sanctioned by the declaration of war and were always overlooked, the occasional inquests or trials nothing but mockery.

So how could anyone speak of the glories of war, except in the name of the State? Do what we say or we'll do our utmost to kill you.

CHAPTER THREE

Colonel John Beauregard Jordan never allowed his slaves to call him "massuh." They addressed him as Mister Jordan, and never would they say, "Yassuh, Massuh." He knew the first names of each one and never broke up families. One born on his plantation stayed on his plantation. He didn't deal in the bodies and souls of human beings.

He instilled these same values in his son Virgil who held them through his law studies and into adulthood.

At community gatherings the other plantation owners would get around to saying, after several mint juleps, "You're coddling your slaves, John."

"They're human beings, just like us," was always the Colonel's reply.

On the rare occasions when one of his slaves did run, he'd let him go and not hunt him down. And under the most scrutinizing search, a whip or a whipping post or leg irons or shackles could not be found on the Colonel's plantation.

No one could remember the last time a slave had run away from the Jordan plantation. It was becoming evident they chose to stay of their own free will, which made a good number of influential people give more consideration to what Colonel Jordan said, "They're human beings . . . just like us." In time and under the light of reason, the South would have abolished the practice of slavery on its own, and the agony and bloodshed, the destruction, devastation, death, and uncontrolled chaotic lust that followed, would never have happened, and Virgil Jordan would still have his beloved young bride.

Knuckle under to our will and our way of life, or we'll kill ya. A simple ideological disagreement reduced to its most basic tenet. Virgil Jordan simply could not reconcile that idea and course of action as having any rationality. But "right justifies might," is how the self-righteous view themselves, singularly or in groups large or small.

Or maybe the North felt that the South had an unfair labor advantage. Maybe it was a mere matter of economics. Maybe the North's championing of human rights was simply a smokescreen for another, more pervasive and hidden agenda.

History books don't necessarily tell the whole truth, and all through history, that's the way it's been.

Virgil had graduated law school at the top of his class from the University of Virginia where he had learned to question and explore, to contemplate and consider, to take sides and decide. And so he knew, boiled down to its essence, war was simple brutality, reducing the most dignified and refined soldiers to commit acts of pure savagery, not willing at first, but relished in the end.

It has a name . . . bloodlust, and like an insidious disease, it rages through a man's veins until it poisons his soul. In the latent sadists and murderers it becomes kill for the thrill, and the poisoning is complete, in many, almost overnight.

Justice? A meaningless word floating about with no weight in reality, he had thought so in the classrooms, and the battlefields had verified the truth of it.

So now he knew the place and the when where he'd slipped off track. It was at the receipt of the news that his wife and infant son had been slaughtered by marauding Blue Coats, after committing their atrocities on her while she was alive. That final stroke completed the picture, and he knew how his heart, that piece of him that once could feel, had turned to a stone lodged in its place.

That was one year into the Goddam War.

The next three years he spent in a red rage of vengeance—bloodlust at its highest level—and he lived for those moments when he was locked in mortal combat with a man in a Blue Coat, and time would cease for one or the other, and if it continued for him, it was only to kill again, and he got very, very good at it.

All in the Name of War declared in the name of God.

And Virgil Jordan adopted his own version of the Twenty-Third psalm, ". . . surely Death and Hell shall follow me all the days of my life, and I will dwell in the House of the Damned forever."

But he was still a man of principles, and believed in justice—that of his own brand. "Punish the bastards as I see fit . . . period," and punish he did. Not many in the country knew his name, but all knew of The Rider.

Chapter Four

Five days back he had left four men lying on the floor of a hotel room in Abilene, gutted and bleeding out.

Over time and by that greatest teacher and gauge of all things, experience, the Rider had established a short list of his favorite ladies. He retained it in the back of his mind, recalling it whenever the need arose. At the top was Lily Francine of Abilene, easy enough to remember.

Lily was from back east, maybe New York, maybe Philadelphia, maybe somewhere in between. Educated and possessed of a sharp wit, two qualities he admired, Lily could carry on a conversation and keep up with him on almost any subject. It often turned out that the time he'd paid to be with her was spent in that engagement, the taking of physical pleasure coming as an afterthought, usually around daybreak.

He never asked her how she had gotten into whoring and she never divulged the information. It probably had something to do with survival in this unforgiving land known in the eastern cities as the West.

But what did it matter? What was, was, and that was all. The fact that he enjoyed her company was all he needed to know.

The bar owner Henry James prided himself on the reputation his hard work had earned him. The Longhorn was the finest, the cleanest, and the most trouble free saloon in Abilene, maybe in all of Texas.

He didn't cater to any particular clientele and welcomed everyone from the mayor of the town to the two old geezers playing checkers by the potbellied stove. Sam and Clem had become fixtures in the place.

Everyone was welcome as long as they behaved themselves and paid cash.

It was a damn cold winter night, just past the hour of darkness, when the heavy oak door, the bat wings removed months ago, swung open letting in a blast of freezing air and swirling snow.

Henry James looked up from the glass he'd been polishing. The icy blast from the open door felt as if it blew across his heart. He offered a quick silent prayer to whatever whimsical gods existed, hoping there'd be no trouble. He kept a double-barreled sawed off shotgun under the bar, just in case.

The Rider's frame filled the open doorway, his shoulders white from the relentless snow as was his Stetson. His hands were into the slits of his buffalo robe overcoat, his right hand resting on the butt of his Colt, the other one on the handle of his heavy Bowie knife.

Glancing left, center, and right from under the shadow of his hat, he stepped through the door and then reached back with his left hand and closed it without making a sound. His reputation had preceded him and the saloon fell into the silence of a funeral parlor.

Eyewitness accounts had told that the Rider could bury his Bowie to the hilt in a one-inch thick piece of hardwood with a flick of his wrist and that the heavy knife, driven by the power of the Rider's arm, could cut through a man's bones as if they were butter. He could place three shots, one on top of the other, or in any pattern he chose before most men were able to clear their pistol from its holster.

Removing his hand from the butt of his Colt, he took his time unbuttoning his overcoat. When finished, he turned, shed himself of the heavy garment, and hung it from a wooden peg embedded in the wall. Turning back he once again surveyed the room at a more unhurried pace, taking in Sam and Clem in the corner. They'd been there his last time through. Panning left, a single drover stood at the end of the right side of the bar. A couple of drifters hung out at the other end of the free standing bar, worn and scarred by a hundred years of use. Left of the drifters was an uncarpeted stairway leading to several dark and quiet rooms above and behind the mahogany behemoth of a bar. Left of the stairway, the sidewall held a field stone fireplace, its roaring blaze keeping the nearby upright piano warm. No doubt a player would show up soon. Left of the silent piano four men sat easy at a table playing a friendly game of poker. Shifting his gaze back to the stairway, he followed them up to the doors down the open hall directly above the bar. No movement, no laughter, no slamming doors, no cussing, only an unwelcome silence.

The barkeep, short, stout, jovial, and starting to show his age, stood relaxed behind the middle of the bar. He still parted his hair in the middle, but it had more streaks of gray than the Rider remembered. His mustache was salt and pepper and his belly had expanded. But he was still Henry James, the ex-Texas Ranger, and a longtime friend of the Rider's, who strode slowly up to the center of the bar, stiff from the long ride in the frozen wintered night.

"Virgil Jones! How are you old hoss?" Henry James blurted out. The Rider tossed a gold coin on the scarred top of the bar. "Shot of whiskey," he said. Then with amused eyes and a slight smile at the corners of his mouth said, "If you can find the time that is."

Henry bent at the waist, reached under the counter, pulled out a bottle of the good stuff, and set it down in front of his new patron, along with the glass he'd been polishing. "Barely able to work you in," he replied with a smile.

Many thought Henry's olive colored skin made him of Mexican descent. He never bothered to argue about it although he was mostly Apache with something else mixed in, maybe Mexican. But even that stout blood couldn't stave off the sagging chin and bulging jowls that give testimony to the accumulation of years in most people, but a few are excepted and appear as walking skeletons from the cradle to the grave. Some of it is in the genes, most of it is in what a person eats and drinks, and the Rider had drank more than his share of liquor since the Goddam War, and as a result had spent a lot of time in oblivion, which suited him just fine, and his body stayed trim.

"What brings you back around to Abilene?" asked Henry James.

"Truth is I was planning on spending some time and no small amount of money visiting Lily Francine. But it appears, suh, that the ladies either moved away or gave up the ghost. It's dead quiet in here. Is this town dyin' out Henry?" The Rider asked.

"Abilene ain't dying, just leveling out some," replied Henry. "We got us a city council now, a couple more churches besides the Catholic Mission, and the marshal has a sworn deputy. We're becoming more civilized you might say," he said with a chuckle.

"City council, eh, you mean men whose wives get 'em to outlaw packing iron and spitting in the street, that sort of thing?"

"That about sums it up."

Not sensing any danger from the drover on his right or the drifters on his left, the Rider tossed back a shot of whiskey, poured another and tossed it down on top of the first.

Sam and Clem continued their incessant banter. "Crown that one you cussed old fart!" Sam wheezed.

"I shoulda crowned you a long time ago, ya flea bitten old coot!" countered Clem.

"Too late now, and 'sides, looky here, I got all your chips right chere under my thumb! I win and you lose!" Old Sam chortled.

"Ya ruthless old goat," declared Clem.

They'd been partners and friends for decades, claiming to be prospectors, but who ever heard of anyone finding gold in Texas?

But they had found what most don't . . . contentment with longevity.

The Rider threw down another shot. Seems all the towns built on spilled blood and guts, on fortunes won and lost, on souls redeemed and souls not found, eventually got around to gelding the men and sooner or later you had city councilmen, he thought. Oh well . . . progress, and wasn't that what war was all about? Like the Goddam War.

"I've noticed the upstairs rooms are either empty or full of some mighty sound sleepers. I suppose they've run all the whores out of town by now, huh? You used to have a pretty lively bunch of ladies in here Henry, what happened?"

"You see that hotel out the front window there, catty-corner to us?" he said and pointed. The Rider twisted at the waist and followed the direction of Henry's index finger.

"Yeah, I see it. Says The Oasis if I'm reading it right."

"That's it. Well ya see, business got so good I had the place built, got a madam, and housed all the girls over there. Figure I've got about five, maybe six years afore the righteous take over and outlaw ladies of the evening in this here town."

"Should be plenty of time to recover your investment," said the Rider.

"And then some, a lot of and then some," replied Henry.

Both men grinned as the Rider tossed back another shot and then asked, "Lily Francine over there then?"

"She is, unless it's her night off. But she'd entertain you even if it is I reckon. She's got the finest room over there at the Oasis, check with Ma Belle first though, before you go looking around."

"Ma Belle?"

"She's the madam I mentioned. She'll greet you in the parlor as soon as you step in the door," Henry paused. "Need a room for the night? I can put you up here."

"Depends on if Lily's over at the hotel or not."

"Of course," replied Henry.

"Keep the gold piece just in case though, I can pick up any change I got coming later on. Buy those two old codgers over by the stove a drink why'll you're at it, will ya?" he said, motioning to the crusty old checker players sitting by the fire.

"Sure thing Virgil," replied Henry.

The Rider turned and walked slow toward his winter overcoat, his boots thudding softly on the plank floor. He had no need of spurs, he didn't like their jingle, might as well announce your comings and goings to the whole world. And his horse, Gabriel, knew what the Rider wanted at his slightest touch, so he had no need of spurs.

Donning his snow free and dry overcoat, pulling the brim of his hat down low over his eyes, he pulled open the heavy oak door. An icy blast of arctic air hit the inside of the Longhorn.

"Hey, you tryin' to freeze us afore we're even in the ground!" old Clem bellowed. The Rider grinned and stepped out, closing the door behind him.

CHAPTER FIVE

A rush of warmth flooded him as he entered the Oasis and closed the parlor door behind him stopping the vicious wind. His senses were overwhelmed by a luxuriousness he hadn't known since Magnolia Hills, the family plantation in Virginia where he'd grown up, a couple of lifetimes ago it seemed. One word fit the scene before him, plush. Red velvet drapes, cream-colored walls, overstuffed couches upholstered in maroon, cream, and light green with matching armchairs set upon oriental rugs over a polished hardwood floor. Two crystal chandeliers, each holding a dozen lighted candles, hung from the ceiling. Oil lamps, secured to the parlor walls, burned fragrant smokeless oil.

A few of the ladies of the evening were seated or reclining, others stood here and there in the parlor, all looked sweet and seductive and as amiable as a man could ever want. He counted seven beauties in evening gowns, all bedecked in jewels and all with alluring smiles. But no Lily Francine.

A soft rustle of satin preceded the apparition of exquisite beauty that floated into the room then stopped in front of him and seemed to hover as she stood still.

"All are welcome here sir. What would be your pleasure tonight?" her musical voice queried, her face and eyes offering a warm and welcoming smile.

He fingered the coins in his pocket. It could turn out to be a very expensive but well worth it night.

"I'm Ma Belle," she said, then laughed, her fingers deftly slipping the bone pegs out from their holding loops down the front of his heavy coat. "Marcelle will take your garment, if you please, sir," she said, undoing the last peg. And then it was off his shoulders, he wasn't sure how, and then it was gone. This wasn't a rowdy bawdy house, but one of refinement and tranquility, of smooth and soothing pleasures.

Ma Belle offered her hand, he took it and the petite buxomly southern belle led him to one of the maroon colored sofas. Gently pushing on his chest, she eased him into its soft, thick, and welcoming material.

"Relax awhile sir. You have all night, n'est pas?"

"Oui madame," he affirmed with a smile. She laughed again, heartier this time and like music from a piano forte'. His smile broadened.

"Would you like something to drink, monsieur?"

The Goddam War had taken away the majority of any refinements he once had, including the names of and taste for fancy drinks.

"Whiskey, sil vous plait."

Ma Belle smiled with delighted amusement. She glanced at one of the ladies and in an instant a blond haired beauty appeared offering a glass of amber liquid perched on a silver tray.

"Merci," he said to the lovely young woman and took the glass. She smiled in return. Demurely? It was possible he supposed in a place as refined as this one appeared to be.

He took a swallow of the whiskey, and beginning with the delicious taste on his tongue, it exploded into his senses like an amber sedative, first spreading into the upper reaches of his head, from there it moved at a perfect pace down into his chest, warming and soothing, until the elixir hit home and settled in his belly. It made Henry's good stuff seem like the worst rotgut this side of St. Louis.

"This is, without a doubt, the finest whiskey I've ever tasted. What's it called?" he asked, the surprise and pleasure of it now aglow in his face.

"Chateaux Le Blanc, monsieur. You like?" asked the blond haired beauty. He nodded and took another swallow, savoring every drop. Somehow, he hadn't noticed Ma Belle disappear.

"We offer only the best for our guests, and now monsieur, what would be your main pleasure for the night?"

"Lily Francine."

"Oui, of course, a very beautiful and talented woman and much in demand, but I do believe she is available at present. If not she soon will be. Relax and enjoy your drink monsieur. If you would like another simply hold the empty glass up and it will be refilled." The Rider nodded his head in acknowledgment as the diminutive woman glided away from him, her silken gown whispering like a soft breeze caressing aspen leaves in the fall, her golden mane swinging back and forth across her lower back.

A lioness, he thought as he watched her disappear around a corner. Make no mistake about that.

A few seconds later, from around the same corner, stepped the Belle of the Ball, Lily Francine. He watched, transfixed, as she appeared to float on the air towards him. Her smile, full and genuine, brought an unmistakable glow to the stunning beauty of her face. Her dark hair, falling to her shoulders, accentuated her large brown eyes, direct and intelligent, and which gazed into his with unmasked and unpretentious desire. Clothed in a dazzling white satin gown, cut low to reveal her ample cleavage, the Rider had to fight to keep his breath.

Before he could say hello, a scream with the force of a lightning bolt pierced the air.

"Upstairs!" Lily hollered, her eyes gone big. It was a directive. His senses, sedated only a split second earlier, snapped back into place on full operative alert. Slamming his hat on his head he leapt over the sofa and hit the bottom stair running, the big bore Colt in his hand. He reached the landing at the top of the stairs in a couple of beats of his adrenaline charged heart. From the stairway landing, one hallway ran straight ahead, another branched off to his left, and a third, an open balconied hallway above the barroom, ran off to his right, the closed doors exposed to the parlor below. Ten rooms straight ahead, five to his left, and five to his right. From which one came the scream of blood being curdled?

Lily appeared at his side just as another shriek of terror shattered the interval of eerie silence. She pushed him toward the open hallway to his right. "End room!" she shouted as he broke into a sprint, Lily not far behind. He stopped in front of door number five.

Turning to her he said, "Better stay over on the landing. This ain't likely to be a pretty sight." Knowing both sides of the Rider's passion, she nodded and then retreated to wait on the stairway landing.

Eyes blazing like molten steel turning hard, he tried the doorknob. It turned. Stepping silently into the room, he back kicked the door behind him, slamming it shut with the cracking sound of a bullwhip.

Ma Belle reached the landing with a sawed off shotgun in hand just before Lily got there, just before the big bore Colt boomed twice behind door number five.

In one quick glance, left to right, the Rider took in the scene and assessed the situation.

A young red haired woman was held spread eagle and stripped naked on the brass bed by four greasy looking men from short, fat, and dark; to tall, thin, and light complexioned; all uglier than sin and twice as mean. He'd run across many of the type in the war and in his travels.

The biggest and greasiest of the four, a man with stringy black hair, a hairy chest, and a back glistening with foul smelling sweat, held the woman's legs apart. She'd been slashed on the underside of her left breast, causing blood to dribble down her belly and onto her crotch. The big greasy sonofabitch had a large potbelly. Underneath that protruded a full hard-on which he was about to poke into the woman's blood drenched crotch.

To the right of Big Greasy, on the far side of the bed, a thin oily weasel faced man with slicked back black hair over his pock marked face stood naked from the waist up, holding a skinning knife to the woman's throat, his eyes holding the maniacal glint of the coward who finally gets the upper hand and isn't quite sure what to do with it.

On the same side of the bed as Pock Marks another tall, thin, scarecrow looking man, his hair the color and texture of straw sticking out from under a floppy grimy hat and fully clothed, held the nude woman's right wrist with his left hand, his eyes glowing a brilliant blue from the heat of his lust. Over on the other side of the bed from the Scarecrow, a dark, short, swarthy man, naked from the waist up, held the woman's right wrist with his right hand. With his left, he fumbled with the fly of his pants as the Scarecrow forced the woman's face toward Dark Shorty's crotch. The woman screamed again. The Scarecrow slapped her across the face then covered her mouth with his right hand, insuring silence.

Pock Marks giggled.

Dark Shorty managed to pull his cock out of his pants. "Deep throat or cut throat, bitch, the choice is yours," he said.

Pock Marks giggled again as Dark Shorty moved his hips closer to the woman's face.

They all turned, wide eyed, at the whip like crack of the slamming door. Time froze . . . mortal combat hung in the air.

The Rider spoke low and even, almost cordial except for the unmistakable undercurrent of deadly intent in his voice.

"Evening gents, party's over."

Pock Marks looked panic stricken at the Big Greasy son of a pig standing between the woman's legs as if to ask, "What do we do?"

The Rider drew his Colt and blew Pock Marks oily face off. His body spun around as his face splattered on the far wall, his arm spinning with the torque of his body. The skinning knife he'd been holding at the woman's throat broke loose from the dead man's hand halfway through the spin and buried itself in Big Greasy's glistening gut, his look a contortion of terror, as Pock Mark's body slammed into the far wall to join his splattered face. The woman screamed as Big Greasy between her legs turned toward the gunman, his eyes huge and disbelieving.

"Believe it," said the Rider, aiming the Colt forty-five at the man's crotch. Fear caused Big Greasy's eyes to grow impossibly large. With a death-dealing smile, the Rider pulled his Colt up and shot the sweaty pig in the gut, the slug tearing a hole just below Pock Mark's knife. The impact sent the big fellow flying backwards. Crashing through the window, he lay draped over the sill, upper body outside, legs in the room, his belly dripping blood down both sides of the wall.

In three quick strides, the Rider was at the foot of the screaming woman's bed, his Colt held belly high and aimed midway between the two remaining bastards.

The Scarecrow had a holstered pistol on his right hip, Dark Shorty had one on his left hip.

"Let her go, now." He spoke low and soft and with ice-cold menace. They did. "Hands behind your heads," he said calm and deadly like a coiled snake sure of its strike. No argument there, it was the gunman's calm that rattled the men's nerves.

To the woman he said, "It's okay now miss, you can go. Wrap that sheet around you and then walk out that door." He waived his pistol toward it just enough to try to entice the two men to go for theirs. No luck.

"Ma Belle and Lily Francine are waiting out there in the hallway for you."

She mewled like a cornered frightened kitten.

"Sh-h-h, it's alright now. These bad men aren't going to hurt you ever again. Ma Belle is right outside that door, waiting for you." He tossed his head in the direction of the door, his eyes never leaving the two men.

Grabbing a handful of sheet, the naked bleeding woman stood up and slapped Dark Shorty full across his bloated face. The Rider cocked his pistol. "Again," he said. The woman slapped her tormentor with all the strength she could muster, then smeared his son of a pig's face with the blood from her body.

He didn't move a muscle, not even a slight twitch.

"Good girl," said the Rider with a note of amusement. She smiled, satisfied, and then sauntered toward the door with the sheet wrapped around her blood-spattered body.

CHAPTER SIX

"Oh my God, Camille . . . sugar . . . are you alright?" screeched Ma Belle, horrified at the site of the red haired woman wrapped in a bloody shroud and walking in a daze toward her. "I'll be fine Ma," she answered. "They cut me here," she dropped the sheet exposing her left breast, "but not too deep. It'll heal up just fine. He's killed two of them. He'll kill the other two soon," she whispered out of that dreamy or perhaps nightmarish state called shock.

Ma Belle handed the shotgun to Lily then grabbed Camille and held her tight.

The night was bloody and it was early.

The Rider bored his steely eyes into the huge brilliant blues of the Scarecrow's. "Over there, by your partner," he said, waving the barrel of the forty-five toward Dark Shorty, causing him to wince. "Real slow like, and keep your hands behind your head." Scarecrow did as he was told, moving over to stand at Dark Shorty's right side, nearest the bed. The Rider kept his Colt belly high, aimed square between the two men.

An agonized groan came through the broken window from the mouth of Big Greasy lying outside. His gut, shot and stuck with a knife, lay dead center on the sill. He let out another groan, this one on the edge of a scream, a reminder of the slow and tortuous death resulting from guts cut and exploded.

Dark Shorty's cock had shriveled and retreated into his pants.

"Real slow," said the Rider to him, "reach down with your right hand and zip your fly. I'll allow you more dignity in death than you ever knew in life. Certainly more than you showed that poor girl."

Dark Shorty, hand shaking, managed to get his fly zipped up.

The Scarecrow didn't so much as blink an eye as his partner returned his hand to join the other behind his head.

"Jesus-jumped-up-Christ mister," whimpered the Scarecrow, "we was just having us some fun with that little whore."

Red hot magma erupted from the Rider's stony heart and spread through his veins like liquid fire. He holstered his Colt.

"That little whore happens to be a human being, a status I'm afraid you gents can't claim. She was kind enough to offer some pleasure and comfort to you even though you're the offspring of swine. Why did you have to try to spread your filth on her? Would you like some sonofabitch such as yourselves to treat your mother or sister, or maybe your daughter, that way? Or maybe you did treat your own kin like that. Well . . . did ya, you scum sucking pigs? Let me hear you say oink oink!"

The words just cleared his mouth when Dark Shorty went for his gun. In the same instant the Scarecrow's right hand dropped to pull his firearm.

Quick as a wildcat the Rider sprang forward as his right hand reached across his midsection and pulled the heavy Bowie from its sheath. Swinging it outward he buried the twelve inch blade in the right side of the Scarecrow's belly, sharp edge up, then he sliced the man's liver in half, cut through his breastbone to halve his heart, then through a couple of ribs and across the man's left lung, cutting off the top of it, quicker than the eye could follow.

Before he could pull the blade free an unearthly peal of terror tore from the throat of the Scarecrow. The blade pulled free, the Rider flattened the arc and swung it into the side of Dark Shorty's neck. The blood heated steel left only a cord of muscle and a strip of skin to keep the man's head from rolling off onto the floor. A crimson fountain spurted from the severed jugular as he staggered back against the brass headboard, the butchered Scarecrow a bloody heap at his feet.

Dark Shorty's left index finger flexed against the trigger of his pistol, putting a bullet through the Scarecrow's head, as if for good measure, making double sure the bastard was dead.

But the Rider had left little room for doubt. He jumped back when his Bowie was finished with its grisly work, a sprinkling of blood on his hand and shirtsleeve, the knife blade dripping with the steamy heat of it.

* * *

A minute after Camille had returned to the balconied hallway from room number five she began to shake as if an arctic wind blew across her soul. Her eyes, wide and glazed and fixed on nothing, were unblinking.

Another shot rang out from inside the death dealing room. Ma Belle, her arm securely wrapped around Camille, exchanged a frightened glance with Lily.

"That was no forty-five," said Lily. "Give me your shotgun Ma, I'm going in there."

Ma stood still, holding on to the weapon. "No Lily, not a good idea," she murmured.

"What if those other two have killed him and come out with blood lust in their veins?" argued Lily.

"Here, you take Camille. I've had more experience with this scatter gun, I'll go in."

Lily nodded and put her arm around Camille's waist, helping her to stand upright. Ma cocked both barrels of the shotgun at the sound of the door to room five opening. The Rider stepped out, wiping the blade of his Bowie on a Union Army Blue Coat. "Burn it," he said as he dropped it on the hallway floor, then sheathed the heavy knife.

Ma Belle eased down the hammers of her shotgun, easing out her breath at the same time. It was over. She lowered the shotgun to point at the floor.

"See, I told you he'd kill the other two," giggled Camille.

The silence was palpable as the Rider walked slow and weary toward the three women.

"Best if you ladies don't go in there, it's not a pretty sight," he said. Turning to Ma Belle he said, "I'm sorry."

"Sorry? For what? You probably saved Camille's life and those of many unknown down the road. We owe you a debt of gratitude at the very least for what you've done. I'd best go in there though, after all, I run this place and . . ."

The Rider cut her off in mid-sentence. "You can start paying off that debt you mentioned by not going in there . . . please," he said, gripping her upper arm like the touch of a feather, ready to restrain her.

"He's right, let the sheriff look into it," said Lily.

"The sheriff," giggled Camille.

"All right, I'll go get the sheriff," Ma Belle relented.

"Give me a ten minute head start will you?" said the Rider. "Otherwise, I'm likely to get tangled up in this mess for a time. Maybe get a murder charge for all I know. Henry told me how this town is changing."

"I'll explain what happened. There won't be any charges," Ma Belle offered.

He looked over the railing at the gawking crowd below. Most were ladies of the house along with a few customers, and who could know what stories they might tell?

"My coat," he hollered as he turned and bounded down the stairs. Black haired Marcelle was waiting at the door with it when he arrived. Grabbing it he flung it over his shoulders, opened and then slammed the door behind him. Leaping over the three porch steps he landed on the frozen dirt street. From there he sprinted diagonal across the street to the Longhorn saloon.

"Be ready to move fast," he spoke in the buckskin's ear as he passed by the big horse. Gabriel tossed his head as if he understood.

Flinging open the heavy oak door, he burst through, letting a twisted gust of wind slam it shut. His sudden and loud entrance caused Henry to fix a startled look toward the door, at the same time reaching for the shotgun under the counter.

"Sorry Henry!" the Rider blurted, moving like a cat across the room to the center of the bar. "But I seem to have baptized the Oasis in blood! Ma Belle can tell you all about it. Here," he said, tossing three gold coins on the bar top, "this oughta cover the cost of clean-up and any other damage done."

Henry just shook his head real slow in amazement. This kind of trouble showed up every time the Rider did. He could only hold out hope that one day it wouldn't.

"See ya Virgil," he hollered at the man's back as it disappeared behind the slamming door.

Uncoiling the buckskin's reins from around the hitching rail, he swung into the saddle, turned the horse's head toward the Oasis and trotted him across the street. The soft light spilling from the parlor windows faintly illuminated Lily and Ma Belle standing on the porch. He pulled up beside them, remaining mounted.

"She gonna be alright?" he asked from atop the horse. Not waiting for an answer, he dismounted and joined them on the porch.

"I think so, hope so, but only time will tell for sure," answered Ma Belle, her concern evident in her face.

"Yeah, I reckon that's true," he said. Turning, he looked deep into Lily's eyes. Seeing the inquisitiveness in them surrounded by sadness, he took her in his arms, wrapped them around her slender waist, and pulled her close. Her arms naturally went up around his neck, her hot breath sweet upon his face.

"I do declare Virgil Jones, death and hell surely follow you wherever you go," she said.

"I want to kiss you," he replied, bending his face closer to hers. Responding, she pressed upward for one sweet tender kiss.

He could feel the wetness of her tears as they found their way down some secret channel between his face and hers.

He pulled back and placed his lips against her ear. "I'm sorry darling Lily."

"Me too . . . so very much so," she returned, her lips brushing his one more time.

Turning to Ma Belle he said, "You wouldn't happen to have a bottle of that fine whiskey I could take along with me would you?"

"I'll check. Be right back."

Her tears now dried, Lily turned to the big man. "Are you ever coming back?"

"It's hard to say Lily. I could be dead tomorrow, you know that."

"I know, I guess that's what makes our time together so precious."

"Lil . . ."

"Here you are Virgil," said Ma Belle coming out of the hotel door. She handed him a full bottle of her special whiskey. He held it up to the light to read the label.

"Chateaux Le Blanc, huh? From France?"

"Maybe," Ma Belle replied, "but I know you won't find it anywhere else this side of the Mississippi," she declared.

"Which way you headed?"

"North," he said as he put the bottle safely away in his saddlebags.

"I'll tell the sheriff you went west."

"Alright," he said from atop the buckskin. He looked long at Lily. "Good-bye Lily Francine of Abilene," he said, touching his right forefinger to the brim of his hat.

"Good-bye Virgil Jones, who rides against the wind."

Looking down the street to the west, he lightly touched Gabriel's ribs with his boot heels. The women watched him head west for a couple of blocks and then turn north into the biting wind. Lily's eyes lingered for a long moment.

"You could have loved him, couldn't you darlin?"

"Yes Ma, I for sure certain could have."

"He couldn't love you, you understand that don't you?"

"Yes . . . I think I do anyway."

"He would never allow himself to honey. It's not so much that he couldn't, he just wouldn't let it happen. A man like that . . . some essential spark of life has been put out inside him, and the only thing he wants, what he looks for, is the day the rest of him dies. The one thing they're afraid of is the one thing they need the most . . . love . . . but they just can't bring themselves to again face the pain that so often comes with it. It's the living that's hard for men like that. Do you understand dear?"

"And they say whores have hearts like ice," said Lily as she embraced Ma Belle with all her heart.

"Maybe I'll see him again someday . . . maybe," Lily mused.

"Well sweetie, I wouldn't doubt it, 'cause you came real close to planting yourself in that stony heart of his." She paused. "Well, I'll go fetch the sheriff so he can start sorting this mess out. In the mean time you should let Henry know what's happened."

"Virgil already told me," said a voice from the bottom of the stairs. It was Henry. "I'll go get the sheriff if you want."

"Oh would you please! Tell him Mr. Jones rode west, in case he's interested," said Ma Belle.

"Will do," replied Henry, a crooked grin playing at one corner of his mouth.

Turning, Ma placed her arm around Lily's waist. "Come on sugar, we better check on Camille," she said as they returned to the silent pall in the parlor of the Oasis Hotel.

CHAPTER SEVEN

Gabriel had stopped. The broken rhythm halted the Rider's deep reverie about where he'd slipped off track. It was pretty easy to see, and deep down he knew it anyway. Slowly opening his eyes, he lifted his head off his chest.

"Drank too goddam much whiskey," he said. His eyes focused, but he couldn't make out the words inscribed on the weather beaten wooden sign half obscured by the swirling snow. But as his eyes focused sharper and the snow and wind became still, he could read it by the dirty yellow light escaping the grimy windows behind it.

THE BURNT DOG SALOON
WITCHITA, KANSAS

Witchita? Well he couldn't expect these transplanted sod-busters to spell correctly, could he?

Looking up the street to his right, it was as deserted as far as the blizzard would allow him to see.

Looking west, he at first glance assumed what he had seen in the other direction, nothing, but as he continued to look he could not deny the presence of a shadow shimmering in the flurry of white, moving indistinct, but ever closer through the blizzard's cover.

He swung down out of the saddle quick as a cat, dropped the horses' reins on the ground, thrust his right hand through the slit of his heavy overcoat, and wrapped his fingers around the butt of his Colt forty-five.

The shadow continued to glide forward, the swirling blizzard making him appear suspended in the air. It finally stopped about three feet in front of him.

"Board your steed at the livery stable sir?" a man's voice asked from beneath the hood of a dark colored woolen cloak.

"Let me see your face," answered the Rider.

The man slowly pulled back the hood that had kept his face hidden in dark shadow, revealing a somewhat distorted but honest countenance. The man's features were of African descent. The Rider had known enough black people growing up on the plantation to recognize the facial structures. The broad nose with large nostrils, the full generous mouth, the forward thrust lower jaw, and the tightly kinked hair, not black, but copper in color. But the man's skin was pale, almost as white as the snow that whirled around it. His eyes were dark in the dim light, but different one from the other. His left eye sagged down on the man's cheek and drifted more to the outside, as if it weren't looking straight ahead, but off to the side. He wasn't more than five and a half feet tall, if that, but had broad powerful shoulders, probably the result of a lifetime of hard work, over which the cloak was draped.

The Rider trusted his instincts and right now they told him this odd little man was one that could be trusted, as far as he would let his trust go, which was about as far as he could see in the swirling snowstorm.

He turned his head back to his horse, who stood as still as stone. "What say Gabriel?" The horse snorted as he tossed his head up and down once.

Turning back to the odd figure of a man, he asked, "How far?"

"A little over a furlong, sir," he replied, jerking a gnarled thumb over his right shoulder back in the direction from which he'd come. The Rider nodded. A furlong, what a strange way to call distance in this time and in these parts, one-eighth of a mile, more or less.

Gabriel's ability to sense danger was almost as acute as the Rider's, and he could place his hooves, both front and rear, with the force of a sledgehammer and with absolute accuracy. The horse had seemed agreeable. He could take care of himself.

To the odd little man the Rider said, "Rub him down; feed him; make sure he's got a clean warm stall. I'll be by to check on him in a bit." He left an open time frame to ensure the stabler's integrity.

The town felt strange and suffocating despite the shrieking of the wind. He'd been here before, in winter blizzards and the blistering summers, had roamed the town in each, and it offered plenty of what he looked for and desired.

But this felt deserted, like a place hanging on the edge of the world, ready to teeter off into some unknown vastness, a black oblivion. Wouldn't bother the Rider any.

He handed Gabriel's reins to the crablike little man, who took them firmly into his twisted, gnarled, ungloved hand. The man turned and led the willing buckskin away, hunching back into a shadow, a pronounced hump on his back, a pronounced limp in his left leg.

He reminded the Rider of a character in a book by Victor Hugo he'd read while at the university, Quasimodo, the hunchbacked bell ringer of the Notre Dame Cathedral.

"Hey mister! What's your name?" he called after the fading figure.

"Casey Mojo," he answered back, his voice strong and carrying over the wind. He turned then, and leading Gabriel, disappeared into the relentless blizzard.

Stepping up onto the covered boardwalk, somewhat sheltered from the fierce wind, the Rider was surprised to feel his hand still loosely gripped on the butt of his Colt. He drew it from its holster, opened the cylinder, and counted the rounds. Two spent, three live. He'd forgotten to re-load after shooting those bastards at Abilene.

"I'm slipping, must be getting old," he muttered to himself, "could end up being the death of me, but then, something will sooner or later," he chuckled at the morbidity of the thought, but no getting around it, and it was oh so real. He could only hope for a quick one, like a lead ball to the head or heart or being disemboweled by a sword, or a knife piercing a vital organ. But not some long drawn out hopeless sickness. He'd cut his own throat if he ever got to that place.

He felt old, and weary to the bone. Not in his body, but in his soul, if he had one, he wasn't sure of that either. Perhaps he did once . . . but now . . . it felt lost forever. Beyond weary, he felt dead inside.

He wasn't more than thirty, counting time from separation from the womb.

Ejecting the two empties, pulling out a couple live rounds from his gun belt, he reloaded, spun the cylinder, snapped it into place with the hammer resting on an empty chamber, and gently holstered the piece, ready to use it in less than a heartbeat.

Chapter Eight

He shook his shoulders and brushed them with his hand, removing the snow off his coat, then he took off his hat and slammed it against his thigh, knocking the snow and ice from off of it. Pulling it snug on his head, he turned the brass doorknob and entered the world of The Burnt Dog Saloon.

The bar, made of solid mahogany, was free standing and spanned forty feet end to end, a lot like Henry's in Abilene and probably as old. A brass foot rail ran the full length along the bottom about half a foot off the floor. Brass spittoons were placed at each end of the foot rail. There were no stools. If you wanted to drink at the century old bar, you stood.

An old geezer with a big belly, short pants held up by red suspenders, the remains of a hat stuck on top of his bushy gray hair, gave the Rider a cursory glance, then mumbled something into a beard that matched his hair and returned to the bottle setting in front of him. He was the only patron at the bar and probably a fixture at the far right end of it.

Three kerosene lamps, lit and burning half strength, were set on the counter behind the barkeep's walkway. Behind those and set in a double row were the bottles of liquor; whiskey and rye, rotgut and red-eye.

A three by five foot painting of a nude woman reclining on a red velvet couch, her head propped up in her right hand and wearing a smile of teasing beauty, hung on the wall over the center of the bar. The Rider figured he'd seen the same portrait, except for the hair color, at least a hundred times by now and still didn't know the name of the artist.

Below the nude and above the liquor bottles was a smoky mirror running the full length of the bar, a place for lonely customers to find some sense of company as they wondered where their lives had run off to. But the mirrors were warped, like the ones they had in the fun houses back east, making the reflections untrue, like the lonely faces that stared into them.

To the left of the bar a wide stairway ascended to a dark hallway, probably with rooms on either side, and probably with whores in the rooms. He could only hope.

To the left of the stairs, setting on a raised platform was a silent piano, kept warm by a blazing fire near it. Further left were several plain pine wood tables with chairs to match.

Looking around for a coat rack, he spied pegs on the wall by the door, as usual. All in all the saloon was like hundreds he'd visited before in all the alike cow towns he'd been through, and it was getting harder to distinguish one from the other after so many. A man could forget himself and where he was if he wasn't careful or if he took a notion to do just that.

But this one felt different, dead or something, like he had felt out on the boardwalk.

The old geezer standing at the end of the bar eyed the Colt forty-five with something akin to fear as the Rider strode to the center of the bar, boots thudding on the scarred and worn floor planks, the mirror above the bottles of liquor flickering his image from fat to thin and back again.

The barkeep waited for him to settle into a spot along the bar. The Rider settled in, giving the barkeep the once over. *I know him, his name's Pete,* he thought and was about to say, "Howdy," until the man ambled over to wait on him. He looked exactly as he remembered him, the front buttons of the white shirt were buttoned clear to the top, the sleeves, buttoned around the man's wrists, were accented by red garters. His build was short and squat, same height and weight, the same handlebar mustache, and the same derby hat, except Pete's hair was black. This man's was fiery orange and his eyes, instead of brown, were very, very blue. Sky blue. Ocean blue. Ice blue. Not a hint of south of the border.

"Evening barkeep."

"Please, call me Pedro. What will it be tonight senor?"

"Whiskey, the best in the house, and you can call me Virgil."

"Si senor Virgil."

Pedro bent at the waist and pulled a bottle out from under the bar. Setting a glass on the surface, he poured the Rider a good stiff double shot.

"Here senor Virgil, I theen you like theese," quipped Pedro, with a broad smile showing sparkling white and perfectly aligned teeth.

The Rider tossed half the drink down. The instant it touched his tongue his senses exploded upward into the top of his head, then, as the liquid worked its way home, warmed his chest on the way down and spread outward from there, he drank the other half. The whiskey was exactly like Ma Belle's Chateaux Le Blanc.

"This is good stuff Pedro. What's it called?"

"El Casa Blanco senor, and you won't find anything like it theese side of the MissSoSloppy."

"The what?"

"The MissSoSloppy. You know, big muddy—the great wide reever senor."

"Oh, sure, the Mississippi."

"Close enough senor."

Strange indeed thought the Rider as Pedro poured him another double shot of El Casa Blanco. He sipped the drink, enjoying the music coming from the piano.

The piano?

Sure enough, a rail thin, balding, mortician looking man sat on the swivel stool at the keyboard. A woman stood alongside it, wearing a rose red silken gown. Her dark hair fell to her shoulders, the tight curls accenting her alabaster skin. Over her dark luminous eyes arched long eyebrows, not prominent, but precise. The left one arched slightly higher than its twin, giving the woman a look between inquisitive and amused. Her somewhat long nose ended in naturally flared nostrils above a full ruby red mouth that conveyed a subdued sensuality.

She stared openly at the Rider. He matched her stare, except for his dropped open mouth. To shut it he downed the rest of his drink, continuing to ogle her, his eyes fixed with the intensity of a hawk that has located its prey.

She didn't flinch.

"Got a fancy for the lady senor? Want I should call her over?" asked Pedro, his white teeth flashing.

"No thanks Pedro. Pour me another shot and I'll go introduce myself. Is she for hire?"

"You'll have to ask the lady senor."

The piano man dropped the mood down into a melodious tune touching on melancholy, playing it in three quarter time and in a minor key. Music that pulled on heartstrings and could put a man deep in his cups, reminiscing over better days for days on end. Days remembered with fondness and yearning, often made hazy by the pain of a once-in-a-lifetime love that is lost, or some other kind of loss, but just as precious, never to be found or seen again.

Chapter Nine

"I know who you are!" a voice boomed from the end of the bar. The Rider whirled toward the sound. "You're that feller they call the Rider. That Johnny Reb what goes around killing Yankees. Didn't you hear they laid Quantrill and his boys in the ground over in Misery? War's over son!"

"I don't reserve my killing for Yankees only old timer."

"I know that. Ya kilt a couple of my own boys down in AbbaLean four, five days ago at the most."

The old geezer turned to square up to the Rider.

"Why'd ya do it?" he asked.

"They were treating a friend of mine like a piece of trash."

"Yep, shore in tarnation sounds like them thar boys. Ya done did the world a favor getting rid of them two," he said, turning his belly back to the bar and cackling under his breath. He tossed down a shot and poured himself another. "Did the world a favor," he chuckled into his beard.

The piano man hadn't missed a beat.

Holding his drink in his left hand the Rider started a slow walk toward the lady in the rose red gown standing by the piano. In between his boots hitting the plank floor, he heard the faintest whisper of a sound behind him. He whirled around and dropped to a squatting position, pulling the big Colt from its holster.

He heard the bullet whiz over his head before he heard the boom of the pistol it came from. Like they say, you never hear the shot that kills you.

His Colt belched fire from hell. The old geezer was lifted off his feet and thrown backwards by the impact of the forty-five slug and lay face up and spread-eagled on the barroom floor, the worn wood soaking in his blood as if thirsty for its taste.

The Rider stood and looked across the bar at Pedro. The fierceness in his eyes, like those of a hawk that had just killed its prey, caused the barkeep to stop in his tracks. Pedro managed a slight shrug along with a weak smile. "You did the world another favor, senor," he said.

The Rider drew in a deep breath of stale saloon air and let it out slow before turning back to introduce himself to the woman by the fire warmed piano. But she was slumped against it, a dark stain spreading down and out from between her breasts, coloring the rose red of the gown to a deep maroon . . . surely death and hell shall follow me echoed inside the Rider's head.

The piano man, oblivious to all the carnage of death, continued to play the melancholy tune, the scene before him now a perfect fit.

"Holy Mary, Mother of God," invoked Pedro as he realized the total finality of the last minute.

Hurrying over to the downed woman with Pedro right behind him, the Rider knelt down close beside her. Hooking his left arm under her shoulders, he held her in a more comfortable position.

Her eyes were tight shut but she breathed, shallow and with long intervals between each one.

"My God, Janice . . . it can't be. But is it . . . how . . . how can it possibly be you?" said the Rider as he held her. If she was not Janice Louise, the love of his life and the bride of his youth, then she had to be an unknown and unmentioned twin of hers, right down to the arched left eyebrow. Her eyes snapped open. She wasn't Janice Louise or her identical twin. Fraternal maybe, but that possibility wasn't in his mind for long. From a distance her eyes appeared soft and brown and of a depth to be explored by many nights of long gazing. But close up they were hard to look into, their burnt orange color with interspersed flecks of yellow, a shade he had never seen, alive or dead, in peace or in war, in love or consumed by lust, were predatory, feline, oddly seductive, and as cold as the raging blizzard that howled outside the heavy oak door of The Burnt Dog Saloon.

But even at that, he'd gotten so close, so goddam close he wasn't ready to give up the whisper of hope he'd heard spoken to what might remain of the soul he once had.

"Janice?

Crooking her index finger she wiggled it outward and then inward, signaling him to bring his face nearer. Softly, with a mere vapor of breath, she whispered, "No Virgil, my dear, I am Jean Loise . . . and I was . . . waiting for you. Oh-h-h," she groaned.

He turned to Pedro hovering over his shoulder. "Better round up a doctor quick as you can," he said to him. Pedro scurried off without uttering a word.

He turned back to Jean Loise. "Please say no more. Save your breath, Pedro went for the doctor and he will be here soon."

"No, my sweet, it is too late for me now. Better me than you, for you must keep on living. Can't you see?" Her eyes closed, her head slumped and she ceased to breathe.

"Any special requests, Mr. Rider?" asked the piano man, poking his head around the back wall of the piano.

The Rider didn't answer, but he did consider killing the silly bastard for a second or two. He stood up, looking dumbfounded at the body of Jean Loise slumped against the piano . . . maybe she would have saved him and in the process somehow healed his broken and stone cold heart.

"What the hell kind of place is this?" he muttered to himself as the piano man broke into *"Look Away Dixie Land"*.

CHAPTER TEN

Turning toward the bar, the Rider stopped, stunned by what he saw.

"What the hell kind of a place is this?" he asked of no one in particular.

The old geezer, who minutes before took the forty-five slug in his chest, stood unperturbed at the far end of the bar, his left foot resting on the brass rail, his right hand tipping a shot of whiskey down his throat.

"What in the . . ." mused the Rider as he once again placed himself at the center of the bar. It had to be hundred years old or better, yet, as he looked up and down it, he didn't spot a cigar burn, a gouge, or any spot where a piece had splintered out from it. No carved initials or curses in the surface aimed at anyone and everyone, not a scratch anywhere.

His eyes slid down the surface to the right, then up to meet those of the old geezer. He was smiling. The Rider's hand went to the butt of his Colt.

"No need for that, Mr. Rider," said the old geezer as he turned to face him. Spreading out his grimy leather vest like the wings of a potbellied bat, he said, "I ain't packin' no iron as you can see," he chortled and then turned and stuck his belly back against the bar.

"I shot you old timer," said the Rider.

"Shore you did, but ya didn't kill me, did ya now?"

"I plugged you straight in the heart."

"Sorry to disappoint you sonny, but ya missed. Just barely grazed my shoulder here, as you can see," he said, turning enough so the Rider had a good view of his right shoulder.

The faded blue chambray shirt had a slight tear in it near the upper arm. It could have been made by a bullet.

But miss by that much at twenty feet? The Rider blinked his eyes hard a couple of times to make sure of what he was seeing.

"Don't worry too much about it sonny. It's all a joke anyways," the old geezer chortled as he downed another drink.

"What's a joke?"

"Why . . . life, that's what. And the sooner you realize that, the sooner you can start having some fun. Live a little! Stop thinking about dyin' all the time. Dyin' . . . hee-hee, that's a joke too."

Crazy old coot, thought the Rider, but the old boy's words had sunk deep. When was the last time he'd been happy or content? He didn't even know the meaning of the words, he had no definition for them.

The joke's on you sonny. Maybe so.

The melancholy tune wafting from the piano pulled him out of his brief reverie. He looked toward the piano and was stunned, by damn, by another apparition. It had to be. Standing, breathing, leaning up against the piano, was Jean Loise, her luminous feline eyes fixed on him.

The Rider wasn't the least bit surprised. Determined to speak with the clone of his broken heart's desire, he covered the distance between him and her in four long strides.

"You were shot in the middle of your chest," he stated.

Were the pupils of her eyes elliptical and vertical?

"Yes, Mr. Jones," she said, taking his left hand and placing it squarely between her breasts.

Confusion spun its webs, cluttering and captivating his mind.

"How do you know my name?" he asked with demanding force.

"We were told you were coming and given a detailed description of you."

"By who?"

"Ah-h-h . . . trade secret Mr. Jones. You were an attorney, surely you understand confidentiality.?"

He couldn't argue that point.

"You were shot. I saw you bleeding," he repeated, noticing the maroon blood stain was gone from her rose red gown.

"But not now, am I," she stated. "Often we see what we expect to see, and if what we see is not what we expect, it is very difficult to comprehend or believe. Do you see, Mr. Jones?"

Her muted laughter puzzled more than angered him.

"I give up," he said. "I'll just take things at face value."

"Would you like to spend some time with me, Mr. Jones, like the entire evening perhaps?"

"Yes, I believe I would, Jean Loise. That is your name, isn't it?"

"It is . . . for tonight."

She was indeed a mystery. In fact, the whole goddam night had been a mystery so far. But he was still alive and that was all that mattered to him at the moment.

Chapter Eleven

"Faith 'n' begora, ladies and gents, faith 'n' begora!" The deep Irish brogue booming across the room caused all eyes to turn toward the open door.

"Damn," said the Rider. Jean Loise gave her most demure smile—a patient kitty.

A short, heavy, dark skinned man with a droopy black mustache and hair to match closed the door behind him and waddled across the barroom floor. Dressed in a colorful serape', wearing a dirty brown sombrero complete with a hatband of silver conchos, the man smiled like it was his first Christmas.

"Peter!" exclaimed Pedro. "Peter O'Malley, good to see you again mi amigo."

"And a hearty good evenin' to yourself Pedro," said the new arrival as he centered himself at the bar.

"And . . . ?" asked Pedro.

"Aye . . . but a little shot o' the Irish first, if ya please."

"Si senor Peter," said Pedro as he poured him a good healthy shot of rye whiskey. O'Malley slammed it down and Pedro filled his glass again.

"Beholden to ya! And may you find the rainbow's end!" exclaimed Peter O'Malley.

"Gracias. And . . . ?"

"Ah yes, the stage . . . she'll be coming 'round the mountain when she comes, she'll be drivin' six white horses when she comes . . . heh-heh. It'll be here any minute now, with just a wee bit o' luck o' course."

The Rider turned his attention back to Jean Loise, her smile stolen from the Mona Lisa. But it was her eyes that captivated him. On the burnt orange background, the yellow specks danced and sparkled with a life of their own. And her pupils! They were neither vertical slits nor round orbs but were narrow ellipses with a long vertical axis. He couldn't read them, which was discomfiting. What was behind them? Humor? Amusement? Kindness? Cunning? Inquisitiveness? Lust? Or were they predatory and it was somehow hidden? He couldn't tell, but there was something . . . feline and he couldn't shake the chilling impression.

"What the hell is this place?" he asked her, hoping for a revelation of truth.

"Why . . . The Burnt Dog Saloon, of course," she replied with the innocence of a child.

"You know damn well what I mean," he replied, exasperated. "There's Pedro, who looks like a large leprechaun, speaking, acting, believing . . . he's Mexican. Then, faith 'n' begora, Peter O'Malley arrives looking like and dressing like a Mexican, but speaking, acting, believing . . . the Emerald Isle is his home. And you, shot in the heart, you pop back up, and you are the exact image of Janice Louise, my wife and the only woman I ever loved, who I lost in the Goddam War and lost my own soul along with her.

So . . . how? What in the double blue blazes of hell is going on? What is so extraordinary about this place?" he implored, his frustration preceding his words.

Her eyes glowed bright from some internal fire, her pupils not elliptical but round and the yellow flecks not dancing but spinning like pinwheels at a carnival.

"Easy. Rest easy Mr. Jones. You aren't seeing what you expect to see, and what you see isn't necessarily the way things are. Do you see, Mr. Jones?"

"The hell with it. Maybe I'll shoot the old codger again, just to see what happens," his frustration bristling like a porcupine with its quills out as he returned to the free standing-brand new looking-hundred year old bar.

A man and woman seated at one of the wooden tables off to the side of the piano were finishing up their meal. Had they been there all along, able to eat with all the excitement going on? The Rider wasn't sure. He wasn't sure about much of anything right now.

He settled himself at the end of the bar nearest the piano and as far away from the old geezer and Peter O'Malley as he could get.

Pedro ambled over, polishing a shot glass, whistling an unknown tune, maybe a Mexican funeral dirge for all the Rider knew. But somehow it complemented the melancholy piano music.

"Another wheeskey?" he asked, his smile broad and unreadable, like Jean Loise's eyes.

"Yeah Pedro, a good stiff shot, por favor."

Pedro chuckled as he moved away and then came back with a double shot of El Casa Blanco.

"Tell me Pedro . . . I've been here to Wichita many times. Didn't this used to be called The Red Dog Saloon?"

"Si senor, many, many winters gone by now."

"So, what happened?"

"Well senor, an old witch lived down the street thataway," he pointed to his right, to the west. "She was performing some sort of ritual or casting some type of spell. She had this huge dog . . .

"Irish Wolfhound," broke in Peter O'Malley, his silver spur jangling as he placed his left foot on the brass boot rail.

"Si, Irish Wolfhound," continued Pedro. "Somehow the bruja witch caught the dog on fire . . . maybe she in a trance . . . anyway, the big dog ran down the street and into this saloon."

"All ablaze, coulda been the Fourth of July, by cracky," wheezed the old shot-but-didn't-die codger at the other end of the bar.

"So the big dog runs in all a'burnin and a'howlin so I throwed a bucket of water on him. Next theeng you know, the bruja witch comes in all screaming and crazy like. "You burnt my dog! You burnt my dog! You will pay. I will curse you . . . I will curse you all," she shrieked.

"Old Charlie over there," the old geezer tipped his hat, "shot and killed the old witch. But he really didn't mean to, it was just a reflex, right Charlie?" Charlie nodded and chuckled.

"Before she die," Pedro continued, "she say, once again, "I curse you all, thees place, thees town and everyone in it." Then she look over at her dog and say, "I'm coming to you my pet." Then I shot the bruja with thees," he pulled a shotgun out from under the bar, "and thees time she lay down and die. We look over at the dog. It is no longer Irish Wolfhound, but had changed, by magic I theenk, into a huge black wolf—a lobo. Snarling and snapping, a vicious and dangerous devil. So I fired a blast of shot at it and old Charlie fired his pistol at the same time and we killed that big lobo. That's him up there," said Pedro, jerking a stubby thumb up and over his right shoulder toward the animal mounted on the wall to the left of and underneath the painting of Miss Nude Everywhere.

Ears flattened with lips curled and fangs bared in a fierce and perpetual snarl, the wolf looked dangerous even stuffed and mounted.

But where was it before? Had he somehow missed seeing the huge animal?

The Rider relied heavily on being alert, his powers of observation, and his attention to detail. Survival depended on it. How could he have missed spotting the big wolf when he entered the saloon? He did forget to reload, yes, but this? Impossible.

What the hell was this place anyway?

He studied the wolf, noticing the taxidermist had used translucent red marbles for its eyes. But should they be glowing?

"El Grande, eh senor? We killed the big lobo and caught the spirit of the bruja witch in the animal's body, all at the same time! Arriba!

"Saints be thanked and praised!" blurted Peter O'Malley.

"I'll be go to hell!" said Charlie the old geezer. They laughed in unison as the piano man started up a lively tune, the kind that no one can name but everyone has heard.

"And so senor Jones . . . we are now The Burnt Dog Saloon you see?"

"Maybe."

But the Rider didn't see. He didn't believe in magic and witches and such goings on. He believed in himself and what he could do with his Colt forty-five. But right now, it seemed on the verge of being shaken, if not shattered.

"So, you just changed the name of this place, nothing else has changed . . . everything has stayed the same, right?"

"Oh, si senor."

"On me dear departed mother's grave!" proclaimed Peter O'Malley.

"Right as rain," chimed in old Charlie who the Rider missed with a shot at twenty feet.

Strange goings on.

The Rider, hearing what he expected, looked over at Jean Loise, and saw what he expected. She had not moved since he last looked at her. Still holding the Mona Lisa smile, she gave him a sly wink he was unable to interpret. A secret she alone held.

"Bartender! Pedro! Check please!" called the man from the square wooden table. He and the woman he was with had finished their meal.

The Rider looked over that way and couldn't see anything distinct or unusual in the looks, mannerisms, dress, or, as far as he could tell, in the speech of either one. His hair was light brown, hers dirty blonde. His eyes were hazel, hers pale blue. He wore jeans and a flannel shirt, she wore a thin cotton dress, his eyes were uninterested, hers were weary.

They could represent the common Everyman and Everywoman.

Pedro sauntered over to the everyday couple's table. He had a white towel draped over his left arm, an unreadable smile spread across his face.

The couple remained seated in their unpainted wooden chairs.

"How was thee deener senor?" asked Pedro of Mr. Everyman.

"Oh my, my, it was delicious, exquisite in every way. I am not accustomed to so many spices though, and am afraid I may suffer a severe case of heartburn when I retire for the evening."

"Not to worry," said Pedro, and reaching into his pants pocket with his right hand, he pulled out a twenty-five caliber over under derringer and shot Mr. Everyman smack dab in the middle of his forehead. Mr. Everyman leaned back in his chair with his head tilted back and dead as the stuffed lobo.

Pedro began stacking the dishes, readying them to clear from the table.

"And how was your deener, senora?" he asked Ms. Everywoman.

"Very, very good Pedro," she lowered her voice, "But I'm afraid I've eaten too many refried beans and later on, at an inopportune moment, I may suffer from, shall we say . . . stomach distress."

"Not to worry, senora," said Pedro as he switched the under barrel of his derringer to the top position and shot her square between the eyes. Her head lolled back and came to rest on the top of the chair's back.

"Such a lovely couple," muttered Pedro under his breath as he carried the dirty dishes through a door behind the bar and into the kitchen.

The Rider couldn't move. For the first time in his life, he was frozen in shock from tongue to toe. Being used to blood, guts, and death, he shouldn't have been; it was the unexpected nonchalance of the violence that held him stunned.

Dishes clattered and water sloshed, the telltale sounds of doing the task of washing them coming from the back room.

The piano man continued playing the Mexican funeral dirge. He hadn't missed a beat yet. Maybe he was deaf.

Slowly, the Rider drew his Colt, spun the cylinder, and saw he had five live rounds. But hadn't he fired one at the old geezer? He placed it on top of the bar. He remembered only one other time his hand had trembled like it did now.

* * *

Sometime during the Goddam War, a gut shot kid begged him to shoot him, to put him out of his misery.

"Please Cap'n . . . please . . . oh God it hurts something fierce." The kid's head wagged from side to side as his eyes rolled up, then down, fixing them on the Captain, begging one more time.

"There ain't no fixing a gut shot Cap'n. You said so yourself. Please . . . oh God . . . don't let the Yanks hurt me no more, don't let them devils play with me!" He grabbed the sleeve of the Captain's coat with a feeble grip, his breathing labored and wheezing, tears running out the corners of his eyes.

Captain Virgil John Jordan, now calling himself Virgil Jones, pulled out his revolver, held it with a shaky hand against the kid's temple and squeezed the trigger and his eyes at the same time. Standing, he waved the pistol in the air and hollered, "Retreat! Retreat up the hill!" at the rest of his men. Then he moved out, walking like he was out for a Sunday afternoon stroll up the hill after his men, his back turned to the Damn Yankees, his back turned on the Goddam War.

As he walked, a rifle ball caught him in the left leg, right above the knee. He stumbled, but he didn't fall, and he just kept walking, limping now, up the hill toward his men who were firing volley after volley at the Blue Coats and cheering their Captain on.

Topping the hill, he grabbed a soldier by the young man's gray tunic. "Come with me son," he said, "let's fire some cannon balls into those blue bellied bastards." The soldier grinned, relishing the thought.

And they did, until the barrel of the cannon was too hot to touch, and the blue coats never stormed the hill, and then there were no more blue coats standing to fire at.

The sun lay low in the west. Ordinarily a beautiful sight, but this night its golden rays turned the bloodied field at the bottom of the hill to the color of rust as the ground soaked up the blood.

"Mine eyes have seen the glory," mumbled the Captain, "and it is most assuredly Hell."

He remembered his hand shaking then, but couldn't remember it ever doing so again, until now. He nodded once. Pedro set the double shot in front of him.

"Does that big lobo have a name?" he asked, motioning toward the mounted beast with the barrel of his drawn Colt.

"Oh, si. We have called him . . . or her . . . since the bruja witch is trapped inside, El Diablo Negro."

"The Black Devil," said the Rider.

"Si. It fits, no? And mucho better than Smokey the Wolf, eh?" Pedro chortled.

"Why'd they put red eyes in its sockets?"

"Senor?"

"Red eyes! In the goddam Black Devil, up there!" he blurted, pointing his pistol at the wolf creature mounted on the wall.

"Senor, look again. I theenk you are mistaken."

He took a close look at the black beast's eyes. Burnt orange with flecks of yellow, that, even though dead, seemed to dance. The pupils weren't quite reptilian slits, but were elliptical, with the long axis vertical. He shot a glance over at Jean Loise. Her eyes glowed red for an instant. At least that's what he thought he saw, he wasn't sure he could trust any of his senses.

The piano man broke into a lively rendition of "*She'll Be Coming Around the Mountain*".

He felt like he was suffocating and needed to get out into the fresh air, to feel the reality of the pure, crisp, cold wind blowing across the northern plains.

Maybe his mind, freshened by the simplest but most important form of life sustaining purity, would snap back into place, and if not his mind, at least his senses.

It couldn't be possible that what was happening inside the saloon could be real.

He looked over at the head shot couple, expecting them to be enjoying their meal, but no, their heads were lolled back on the chairs, a neat little bullet hole in the forehead of each, and dead still.

The Rider holstered his Colt.

"I need some air, Pedro. I'm going to step outside for a minute or two, but I'll be back. Don't stash that whiskey too far under the counter."

"Si, senor. Buenos Noches senor."

"I said I'd be back."

"Si, senor."

He turned, looking neither right nor left and moved unsteady toward the door. Too much whiskey or too much assault on his psyche, it didn't matter which, what mattered is he didn't remember feeling this way since the Blue Coats embedded that lead ball into his left leg, just above the knee. Pulling his buffalo overcoat from off the wall peg, he draped it over his shoulders.

"She'll be driving six white horses when she comes," sang out Peter O'Malley in a fine Irish baritone despite looking and dressing like a Mexican, the waxen piano man accompanied him. Charlie the old geezer cackled like a hen laying an egg as the Rider stepped out into the cold refreshing air.

The weather hadn't changed a bit nor had it let up any. The high velocity wind still came out of the north and curled up the east-west running street blowing swirling snow and ice pellets in an easterly direction and bringing in a light misty fog in contrast to the black density of the frozen sky. It for sure was real, and it felt good, cleansing. He drew in a deep breath and then another, not trying to figure out what happened back there in the saloon. All he needed to know was that it was sometimes subtle and sometimes blatant, but always madness manifested in varying degrees.

Maybe he'd been dreaming. Maybe some kind of drug had been slipped into his drink. No, not too likely, not here in the constant crystal clarity of the Great Plains, could it?

CHAPTER TWELVE

Nothing moved on the deserted and frozen street, but something was moving towards it, and fast. A low rumble, faint at first but growing louder by the second, headed toward the town. The sound drew nearer, dissipating into sounds more distinct than a rumble, but he still couldn't quite identify them. Visibility in any direction was near zero. The sounds grew louder and more distinct, the slapping of leather on horseflesh, the creaking of wood, the clanging of metal. He wasn't sure if he could trust what he was hearing, though he'd heard the same sounds hundreds of times before. But this was one weird place. Wait and see, he told himself, and rested his hand on his Colt.

The pounding of hooves . . . maybe.

A loud crack, perhaps a whip, perhaps a small caliber gun shot.

A loud "hee-yaw" spewing forth from a hoarse raspy voice.

Another crack, another slap of leather, the pounding—creaking—clanking of what, he wasn't sure. He strained his eyes against the blizzard, but saw nothing to validate the sounds he was hearing, nothing at all, just the sounds alone, growing ever louder.

Then two huge black horses exploded out of the whiteness, feathered black plumes bobbing on the tops of their heads, flared nostrils blowing steam from their muzzles, sparks flying from off their giant hooves, reins pulled back against the power of their thrust. They slowed as they passed in a blur, followed by two more pairs of matched blacks, six black horses pulling a glossy black coach that could be mistaken for a hearse. Or was it one in fact? The horses and coach came to an abrupt stop, straining against its forward momentum, and then recoiled backwards before settling still and silent. At least that appeared as cause and effect, but at the same time the scene could be from a macabre circus that had lost its way.

The Rider stood transfixed in the street, stunned into immobility, doubting all his senses. He waited.

The driver, whose black cloak and long white hair had been flying back from the wind, laid down his whip and clambered, spider like, from his bench to stand on the frozen ground. He turned and gave the Rider an intent look. His face was ghastly pale, white as any full moon, and frozen in a grimace, whether diabolical or comical, it was hard to tell.

His eyes though, wide and wild, suggested diabolical. Then quick as a scampering insect, he was at the coach's door.

The Rider put a firm grip on the butt of his firearm.

"Witchita," hollered the coachman, opening the door with a pronounced flourish.

The Rider walked over to him and stood as close to the man as the nausea in his stomach would let him.

"Where ya from?" he asked the skeletal driver.

"Why . . . where we're always from," he replied with a note of sarcasm. "D'Odds City," he answered, managing to light a lamp he'd hung on a hook by the coach door.

A diminutive figure stepped out of the dark interior of the coach, clad in fringed buckskin leggings, a beaver hat with a round top and wide brim, a band of colorful beadwork circled the hat, the design anywhere from Sioux to Apache. The wind blew open the white buffalo robe overcoat to reveal a buckskin shirt underneath. One foot touched the step, and then both feet were on the frozen ground, quicker than the eye could follow. Standing straight up in the wind, the person held a Winchester rifle. Hair, the color of copper or bronze or gold, was long and loose and fell to the person's shoulders. Wide set eyes, the color indescribable in the swirling snow, were set in a strong and determined face. Underneath high cheekbones, a smile curved upwards at the corners of a full mouth.

The woman was about a foot shorter than the Rider.

She was no lady, at least not by the standards of appearance he had known, and he saw no daintiness in her mannerisms.

She looked, without flinching, into the eyes of the Rider, her amusement apparent, as if she knew his thoughts. She turned her head and spit a stream of tobacco juice onto the street. The wind, catching her overcoat, blew it open, revealing a pearl handled revolver riding low on each of her hips.

A bag thumped onto the street beside her, thrown from the top of the stagecoach. The Rider looked up. Casey Mojo waved to him, his grin lop-sided.

He looked again at the woman. He'd never seen her that he could recall, and yet there was something . . . familiar. No, don't trust your senses, he told himself, not in this place. She stepped closer to him as Casey Mojo scampered down from atop the coach to pick up her bag.

"Want it in the saloon, ma'am?" he asked.

"Uh—huh."

She stepped even closer to the Rider and into the reluctant dim light that spilled from the saloon windows.

"Ma? Ma Belle, is that you?" he asked after getting a better look at the frontier woman. She stopped and looked up at him, the amusement still on her face.

"You got the wrong person, mister. I ain't nobody's ma, and I ain't no one's long lost love come to mend your poor broken heart, and I sure as, by goddam, ain't no country sweetheart.

Name's Pistol Ann and I'd shake your hand 'cept I'd have to set down my shootin' iron, which I won't do. But come on inside, Mr. Forlornly, and I'll buy you a shot or two of whiskey."

She spit in the street, winked at him, and bold as brass strode on in to The Burnt Dog Saloon, Casey Mojo hunching along behind, carrying her single bag.

The Rider stood still as bone staring after the whirlwind he'd just encountered. The sound of leather slapping flesh pulled his attention toward the coach.

The Rider looked up at the black cloaked figure as the coachman turned and looked at him. He had no eyes, just flat black holes pinned against the pale skin of his skull. His mouth curled in a mirthless smile as he slapped the harnessed beasts one more time and cracked a whip over their heads.

"Giddap, ya hell bound hosses!" he screeched. The blacks broke into a dead run, the feathered plumes attached to the tops of their heads flattened by the shrieking, twisting, north wind.

The Rider watched the coach disappear as a wary uneasiness stirred inside of him. Uneasy because the absurd, the macabre, the utterly twisted comedy that had been unraveling tonight was beginning to be expected and seem normal.

Casey Mojo stepped through the doorway of the saloon, its dim light falling on the dimmer lit boardwalk. The hunchback paused, and from under the shadow of his cloak's hood, regarded the solitary figure standing alone in the deserted street.

The Rider stared after the stagecoach whose creaking and rattling faded into the blackness of the night, blackness close to the dark that shrouded his stony heart.

"Perhaps she brings my death," he muttered, pondering the strange arrival of Pistol Ann.

"Your steed is at rest sir."

"Huh?" Dumfounded he turned and focused on Casey Mojo, standing still as a stone on the boardwalk.

"Your steed, sir, he is well fed and at rest," the hunchback repeated.

"Oh yeah, Gabriel. I think I'll walk on down to the livery and say hello. Bring something normal into my life for a while, maybe."

"I'll walk with you, if you don't mind, sir."

"No, I don't mind, and please, call me Virgil."

"Virgil, right sir."

Maybe this man is normal. Perhaps the only person that is in this skewed town, thought the Rider, his mind beginning to pull back together by that one thought dropping into place.

Chapter Thirteen

Pistol Ann braced the Winchester against the wall within arm's reach behind her, shed her white buffalo overcoat, hung it on a peg embedded in the wall, spun around on the ball of her foot, hollered, "Evenin' gents!", drew her pistol and shot El Diablo Negro just above the shoulder. The slug made a smacking sound as a small cloud of dust rose from the animal's hide.

"Well, faith 'n' begora, if it isn't Pistol Ann!" exclaimed Peter O'Malley, a look of delighted surprise etched in his distinct Hispanic features.

"By all that is and all that ain't, by all the sinners and all the saints, by all that can and all that cain't Pistol Ann, good to see ya lassie!" exclaimed old Charlie.

"By damn Charlie, you old coot, ain't you never gonna buy the farm?"

"From the cradle to the grave, I'm here to rant and rave. Hell no. I ain't payin' fer no three foot by seven foot by six foot deep farm. I got too much rantin' and ravin' fer that!" Charlie roared back. The bar patrons broke out in laughter at the verbal antics.

"Drinks are on me boys! Set 'em up Pedro!" she hollered, and then moved lithely up to the bar, settling in on Peter O'Malley's right side, within reach of her Winchester.

"Too short to belly up to the bar, reckon I'll have to settle for tits up!" exclaimed Pistol Ann.

Laughter roared all around.

She's a firecracker, that one, thought Pedro as he busied himself pouring drinks for the patrons. He set the last one in front of Pistol Ann.

"Mucho gracias," she said and dropped a gold piece on the bar.

"Uh . . . senorita, it's not such a good idea to be shooting holes in El Diablo Negro. The bruja witch is trapped inside the animal's hide. Too many holes and one day . . . pfoot . . . out she'll come," Pedro explained.

"Ya mean like a fart?" she responded.

Old Charlie's drink almost spewed out of his mouth, he laughed so hard.

"Bruja witch my ass. I reckon that was the first hole put in that mangy critter, other than the one that killed him. So, just for you Pedro darlin' I promise not to put any more holes in his hide . . . tonight."

"Si, gracias senorita," said Pedro and shuffled off.

"The bruja witch, she be worse than any banshee bitch, and saints alive lass, we wouldn't want that loose on us now would we?" said Peter O'Malley.

"Bruja witch, my ass," replied Pistol Ann, sticking her ass out at the Irish speaking Mexican and slapping it with her right hand. "When Irish eyes are smiling, eh Peter," she said with a wink.

If his skin hadn't been naturally dark, his blush would have shone like a beacon in the night.

Pistol Ann looked around the room, her glance not landing in any one place or on any one person—dead or alive—for long.

"Say, where's that tall fella wearing the black buffalo robe overcoat, old Mr. Forlornly? I offered to buy him a drink too."

"You must mean Virgil Jones. He said he was going out for some fresh air and that he'd be back soon," Jean Loise said from her spot by the upright piano.

"You mean . . . the Rider?" asked Pistol Ann.

"That's exactly who I mean."

The piano man started up *"Look Away Dixieland"*.

CHAPTER FOURTEEN

Virgil walked along with Casey Mojo in silence, their heads bowed down against the blizzard's wind; Casey's more naturally inclined that way. He hustled ahead the short distance to the livery stables, opening the man door for himself and the Rider. Just to the right of the man door were two double wide and double high doors that swung inward, giving easy access to both animals and carriages.

The interior of the livery was warm, with no wind finding its way through the small cracks in its well-constructed plank walls. It was dim inside, but not dark, except for the far corners. Its light was provided by four oil lamps hung on support posts at twenty-foot intervals. Two stalls were between two posts, each ten feet wide and located off to the sides of a twelve foot wide course-way, intersected in the middle of the building by a ten foot wide course-way. In the intersection was a huge brick fire pit with a metal hooded vent hung over its top allowing the smoke to escape through the roof.

A fire blazed in the pit, keeping the stables warm against the icy blasts of the north wind. An anvil secured to a bench on the left side of the pit waited for red-hot steel. A few blacksmithing tools lay beside it. Along the side of the fire pit facing Casey and the Rider were three plain wooden chairs set there for warming.

Gabriel whinnied from the fourth stall on the left as the two men were about to pass by it. Casey Mojo stopped and unlatched the gate, letting the Rider in to see his mount.

"Hello old hoss," he said, patting the big buckskin on the neck. "Casey treating you okay?"

"Hello yourself," replied the horse. "And if he weren't, I'd kick a lung out of him."

The Rider jumped back in an amaze bordering on shock, and by instinct drew his Colt as his left shoulder smacked hard against the top plank of the stall.

"What in the name of sanity is going on here?" he said to no one in particular, as his gray eyes darted around the stall, his Colt automatically following along with them.

"Wouldn't shoot an unarmed horse now, would you?"

"Gabriel?"

"Yup, it's me, old boss."

He holstered his Colt but remained with his back against the sideboards of the stall for support. Rubbing his banged up left shoulder, he once again asked, "What in the double blue blazes of hell is going on around here?"

"Don't ask me pard, I showed up the same time you did," replied the horse.

The hunchback scurried over from tending the fire with surprising quickness and agility. One look at the Rider told all.

"Did the talking horse spook you, sir Virgil? My apologies for not telling you to begin with. All animals are able to speak here if they choose to. It can be quite the comical circus at times, it can," he laughed, just a little.

The Rider stood stunned and speechless. What little—if any—sanity he thought might remain was now torn and shredded, gone into the realm of what once seemed impossible.

"Casey Mojo, I have a few questions," he said in a stern voice.

"Yes sir?"

"For starters, what exactly is this place? And call me Virgil."

"Why, it is Right Here and Now, Virgil sir!"

"Right Here and Now?" questioned the Rider.

"Of course. Is there any other place? Come, sit with me by the fire, and as to your other questions, I'll give it a jolly good try to answer them, after you've tried my whiskey that is. Nothing like it anywhere and I'd be willing to wager on that statement. There's nothing quite like the White Castle to put a man at ease. Comes all the way from the Queen's Land, it does!"

Like a zombie in a dense fog, the Rider walked stiff and dreamlike out of Gabriel's stall to plop down on one of the chairs by the fire.

Casey Mojo came scuttling out of the intersecting course-ways, carrying two shot glasses and an unopened bottle of the bragged up White Castle. Setting the glasses on the rim of the brick fire pit, Casey sat himself in a chair, opened the bottle and poured the glasses full.

He was right. The taste, the sensation, the feeling, was exquisite, better than any Kentucky bourbon he had ever tasted. Its only equal was Chateaux Le Blanc. The Rider didn't say a word, but stared into the fire as if the answers to his many questions might reveal themselves in the flames. He felt a light touch on his bruised left shoulder, causing him to wince.

"Sorry Virgil sir," said Casey.

"It's alright. Good whiskey, may I help myself to another?"

"Be my most welcome guest, sir Virgil," he replied.

Pouring himself another drink, the Rider turned to the mysterious deformed man on his left.

"What is this place, this town called? It must have another name besides Right Here and Now. Can you not tell me?"

"Why . . . it is Witchita sir, spelled W-I-T-C-H-I-T-A, as the sign hanging in front of The Burnt Dog Saloon says, and very indeed, it is Witchita."

"It's like the Wichita I've known in the past, but everything is warped, and somehow seems a mockery of the real Wichita, but how, and why?"

"The REAL Wichita you use as a reference sir, is the very cause of your confusion. For that Wichita and this Witchita are both real and both exist. One exists Over There and one exists in Right Here and Now. And if you were Over There it would become your Right Here and Now and, of course, vice versa."

"So Right Here and Now would become Over There?"

"Exactly. And so you see, you are always in Right Here and Now, and so it can never really change."

"Okay, but where then is Over There?"

"Where you came from sir Virgil."

"So . . . how did I get from Over There to Right Here and Now in Witchita?"

"Somehow sir Virgil, you and your steed passed through The Other."

"The Other?" quipped the Rider.

"Yes sir, The Other."

"Joke's on us, eh, old boss," Gabriel commented from his stall.

"Maybe so old hoss, maybe that's all it amounts to is some kind of twisted joke."

CHAPTER FIFTEEN

A rifle shot rang out from somewhere up the street, followed by another.

In an eye blink, the Rider was up and headed for the man door, throwing on his buffalo robe overcoat as he opened it.

Casey Mojo remained seated by the fire, not wanting to leave its comfort, and not interested in gun play at the moment.

The Rider hurried along the frozen street, his slight limp from the goddam Yankee lead ball much more pronounced because of the cold in the air and the urgency in his insides.

The snow drifted and then didn't, swirling horizontally across the street like a mist refusing to rise.

Getting a firm grip on his forty-five, he leaped up onto the boardwalk, took a long stride forward and flung open the door of the Burnt Dog. Bursting through, the first thing he saw was the alarmed look on Pedro's face. All other eyes were fastened on him, curious as to who would make such a reckless entry into the saloon.

One quick sweep of his eyes told him the whole story.

Pistol Ann, her hat hanging down on her back, her hair shimmering in that odd color somewhere between copper and honey, held the smoking Winchester in her left hand. She was facing toward the piano. Looking in the direction the rifle was pointed, he saw that the baby eating couple each had another bullet hole in their foreheads, twice as large as the first ones. She'd shot them again, but why?

She looked his way as he slammed the door behind him against the fierce shrieking of the wind.

"Well, Mr. Forlornly, glad you could join us," said Pistol Ann.

Pointing her smoking rifle at a table two removed from the twice-shot couple, she said, "Join me at that table yonder and I'll buy you the drink I promised."

Removing his hand from the butt of his Colt, he tipped his hat to her and headed for the indicated table. He didn't pull a chair out for her to be seated on, knowing she was the independent kind and wouldn't want it that way. But, she could turn out to be a fine lady, here in Witchita.

Seating herself across from him, she leaned her rifle against the table top's edge and gave him an inquisitive and amused look, her soft brown eyes aglow with, what . . . anticipation maybe?

He glanced over at Jean Loise standing by the piano. She was hard to read, but guessed she was in neutral, except for that mysterious Mona Lisa smile of hers and her eyes . . . they glowed . . . red. A touch of jealousy perhaps, but blood red?

Turning to Pistol Ann he asked, "Why'd you do it?"

"Do what?"

"Shoot those dead people," he pointed, "over there."

"Oh, they got up and wanted to leave. Couldn't let 'em do that you know, they're supposed to hang in the morning."

"But they were already . . . DEAD!"

"Well, I guess they were at that, Mr. Uh-h . . ."

"Jones, Virgil Jones."

"You're the one they call the Rider."

"How can you know that, here in, wherever and whatever this crazy place is."

"Right Here and Now is not that far removed from Over There, Mr. Virgil Jones Rider, and what goes on Over There is known here."

"Okay, so what about those cadavers over there?"

"People don't stay dead here. They can come back any time."

Remembering the incidents with the Old Geezer and Jean Loise being shot, he had to accept what she told him, no sense in trying to make sense of it, but how he had gotten from Over There to Right Here and Now was a mystery he intended to unravel.

Pistol Ann twisted around in her chair toward the bar. "Pedro, two shots of El Casa Blanco, sil vous plait!" she hollered.

"Si, mademoiselle," he answered as they shared a moment of laughter. The Rider ignored it, thinking non-involvement might be the best way to help solve the riddle of Right Here and Now.

Pedro ambled over with a fresh bottle and two glasses, setting one glass in front of her and one in front of him. Opening the bottle, he first poured for her, and then the Rider.

"Merci, Pedro," she said.

"Gracias, and bon soir, senorita!" he responded, their eyes dancing with a mirth known only to them.

The Rider took a sip of his whiskey, and the El Casa Blanco elixir had the same effect as Chateaux Le Blanc, and the White Castle Casey Mojo had served him in the stables. Ma Belle had told him, "You won't find anything like it this side of the Mississippi." Pedro had quipped, "Nothing to compare to it this side of the MissSoSloppy."

"Wait a minute!" he exclaimed out loud, "they all make reference to a white dwelling of some sort!"

"Mind sharing your sudden enlightenment?" asked Pistol Ann from across the table.

For the first time, he looked . . . really looked, at her. She shined . . . reminding him of a time long ago, Over There, which he now realized wasn't a matter of distance. But this was different, her shine came from within. No glow surrounded her. Maybe that was due to her tough exterior and the buckskins she wore. He was certain that she was indeed a lady, in the fullest sense of the word . . . no exterior trappings or polish needed.

"Huh? Oh yeah, I was just trying to fit some pieces of a puzzle together in my head."

"What puzzle, if you don't mind me asking. And if you do, answer anyway. You've gotten my curiosity all fired up."

"I've somehow broken through The Other. I don't know what it is, where it is, or what it's made of. And so, I have come from Over There to Right Here and Now."

"Sounds like we got us some serious talking to do, Mr. Jones," she said. Taking a gulp of her drink, she slapped her glass down on the tabletop. "A-h-h, that's mighty good stuff!"

Tossing her head in Pedro's direction, sending her copper—gold—honey blond mane flying across her back, she hollered at him. "Pedro, will you put those two cadavers out back? That way if they decide to try going for a little stroll, they'll be stuck frozen and I won't have to shoot 'em again."

Old Charlie wheezed out a chuckle.

"I'll lend ya a hand Pedro," offered Peter O'Malley.

Turning back to the Rider she asked, "So, Mr. Jones, let's get down to business."

"You can call me Virgil."

"How'd you learn about The Other?"

"From Casey Mojo, just before I came in here because of the rifle shots I heard. Do you know him?"

"I know who he is, the hunchback of Notta Damn. I've spoken to him a few times."

"Notta Damn? Right Here and Now is one helluva strange place."

"It depends on your perspective, Mr. Virgil Jones Rider. If you've lived all your life here, it is . . . you know, normal.

I'm sure if anyone from Right Here and Now wound up Over There, it would seem quite strange to them, don't you think?"

"You're making my head hurt, but of course you're right. But that still doesn't answer my question."

"And what is that?"

"How in the blazing blue hell did I get here, and how do I get back?"

Pistol Ann took another gulp of her whiskey, very unladylike, but not in The Burnt Dog Saloon or in the eyes of the Rider.

"I'm not sure. Maybe it's just your As—Is," she replied.

"As—Is?"

"Your u-m-m . . . what would you call it . . . your Fat?"

"Fate."

"Yes, that's it, Fate. Isn't that how you try to explain the unexplainable Over There?"

"Well, when any rational explanation can't be found for some event that occurs and is unwanted but must be endured, either on a personal or social level, we resign it to Fate, yes."

"Bad things happening for no apparent reason," she said. "And so Fate is all powerful Over There."

"In a sense, yes. But, we also have Destiny," he said.

"Okay, let me guess. Destiny occurs when something good happens, or some desire is fulfilled, personally or socially."

"In a sense, yes," he repeated.

"Big, slick, fancy, evasive words, Mr. Virgil Jones Rider. Eloquent for a man who is from everywhere and nowhere, so I've been told."

"Is that what you've been told about me?"

"In a sense, yes."

The Rider laughed and took a swallow of whiskey.

"What did you do before you decided to become a wandering executioner? Let me take another guess. Over There, at one time, you were . . ." she pursed her lips and furrowed her brow, studying him for a long moment, "an attorney."

"Right." His head spun, crazy. No words came to his mouth with which to dazzle or baffle or surprise or evade this woman.

"My horse talks," he managed to mutter.

"That's normal, and don't change the subject," she said. "Speaking of subject, wouldn't it be easier to have said, Fate is for bad stuff, and Destiny is for good stuff. I understand big fancy words Mr. Virgil Jones Rider, but not all people do. You should use simple words, don't you think?"

"Will you stop calling me Mr. Virgil Jones Rider."

"Alright, Mr. Rider."

"Gawd!" he exasperated.

"Gawd? I thought it was Fate or Destiny. You people Over There need to land on something, seems to me. In Right Here and Now, we only have As—Is. Do you see that to be true, Mr. Rider?"

"Gawd!" he exclaimed. She ignored him.

"That should be self-explanatory. Okay . . . what it is, is what it is . . . but that depends on what your definition of is . . . is. Savvy? Whatever happens, happens, eh?"

"You're making my head hurt. But I do get the main idea, and it's no different than Fate or Destiny."

"Bingo! Except no past or future is involved," exclaimed Pistol Ann, drawing her namesake and firing a shot into the ceiling to celebrate the enlightened occasion.

"Saints alive, ya near made me spill me drink, lass," said Peter O'Malley.

"Hee-hee, better luck next time, miss," said Old Charlie.

Pedro shook his head as the piano man started up with *"Buffalo Gals"*.

Jean Loise remained unmoving over by the piano. The Rider noticed her eyes. They had returned to burnt orange with yellow flecks. Turning his gaze to El Diablo Negro, he saw the big wolf now had the blood red luminescent eyes. He shrugged and turned back to Pistol Ann as she holstered her pearl handled revolver.

"As—Is it is then," he said to her. "But you know, one of our prominent ancient civilizations, the Egyptians, had a deity named Isis. I wonder . . . the name could be a derivative or mutation of As—Is I suppose."

"There you go using them big fancy words again! If you want to continue being a wandering executioner, you need to tone down your speech. Don choo theenk, senor?" she said with a chuckle. "But of course, As—Is was mutated into Isis in ancient Egypt."

"How do you know that?" he asked.

"I read. We have history too, sort of. Anyway, the Egyptians, Over There, missed the point and gave Isis god status, which neither Isis or As—Is have. Do you see, Mr. Virgil Jones Rider?"

Before he could answer she continued. "The first key to understanding the difference between Right Here and Now and Over There is that they run parallel to each other and reflect each other, but not perfectly. Through a glass darkly, if you will."

"I will," he replied.

She smiled. It lit up her entire being and was a delight for him to behold.

"Gawd, now I'm using big fancy words," she said.

The Rider finished off his whiskey and poured himself another, without offering Pistol Ann one. She was quite capable of taking care of herself, and that he knew . . . right well.

"Okay, I got the first idee stuck in my haid now, I reckon. Does ya got anymore to tell me Pistol Ann, ma'am?"

Her head tilted back in laughter, exposing her long delicate throat and surprising white teeth, considering she was a tobacco chewing mama.

"Please, call me Ann," she said. He didn't know if she was playing or serious. He did know his store of patience was near to being depleted.

"Alright, Ann. Can you tell me anything else I should know about Right Here and Now?"

"Pedro!" she hollered as she twisted around in her chair, "You gonna remove these fake cadavers before they start stirring around again and I gotta waste a couple more bullets on 'em?"

"Si senorita." Peter O'Malley left his place at the far end of the bar to help. Pedro grabbed the man under the arms while Peter grabbed the woman likewise. As they were being dragged away, the Rider thought he saw the woman flash him a smile as her heels scraped across the floor. Apparently, they didn't feel any pain.

A blast of icy air filled the saloon as Pedro, the Irish Mexican and Peter, the Mexican Irishman, dragged them through the back door to the outside, giving the Rider a shivery chill. He turned to Pistol Ann. "And . . . ?" he asked, coaxing her to tell him more about this strange place.

"Right, I'll tell you all I'm able to, maybe all you can take for now. I ain't never been Over There, but we do have records of its history from ancient times, until the very end of time, as you know it, Over There."

"Impossible."

"Perspective, Mr. Virgil Jones Rider, perspective. Maybe we'll get into that. As I said, I will tell you all you are able to bear for now. May I continue?"

He pinned her with an intense look, refilled his shot glass and threw down the drink. Nodding his head once he said, "Shoot straight."

"I always do, and I always hit my mark," she replied.

Why did she seem so amused? Or was she one of the few fortunates in any world blessed with an innate joy? She for sure was becoming more enigmatic to the point of fascinating. His resistance to her waned as his trust in her grew, and he couldn't put a finger on the reason why. Maybe he didn't need to.

"Over There, time is, in reality, an illusion, because it is viewed as a linear continuum . . . pardon my Big Fancies. And that is the second truth you need to understand about the difference between Over There and Right Here and now."

"How else can time be viewed?" he asked.

"As an illusion, like I said."

Taking a swallow of the amber liquid from her glass, she continued. "Over There is a place of confusion and chaos, of illusion and disillusion, of loss and isolation," she paused, giving him a long hard look as if trying to see into his cold and stony heart, "and one of death and destruction."

"I have to agree with that, and it keeps circling back on itself. And Right Here and Now?"

"It is a place of memories and haunting, of daydreams and nightmares, of possibility and magic, of life and continuance. Do you see, Mr. Virgil Jones Rider?"

"I ain't got near 'nuff experience in this here place to give an accurate yes or no . . . ma'am. And please, call me Virgil."

Then he tipped his hat, her face lit with a smile, and her smile lit his face.

Magic.

"How do you know so much, or anything at all, about Over There?" he asked.

"Like I said, we keep records, both of your world and of ours, and I read them. But your world is locked into the idea of a continuum—remember?—and we are not."

"And that idea causes fear, believing, spoken or unspoken, that someday it will end."

"Exactly. Our records go far into what you believe to be the future of Over There, and one day your people will realize that they are not alone in the universe, nor the center of it."

He observed her with sharp intent, as if he were trying to look into her heart.

"And no, you will not be allowed to see what will happen in your world," she said. Was she also able to read his mind?

"Why not?"

"Because you want to find your way back, don't you?"

"Yes, of course, but how do I get back?"

She placed her hand over his and with genuine regret said, "I don't know, Virgil. I wish I did. I'm not sure anybody does. Just once in a while somebody somehow manages to break through The Other, from there to here, or from here to there. No one has discovered the key to that door."

"Those are words I didn't want to here, but I guess that's all part of As—Is," he said and smiled. She gave his hand a gentle squeeze, a gesture unexpected but welcome.

"Now you're learning," she said.

CHAPTER SIXTEEN

His mind wasn't reeling as much as it had earlier. Still, the idea of parallel worlds with similar reflective people, but not always synchronous events, was a concept hard for him to grasp and accept, but he had to because that's how things were in Right Here and Now.

"Oh, and one more thing Virgil Jones, if you get killed while in this land, you will stay dead."

"Unlike the people born here, huh?"

"Yup, that's true."

"Well, that doesn't bother me all that much, but how do the people born here stay dead, if at all? There must be something that keeps them in their graves."

"There is. We must cut off their heads," she replied with blunt force.

His face lost any softness, indicating his senses had snapped into their usual place and now held an alert hardness.

"Why hang them then?"

"A method used Over There that we reflect. But there is a guillotine at the western edge of town, by the bruja witch's shack, that we use to finish the job."

"A guillotine, and that was reflected in our world?"

"Yes."

"And what about the people from here that cross to Over There?"

"The same. They can only remain dead if decapitated. And, if they go over at night, they cannot live in the light of day. Some, on either side, become shape shifters, like that stuffed wolf on the wall. I don't rule out the possibility that the bruja witch is trapped inside of him, because he did shape shift just before he was killed. Animals do not need to have their heads cut off to stay dead, although in your world, they are often cut off and mounted on walls. Why?"

"I don't know for sure. It is kind of grisly isn't it?"

"Perhaps it's an intuitive act influenced by Right Here and Now."

"Could be. But back to shape-shifters. It makes me think of tales I have heard of creatures of the night and humans that change to some sort of animal are a fact and not merely flights of the imagination."

"Very likely, Mr. Fancy Wordsmith," she said.

"You do alright yourself Miss Polished Pistol Ann."

The anger inside him simmered down to below the boiling point to become a comforting warmth, a warmth he hadn't felt in many long, lonely, and lost years.

As if reading his thoughts again, she asked, "Are you sure you want to die so soon, Mr. Virgil Jones Rider?"

The question stunned him, not because it came out of the blue, but for the first time since the Goddam War, he couldn't respond with an automatic yes.

He poured himself another drink and one for Pistol Ann as well. She thanked him with her eyes and asked, "Will you drink with me to life . . . and continuance?"

"I will." They clanked glasses and drank deeply of the amber liquid and of each other.

"So tell me Ann, do you know of anyone who has passed through The Other and found their way back?"

"Only one, Casey Mojo."

Chapter Seventeen

He sat staring into the fire that blazed in the brick fire pit. Seated in one of the nondescript wooden chairs in the center of the stables, the solitary figure didn't feel lonely or overwhelmed by the vast empty space. It was nothing compared to what he once knew, when he dwelt in the nether regions of the Notre Dame Cathedral Over There in France, and was known as Quasimodo.

Casey Mojo took a sip of White Castle. It never got him drunk, so he suffered none of the misery that accompanies drunkenness. It did not bring on moments of euphoria followed by unremembered and torturous times of unpredictability. No weepiness, or belligerence, or wallowing in self-pity. No deep sorrow, or an emptying of self into oblivion for a time. None of that. The nectar of White Castle soothed and stayed there and caused pleasant drifting daydreams. Maybe it was different Over There. He never found out.

Lost in the captive fire, adrift in contemplation and the memories of the woman Esmeralda, in Paris Over There, he didn't hear the Rider come in, or notice that he sat down in the chair next to him.

"Casey Mojo," the Rider said softly, yet strong enough to pull the hunchback into the now. The hood of his woolen cloak up over his head, Casey Mojo turned his shadowed face in the direction of the voice.

"Sir Virgil! Where have you been?"

"We were talking about The Other before I went to check on those rifle shots, remember?"

"The Other? Oh yes, we touched on that subject for a short while, yet it seems very long ago."

"I've met Pistol Ann. Do you know her?

"Oh yes, everyone does here in Witchita."

"She told me you had once broken through The Other, and then somehow had returned to Right Here and Now. Is that true?"

"It is indeed sir, and you would be curious as to how I accomplished that feat?"

"Of course. Can we continue then?"

"Certainly sir, but I must tell you first off that I am not exactly sure how it happened myself, and so there will be gaps in my story which I cannot give an answer to."

The Rider was not surprised. The transition from Over There to Right Here and Now had been nothing but a mystery from the get go, but he wasn't ready to give up yet, and never would be if he stayed true to himself.

"I figured you'd say something like that. It has to be the way it is or people would be jumping from one side to the other trying to change their own or someone else's life," he said to Casey.

"Yes . . . or history in some way. But, I did say gaps, and some don't seem so very wide. There are clues and I have some hunches if you would care to hear them. It could get tedious after a while sir. Do you feel up to it?"

"I know I'm all ears," said Gideon from his shadowy stall, ending his comment with a whinny. An answering whinny came from the first stall on the other side of the intersecting course-way where a beautiful chestnut mare was hosteled.

"Where to begin, how to begin," agonized Casey Mojo. He pulled the cloak's hood off his face, exposing his African features to the light of the fire. His heavy brows so furrowed they almost knit together over his deep set dark eyes. His light complexioned skin glowed gold in the fire's light, the dancing flames wiggling shadows across his face, his lazy, sagging, and wandering left eye held in the deepest of the shadows.

Just by looking at him few would realize the amount of great intelligence or the brave heart that dwelt within him, if, as is so often the case, the book is judged by its cover.

"Begin at the beginning, as the saying goes.

What can you tell me about The Other? Is it a living thing? An ethereal thing? An unknown or unknowable substance? A figment of everyone's imagination here? What?"

"I dare say, sir Virgil, slow down some. The Other is all that and much more. It is where dreams come from and are made manifest. It is where thoughts are transformed into substance. It is a membrane, a placenta, giving birth to all the things in your world and in ours. Both are very alike, but not the same, skewed one from the other, if you will."

"I can see that, but how . . . ?

Casey Mojo held up his hand, stopping him in mid-sentence.

"Please, sir Virgil, no questions yet, for I will be unable to answer them with even a small degree of accuracy.

How does one get from Over There to Right Here and Now and then back again, or vice versa? I reiterate, sir, I do not know. But, let us establish one thing."

"That is?

"The Other is obviously some kind of door or passageway between our worlds, and we don't know who has the key, or if there is a key at all that will open it."

"Agreed," said the Rider.

"Do we have a choice anyhow?" Gabriel said. The Rider chuckled under his breath. Casey Mojo smiled, ever so slight, but it was a smile.

"No, I reckon not," replied the Rider to his horse.

"Shall we continue then, sir?

"Yes, and please, excuse my, uh, steed over there."

"Certainly, sir."

It didn't seem possible, but the storm outside increased in fury, hammering the livery stable with ice pellets that sounded like pebbles striking the roof and the sides. An occasional gust of fierce wind penetrated the walls that until now had been impenetrable, the rush of cold air fanning the flames of the fire, sending grotesque shadows twisting and dancing along the walls.

The chestnut mare whinnied and stomped her front hooves in nervousness. Gabriel whinnied back, offering as much assurance of safety as he could.

"I'll tend the fire. You just continue on," said the Rider.

"As you wish, sir Virgil." He drew in a deep breath, and as he let it out, poured himself and his companion another drink.

"You were a barrister, I mean, an attorney, I beg your pardon sir, Over There, correct?"

"At one time, long ago,

"Then you have probably heard of Victor Hugo's novel, "*The Hunchback of Notre Dame?*"

"Yes, in fact I have read it. I remember it well."

"Well . . . I am . . . was, Quasimodo, the bell ringer in the book, at your service."

The Rider's mouth dropped open, his spine stiffened, and his eyes widened with disbelief.

"But . . . but . . . Quasimodo died in the story!"

"In the story, yes, and it made for a good one too, but that was Mr. Hugo's imagination. Obviously, I wasn't beheaded Over There." He paused for dramatic effect, being the central figure of a classic novel he thought it would be appropriate, and it was.

"And now we can begin," said the hunchback. "What do you think was the theme of the novel, sir Virgil?"

The Rider paused long, staring into the dancing flames, thinking of the dancing woman of the story, Esmeralda, and how society and its established power had abused her to the point of death. But that was not it.

"It is the story about a man whose love for one woman was so deep, so pure, that he would sacrifice his life for her, and he did so in the end."

"Precisely sir Virgil, and now we may continue," said Casey Mojo. "I was born and have lived most of my life in Right Here and Now, except for my short jaunt to Paris, of course.

As I grew to manhood, I realized my misshapen body would never change. Bitterness and anger and no small amount of self-pity filled me with more loathing for normal people than I'm sure they had for me."

He paused, this time to look long and hard at the Rider.

"My heart had turned into a stone and had no room for love of any sort in it. No kindness, no compassion, not even everyday civility. All I wanted was to wallow in my own misery, cursing As-Is every day of my life, shunning people much more than they would ever have shunned me, had I given them the chance, you see."

The Rider stood up slowly from his chair, went around to the other side of the fire pit to the intersecting course-way and disappeared into the right branch. In a few moments he returned carrying a couple of chunks of wood. He tossed them on the fire, a shower of sparks exploded like fireworks. Casey Mojo ignored them as they were trapped by the metal hood hovering over the fire pit and were sucked up the flue to die.

More shadows spun on the far wall, the Rider's making a caricature of a herky-jerky stick man as he moved around the fire pit to the other side and returned to his chair, waiting to hear the rest of Casey's story.

"I have a special purpose in Right Here and Now," the hunchback continued.

"And that is?"

"I have the ability to detect when The Other has been disturbed, and someone or something has broken through it from Over There."

"Do they force their way through?"

"No, not by force, a passage seems to open at random, and we've gone over it a few times already that we don't know how or why, but it does cause a disturbance. Anyway, when I detect one, I climb those stairs . . ." he said, pointing to an opening in the wall on the other side of the intersecting course-ways and to the right, an opening the Rider hadn't noticed until this moment.

". . . to the top of the tower. You've seen it from the outside?"

The Rider nodded.

"Up in the tower is a bell I ring to alert the Land that someone or something has passed through The Other."

"Something?"

"Once a very large, flesh eating lizard found its way through, I believe from your Jurassic period. We finally managed to send it back."

"Jurassic! That was millions of years ago! You couldn't possibly have done . . ."

"Pardon me sir, but let me remind you, time has no meaning here."

"Right, I think Pistol Ann mentioned that."

"Quite certainly sir. But we're getting side tracked here, back to the story.

So, as a young man and liking the attention I received when I rang the bell, and as a way of ruffling up the physically normal people, I often rang the bell under false pretenses. So often in fact, that eventually the people paid no attention to the ringing bell."

"Like *"The Boy Who Cried Wolf"*, in our story Over There."

"Precisely, sir. So . . . the villagers told me to ring the bell as often as I wished, because they did not give a damn. Thus I got the name the hunchback of Notta' Damn."

"And it became a story . . . Over There!"

"Yes, it was the core of it sir."

"Fascinating!" replied the Rider. "And so you wound up in Paris, France as the actual bell ringer of Notre Dame Cathedral."

"Exactly, old chap! Oh my, forgive my impropriety sir Virgil, I seem to have gotten carried away."

"I consider you my friend, Casey, no need to apologize."

"Thank you, sir. And now that I have changed, the townspeople know and trust that I ring the bell only when the need arises."

"So that's how Jean Loise and the other folks knew I was coming and were expecting me," the Rider mused. "But you said you changed. How?"

"That is later in the story if you wish me to continue." The hunchback refilled their glasses and asked, "Are you bored to tears yet sir?"

"Not even close. Please continue."

"So one day, after drinking a bottle of White Castle, and tired of being teased as the hunchback of Notta' Damn, I decided to leave town for good, and rode away on that chestnut mare, over there." He pointed to the first stall on the left, across the course-way intersection. "I didn't care where I ended up. The whiskey caused me to doze off as the mare walked along, picking her own route. The next thing I knew, I woke up in a stable, settling the mare into one of the stalls, when a priest in a frocked black robe burst through the door in a panic and hollered. "Quasimodo, hurry! You've been too long on your ride. It's almost time for evening mass. Be quick now! To the bell tower with you lad." Well, as you can guess, reality preceded Mr. Hugo's *"The Hunchback of Notre Dame"*, and I had fallen in love with Esmeralda, and I did lie by her in death, for . . . I don't know how many days. Eventually, I struggled up and left her, found my horse at the stable and rode back the way I remembered, as best I could anyway."

He paused, taking in a drink of whiskey and a large gulp of fresh air and then continued.

"I dozed off again as the mare was plodding along, and somehow I had returned to Right Here and Now."

The Rider's attorney wheels turned in his head. "Wait a minute! What about the mare? She can talk can't she? Did you ask her?"

"Yes and yes, but she can't remember anything unusual or more specific either. But what did happen was I returned a changed man."

"And how were you changed Casey?"

The hunchback had been staring into the fire as he told his story. He turned now and looked in the Rider's steel gray eyes.

"I knew I could love again and that my heart need not remain a stone. And that is all I can tell you sir. I do not know of any key."

"Maybe not just yet, but you've given me quite a bit to think about, my friend."

"Glad to be of service to you sir."

The Rider set his empty glass on the rim of the fire pit, stood and stretched his arms full length above his head, his backbone giving an audible crack. "I'd better stop off and say good-night to Gabriel before I go," he said.

Lost deep in the fire and in his own thoughts, Casey Mojo heard the Rider speak, but it was muffled like a voice from far away. Turning slowly, he looked up at him. "Maybe you can backtrack and somehow retrace your steps," he said.

"Put myself in the same scenario, like you did, if I can."

"Yes, exactly, sir."

"It'd be worth a try I think," he said, then turned, walked over to Gabriel's stall and leaned over the top rail of the gate.

"Whaddya think old hoss? Would it be worth a try to return to Over There?"

"Sure, but not tonight, eh? I've got my eye on that little filly across the way. I can't remember the last time I spent . . ."

"Alright, I get your drift. I reckon we'd have to clear it with Casey and the mare of course."

"Why don't you come over and see me sometime big boy?" came a voice sultry and oozing like honey from the chestnut mare.

"Casey Mojo, you hearing all this lovey-dovey talk going on?" said the Rider, his face a mask of mock puzzlement.

"That I do, and it has got me wondering if a foal should come out of this, shall we say, union, and it were dappled or a pinto with buckskin and chestnut coloring, what would we call it? Bucknut? But if these horses want to do a bit of cavorting, that's fine by me mate."

Chapter Eighteen

"Well, I'm going to say good night good friend"

"Yes. It has been a good night," replied Casey.

The Rider stood up, grabbed his buffalo robe overcoat from off the top rail of the stall next to Gabriel's, and headed out the man door into the unrelenting blizzard. The wind had twisted around from the north to blow out of the east, causing the dry powdered snow, as fine as confectioner's sugar, to drift up against the store fronts on both sides of the street.

His limp more pronounced due to the arctic air, his mind swirling in cadence with the wind driven snow, the Rider canted up the street, a singular shadow in the whitened darkness of the night. Unlike the snow, his thoughts didn't gather themselves in drifts as he hitched along. Nothing of much use had materialized out of all the information the hunchback had given him.

Chuckling at the thought of Gabriel and the chestnut filly, he realized he couldn't remember the last time he had the pleasure of a woman's company. "By god," he said to no one there, "I do believe I will spend the evening with Jean Loise." He turned the knob of the heavy oak door and stepped into The Burnt Dog Saloon, closing the door behind him without a whisper of sound.

More from habit than curiosity, he wondered what time it was. A purposeful glance around the room told him no clock was on any of the walls. Right . . . time didn't exist in Witchita. He still couldn't grasp that idea, it was one of those things to accept, like the word fair meaning an event that happens in counties, in late summer, back home. Hanging his snow powdered coat on a peg by the door, he turned around only to be greeted by Pistol Ann.

"Pull up a chair Mr. Forlornly, set a spell, and I'll buy you a drink or two."

Maybe he would by-pass Jean Loise. The unfolding of the evening would tell the outcome of that idea. Slipping his Colt out of and then back into its holster, he made sure it would pull easily-just in case. He did the same with the Bowie on his left hip, acutely aware that danger often came in subtle forms and being taken by surprise was always a possibility if you let your guard down.

That done, he sauntered over to Pistol Ann's table, pulled out a plain wooden chair and settled himself into it as she poured him a glass of El Casa Blanco.

"Did you find out anything from Casey Mojo?" she asked.

"Huh? Oh . . ." His mind had been on Jean Loise who stood sultry by the piano, the intrigue of a Mona Lisa smile still playing at her mouth. Her burnt orange eyes with the mysterious yellow flecks danced and sparkled as she looked directly at him.

"Yeah . . . actually quite a lot, but nothing I can put my finger on or use just yet. He couldn't come up with a definitive key as to what allows a body to pass through The Other."

"Did you ask your horse?"

"By goddam, that never occurred to me! I was too busy hooking him up with that chestnut filly stabled with him."

"That'd be ReeBa, she's a slut."

He almost spewed out his drink at her remark.

"Not that that's a particularly bad thing, just wouldn't want your horse feeling too flattered," she said, clarifying her choice of words. He drank in the sparkle that was all around her. Together, they broke into a-good-old-fashioned-belly laugh.

"A slut horse, that's damn funny Pistol Ann!" he declared.

"Well, the male is called a stud isn't he?"

"I get it, fair is fair, huh?"

"Exactly. And . . ." she said.

"And what? Oh, The Other. No not much, in fact nothing except it's still a mystery. It may be alive, or not. It may have substance, or not. It may be malleable . . ."

". . . or not" she added.

"And so I learned nothing of real value, but I'll ask Gabriel. That sounds so absurd."

"As-Is."

"Yeah, he's probably busy right now, so I'll wait awhile."

She gave him a wink. Pistol Ann wasn't stop-you-in-your-tracks beautiful, and probably wouldn't be even if she were all fancied up. But she shined. Something about her . . . her spirit, her soul, her openness, her honesty, her straightforward manner, her . . . rightness caught him. And she sparkled. Her smile always made it into her soft brown eyes; clear and bold, inquisitive and fearless, kind and compassionate all rolled into one. Pistol Ann's beauty went deep. So deep it would take a lifetime to fathom, like a finely cut multi-faceted diamond to be turned and explored in broad daylight; at sunrise and sunset; under the moon, full or waning; or by the light of billions of stars in any of the four seasons. And it scared him because it felt so right, and the rightness of it would touch his heart, if he could find the courage to take that chance.

He'd forgotten about Jean Loise until a soft silky voice broke through his pleasant reverie. "What's a lady got to do to get a man to buy her a drink around here?"

He looked up into her large odd colored eyes. Captivated by their mesmerizing glow, it was a captivation he did not struggle against, for he was now in familiar territory where his loins surged, instead of his heart.

"Jean Loise!" he exclaimed as he stood and moved around the table to pull a chair out for her. "Please, have a seat. Join us and I'll be happy to buy you a drink or two."

Sensually accenting her every move, she took the proffered chair, and allowed the Rider to seat her as she gave Pistol Ann a winsome, knowing smile.

"I assume you ladies know each other?" he asked, looking first at Pistol Ann and then at Jean Loise, her eyes still holding him captive.

"From a distance, which is how I like it," replied Pistol Ann.

"Why Pistol Ann, I was hoping we could be good friends," replied Jean Loise her tone laced with heavy sarcasm. Surprised to find her hand resting on the pearl handle of her revolver, Pistol Ann returned it to her lap. Not unnoticed by Jean Loise, her short but penetrating laugh was filled with mockery. *Did the woman have a death wish or something,* thought Pistol Ann. *I could blow her to hell before she drew another breath.*

"Do you mind?" said the Rider, pointing to the bottle of El Casa Blanco in front of Pistol Ann. "Be my guest," she replied to him and turning said, "I've always had a soft spot in my heart for stray cats, and you have worked in a cat house, haven't you Jean Loise?"

Smiling at her sudden antagonist, masking her determination to not let herself get rattled, Jean Loise chose to remain silent, knowing she would have the upper hand by evening's end.

She knew what men like Virgil Jones wanted, and what they wanted was all they knew. What they needed had to be slowly revealed to them.

He poured her a shot glass full of the amber elixir. "Thank you, Mr. Jones."

"Call me Virgil," he replied.

Her resemblance to his bride Janice Louise caused him to marvel, not only at her looks, or the sound of her voice, or the way she moved, or her expressions, but at how it took him back to a time when he could feel. And he marveled at how poignant and how strong the memory of her still remained within him. How could he, how would he, ever forget her? Would the pain of losing her ever subside, let alone go away?

He sought oblivion, still.

"You have an uncanny resemblance to a woman I knew, and loved, and married, a long time ago," he said. She smiled thinly, lips together, and placed her hand over his. "I know, my dear," she said with gentle certainty. The impact of her remark didn't register. All he saw was Janice Louise and all he felt was his longing for her.

He raised his glass to take a swallow. Quickly, but gently, she grasped his arm, halting it in mid-air. She clinked her glass to his. "To us," she said and they drank to each other.

"Well ya'll, I think I'll go tits up to the bar," Pistol Ann broke in.

"Ann, no, you don't have to go," he said.

"Hush, Mr. Virgil Jones Rider, although I don't know why you'd want to pay for something that could have been yours for the asking." Standing, she headed toward the bar, Winchester in hand, leaving the bottle of El Casa Blanco on the table. Virgil watched her walk, a vague regret stirring in him as she moved further away.

Jean Loise had ignored Ann's dramatized exit, keeping her attention fully focused on the Rider. "Are you planning on staying the night?" she asked him.

"I am, if Pedro's got any rooms to let."

"He does, but I have one already," she paused, "you can stay with me . . . if you'd like."

"That I would like," he answered without hesitating. Direct and to the point, he liked that in a woman. They clinked glasses as he lost himself further in her mesmerizing eyes.

"I've never been Over There," she idly commented. "What's it like?"

"It's a chaotic, dangerous place trying to find itself after a long, devastating, and bloody civil war."

"It sounds absolutely horrid," she declared without emotion or passion of conviction, just a-bide-your-time comment. "I think you're much better off in Right Here and Now . . . Virgil."

"Yeah, I do too, especially when we can quit talking."

Direct and to the point, she liked that in a man.

"Shall we?" she invited.

Quick as a hungry cat he was behind her pulling out her chair as she stood. Hooking his right arm with her left, he grabbed the bottle of whiskey and they proceeded toward the stairway. They had no more than placed a foot on the first stair when the saloon's outside door flew open.

Two young cowboys burst through letting in the shrieking wind. Hats off, brushing the snow from them, they bellowed out a "yee-haw." One back kicked the door, slamming it with a resounding thud against the storm. The other one hollered as loud as the wind that brought them, "Whiskey barkeep, and lots of it!" Striding up to the bar, their boot heels pounding solidly on the plank floor, their spurs jangling, it was easy to see these boys liked attention, or trouble, or both.

Splitting like a rushing stream that suddenly forks, one settled in on Pistol Ann's right, the other on her left, and both with one boot hitched up on the brass foot rail. Peter O'Malley and Old Charlie were situated off to the right of the trio, the old geezer the farthest away.

Stopped in his tracks by the sudden commotion, the Rider didn't take another step up the stairs. Jean Loise halted with him.

The cowboys were lean, range tough, and looking for excitement. The one on Pistol Ann's left had black hair, slicked back and oily, like his pock marked weasel's face. He wore a heavy pistol; low slung on his right hip, and was shorter than the scarecrow looking man on Pistol Ann's right side. His boyish looking face and scraggly hair sticking out like straw from under his floppy hat were accented by brilliant but wild blue eyes. He pistol was holstered on his left hip.

They were so familiar; the Rider thought he had seen them before. Ah, Pock-Marks and Scarecrow in Abilene? What in the hell?

"Please Virgil, let's go on upstairs," urged Jean Loise, sensing the danger as it brewed with the heaviness of an oncoming prairie cloudburst.

"Not just yet. I don't like the looks of those two at the bar."

"Do you know them?"

"Maybe, they look like a couple of boys I knew, very briefly, Over There."

"The dark haired one is called Jesse James Jackson, the blond, boyish looking one is none other than the Billy Goat Kid, two of the baddest boys in the country. Come on, let's go upstairs."

"Not yet darlin', you can wait for me if you want, or not."

Jean Loise had lost the upper hand she had gained only a few moments ago. Perhaps she had underestimated Mr. Virgil Jones. Maybe his lust for blood was stronger than his lust for the pleasures she offered. Or . . . perhaps he was the silly chivalrous sort and felt protective of Pistol Ann. She decided to watch the scene play out from over by the piano.

The piano man, wide-eyed and not sure what to do, started playing some standard dance hall tune; light, bouncy, and very lively.

The Rider stepped back from the stairs, walked slow and easy over to Pistol Ann-sandwiched between the two cowboys-and asked, "Join me for a drink at the table, ma'am?"

The Billy Goat kid, on her right, glared a strong and scornful look at the Rider, and then softened as he turned to Pistol Ann. "Thought we'd have us a party tonight, little lady," he said. "You're not turnin' fickle on me already, are yuh?"

From the left, Jesse James Jackson snickered, its sound like a mirthless hiss. "I don't think she'll be wanting that drink with you mister," he said to the Rider.

The dormant molten lava in the Rider's heart was rising fast. These may not be the same men he'd met and killed in Abilene, but they were the same type—the wandering damned—whose only purpose was to plague the land in which they wandered.

"I'll be the one to choose when and if I party," broke in Pistol Ann, looking up at the Rider, "and who I party with," she added. He was taken aback, not by what she said, but because what he saw in her eyes wasn't anywhere close to fear, but dark amusement backed by deadly intent.

Yeah, she can take care of herself, he thought, and that he knew . . . right well.

"Certainly Mr. Jones, I'll join you at your table," she chirped. Grabbing her Winchester, she turned and started toward the group of tables near the piano. A strong hand grabbed her left shoulder and spun her around to look into the blue eyes of the Billy Goat Kid. "You're staying here, with us, pretty thing," he said.

Quick as a rattler, she planted the heel of her left boot square on the man's shinbone. Yelping at the pain, he released his grip on her shoulder.

"You ever touch me uninvited again mister, you'll have a bullet hole where your pecker used to be!"

Charlie the old geezer cackled loud and wheezy, he just couldn't help it.

The Billy Goat Kid's face flushed red, in part from embarrassment, but mostly from anger.

The Rider kept a close eye on Jesse James Jackson.

"You're a regular wildcat now, ain't ya, just my kind of woman. I'll get around to ya later, sweet cheeks," said the Billy Goat Kid, glaring hard at the Rider. *If looks could kill,* thought the Rider.

"Ready?" he asked Pistol Ann, keeping the Kid in the corner of his eye. Taking his arm, they sauntered over to a table, their backs turned to the cowboys. She moved out ahead of him and seated herself. After he sat down she said, "You didn't have to think I needed rescuing. I can handle myself." She wasn't much for pretentiousness.

"I have no doubt of that, but those two are special types. I had a run in with what could be their twins—Over There—for the same reason; they were abusing a friend of mine."

"Am I your friend then, Mr. Virgil Jones Rider?"

"Yes Ann . . . I'd sure like you to be my friend."

"Done!" she exclaimed and stuck out her hand. They shook.

Damn it felt good to be in her company. He knew he could spend hours with her, each moment an awakening treasure, and not even think of taking off her clothes.

"Do you know those gents over at the bar?" he asked.

"I wouldn't exactly call them gents, but no," she said.

"Jean Loise told me their names, and who they are."

"Oh."

"Pretty bad boys, huh?" said the Rider.

"Just about the baddest in these parts, but how did that bruja witch know?"

"That who?" he asked.

"Jean Loise . . . I figure if the bruja witch lives, as Pedro claims, she'd inhabit Jean Loise," said Pistol Ann, and then, "Listen, Virgil Jones, you get shot and killed, in Right Here and Now, you'll stay dead you know?"

"Yes, I know."

"Well then, take it a little easy. Those two boys at the bar are high strung and trigger happy."

Without warning she changed the subject. "That had to be the quickest quickie in the history of quickies!" she said.

"What?"

"You and the bruja witch. You know, doing it, getting it on . . . do I need to go any further? How much did she charge you anyway?"

"We never made it upstairs before those boys blew in. Besides, I think you're poking your nose in where it don't belong . . . need I go further?"

"No, Mr. Forlornly, you sure as hell don't."

He poured them each a drink, he gulped his and she sipped hers as they stared into each other's eyes for a long lingering moment. His desire to kiss her was overwhelming as he watched her lips part very slight and very slow. As if reading his mind she said, "I think I'll get rid of my chew."

He burst into laughter; she was so full of surprises.

Leaning over, she spit her chew into the brass spittoon Pedro had placed by the table. Taking a swig of whiskey she swished it around in her mouth and swallowed it down. No pretense with this woman.

"Hey you, pretty lady, come on over here and join us for a drink, whatta ya say?" Jesse James Jackson hollered over at Jean Loise.

"Bet you a dollar she does," quipped Pistol Ann. Before the Rider could respond, Jean Loise was gliding across the floor toward the two young cowboys.

"I told you, she'll do about anything for money."

"You can ease up Ann. I don't consider her close to being a friend."

"Oh," she said, leaning back contentedly in her chair.

The Rider had positioned himself so that he could keep an eye on the two men. He'd made sure Pistol Ann was seated to his left so his view or his line of fire, if need be, wouldn't be blocked.

"You smell trouble, don't you?" she asked him.

"They've made a stench from the minute they entered the saloon."

"Well, yeah, they're that type all right. And of course, their reputation precedes them, which is usually enough to let them have their way. They ain't gonna forget what you done."

"I reckon they won't."

"So . . . when the trouble starts, don't count me out, okay?" Seeing she was dead serious, what could he do but agree?

"How'd you come to be called Pistol Ann anyway?" he asked.

"I have a hunch you'll find out shortly," she replied.

CHAPTER NINETEEN

"Ouch! You're hurting me! There's no need for this. Please, let go of me!" It was Jean Loise. The Rider tore his eyes away from Ann's to look over at the bar. They had her sandwiched between them, the oily bastard had pinned her arms while the rail post was trying to plant a rancid kiss on her mouth.

"Please . . . don't," she implored them again. But they were the kind of men that liked to hurt people and grinned like ravenous wolves.

"No reason to treat the lady that way friends," said the Rider from his chair, his voice low but loud enough for them to hear. Like water thrown on a flame, they stopped their horseplay, both staring in the Rider's direction.

"Ya know what mister," said the Billy Goat Kid, "you've gotten into my business once too often tonight and you're starting to get under my skin. And believe me, Jesse and I ain't your friends."

"You are absolutely right. I was just trying to do this smooth and civil like. But I can't help thinking of you as nothing more than a shit-eating dog and your partner as the first cousin to the ass-end of a skunk."

That stopped them, dead and cold. They let the woman go.

"Uh-oh, you'd best go over by the piano," Pistol Ann said to Jean Loise. She didn't need any further coaxing and scurried over to the now silent upright.

Slowly pushing back his chair, the Rider stood up, his eyes never leaving the two cowboys, who by now had squared around to face him.

"Maybe you should go over by the piano yourself, Ann," he suggested, not moving his eyes off the two men.

"I told you not to count me out," she said with flat refusal.

The boys at the bar were as fixated on the Rider as a rattle snake on a rabbit, their eyes huge, their hands loose near the pistols hanging on their hips, Jesse James Jackson's on his right, the Billy Goat Kid's on his left. Nothing moved except for a slight twitch in Jesse's lips, the tension in the room thick enough to slice with a knife.

"I think it best if you boys leave now," said the Rider, low and soft and dripping with danger.

"Leave? Why, we're gonna kill you mister," replied Jesse, the twitch in his mouth more pronounced.

"Alright then, but it's only fair to warn you that after I shoot the both of you, I'm going to cut off your son-of-a-pig ugly heads."

Jesse's lips twitched faster. Billy's eyes grew impossibly larger. The kind of treatment they were receiving was unnerving them and the Rider knew it.

Pistol Ann stood up very slow, keeping her hands in plain sight. She glanced quickly over at the Rider and he couldn't believe what he saw. Had she gone loco? Utter amusement danced in her eyes and then she dared give him a wink before turning to the bar!

"Now gentlemen," she implored, "there's no need to do things this way," she said, holding her right hand, palm out, toward the Rider, her other hand toward the cowboys at the bar, as if doing so would stay the violence. She shot the Rider another amused look, this one cloaked in mischievousness.

"No need to trouble yourself any further Mr. Jones," she said. "Allow me to blast the balls off these two low-life sonso'bitches." Squaring away to face the outlaws, dropping her hands to her sides as she did so, she asked, "Which one of you manure eaters wants to be a eunuch first?"

In a single blur, both men went for their guns.

Pistol Ann's guns belched fire, turning Billy's crotch into a blood spurting fountain, at the same time, a hole was blown open in the middle of his chest. In the same split second, Jesse's crotch burst crimson as did the middle of his chest.

The four shots boomed with the ear splitting force of a cannon, reverberating across the room as a single sound. Four shots fired, two men dead, in one heartbeat.

The shock of disbelief etched itself on the outlaw's faces as Billy's gun fired into the floor, adding another bullet hole in the riddled planking. Jesse's finger reflexed closed on the trigger of his gun, sending a bullet smacking into the side of the black wolf mounted on the wall behind the bar.

"Santa Maria!" exclaimed Pedro, crossing himself, and then pulling his shotgun out from behind the bar. "Saints preserve us," breathed Peter O'Malley, his mouth dropped open in awe. Their mouths weren't gaping at the swiftness of death brought to the outlaws lying face down on the wooden floor, the worn planks thirstily soaking up their blood. They were staring, horrified, at the black wolf, El Diablo Negro. The beast had come alive! Ears laid flat, lips peeled back in a vicious snarl to expose blood red gums and fangs the size of a man's index finger, its massive jowls snapped, its eyes glowed red as saliva flew from its muzzle. The huge lobo strained to free itself from its mounting as it let loose with an unholy wailing.

Jean Loise shrieked an ear splitting, soul piercing, scream no demon could match. She had loosed it not from terror, but at the joy of being reborn.

All eyes in the place spun over to her. Standing like a statue, a ribbon of black mist twirled around her, moving counter clock-wise from her feet up to her head, rendering her into a shadow. Opening her mouth, she breathed deep, sucking in the misty ribbon as if it were smoke. No longer shrieking, she opened her eyes, which now glowed and glistened like blood red rubies. Panning the room with a malevolent smile that twisted her mouth, she levitated and rose to hover a foot off the floor.

"I warned you I would return, you silly fools!" she snarled as she glided forward, her rose red silken gown as silent as the incoming night.

"The bruja witch, I knew it," shouted Pistol Ann aiming her pearl handled revolver at the oncoming apparition.

"You can put that away dearie," said the witch, moving ever closer. "Oh, and I do have a name, Mesmerala. I'll deal with you later on, my sweet."

Pistol Ann put a bullet where the witch's heart should have been, but she might as well have shot through a wisp of smoke. Her eyes boring into Pistol Ann's, the witch cackled, "I told you to put that away, silly girl." Turning to the Rider, who had already holstered his Colt, she screamed, "And you my dear, don't you know, hell hath no fury like a woman scorned."

He reached across his belly for his Bowie knife, but before he could pull it, she was on him quick as a demon-cat, striking him square on the jaw with her right fist. He flew backwards and landed on top of a table, breaking it into splinters, as he and the table hit the floor with a loud thud. He shook his head, trying to clear it.

Calmly gliding toward the door, the bruja witch stopped, crooked, and then wiggled her index finger at the black wolf, still howling and struggling against his restraints. "Come, my pet," she spoke, and the brute broke free of its wall mounts, leapt over the bar, and landed with one forepaw on the Billy Goat Kid and the other on Jesse James Jackson's blown out back. Snarling and snapping with saliva flying from its mouth, the wolf opened its massive jaws, took the Kid's head in them, bit down, jerked upwards, and with a red, popping noise, ripped the head off the body. Opening his jaws wide the big lobo tossed the head left and rolled the grisly object across the floor.

Laughing with maniacal delight, Mesmerala opened the heavy oak door and entered the darkness beyond, the black devil turned to follow close on her heels.

Pistol Ann spun her weapon into its holster, took two long strides to where the Rider was sprawled amid the splintered table and offered him her hand. He took it and stood upright. Rubbing his jaw, he said, “I can’t remember ever being hit so goddam hard.”

“We better try see where the bitch and her monster wolf go off to. Probably her old shack but I’d like to be sure.”

“Let’s go,” he said.

They crossed the room, stunned into silence, and grabbed their heavy overcoats off the wall pegs, throwing them on as they went out the door.

The piano man broke the silence, starting up his Mexican funeral dirge once again.

CHAPTER TWENTY

Casey Mojo led Gabriel across the course-way from ReeBa's stall when he heard what sounded like a cannon boom not too far up the street.

"Gotta go boy," he said, closing the gate to the horse's stall. Hurrying to the fire pit, he grabbed his cloak off the back of the chair and flung it over his broad stooped shoulders.

Stepping out the man-door, the ice pellets stung his face like angry bees. He paused, adjusted to the force of the blizzard and the black of the night, then lowered his head and hitched along toward The Burnt Dog Saloon as the powerful wind strove to drive him backwards. Under ordinary circumstances, he would have used the boardwalk, but because of the high thick snowdrifts, he kept out of their cover and comfort of shadow, and hunched along up the middle of the wide street. If daybreak ever came, the shop keepers would have near half a day's work clearing away the snow that blocked the entry doors to their shops . . . if daybreak ever came.

One could never be sure in Right Here and Now. Sometimes long nights were needed, sometimes long days. It all depended on what needed doing. The hunchback figured it was going to be one helluva long night.

A shadow materialized before him. Squinting against the swirl of snow and ice granules, he couldn't discern who or what it was. Now there were two. One of them said, "Nice to see you again, Casey Mojo."

"Mesmerala," he said, recognizing her voice, "so you finally escaped."

The blizzard abated around her, bringing the witch into clear view. The other shadow remained obscure. About waist high to Mesmerala, it emitted low, rumbling, threatening growls.

"Your new familiar?"

"Yes. Casey Mojo meet El Diablo Negro, as they have called him. But his true name is El Sangre Derramar—The Blood Spiller—and believe me little man, his name is true to his purpose." The resurrected animal growled with threatening menace and bared its fangs; its red eyes aglow with the piercing light of molten steel freshly hammered on an anvil.

Casey Mojo floated up and then suspended six feet above the frozen ground, invisible hands holding him in place, as he stared at Mesmerala down below on the street. He jerked a short-barreled shotgun out from under his cloak pointing it between the witch and her familiar.

She laughed, if the sound coming from her throat could be called that. It was more a shrill, bitter, trilling; a cry that mocked not only Casey Mojo but everything in the world of Right Here and Now.

"I see you are still the sorcerer," she said. "But you should know that mere bullets cannot harm me."

"I'll blow the big lobo's head clear off," he said, shifting the barrel of his weapon to point at the wolf. Mesmerala shrank back, hissing through her teeth.

"I see that bothers you. Why? Because I would cut your power in half by killing the big wolf, would I not?"

She didn't answer direct but gave a slight nod of her head, glaring at him through eyes now the color of the black wolf's; blood red and lit with the light of hatred.

"You cannot trouble me anymore, you know that, don't you witch? When you misshaped my body, you also poisoned my heart. But you know that too, don't you . . . witch. But my heart has since been healed and the toxins have been removed," he said as his feet touched the ground.

Pistol Ann and the Rider stood outside on the saloon porch. Seeing Casey Mojo standing in front of what once was Jean Loise and the stuffed but now alive wolf, they bounded down the steps and hustled up the street to offer help.

"And how was the toxic poison removed?" asked Mesmerala.

"I found out I was able to love again. No, you are not able to touch my heart with your poison . . . witch."

"Tell you what, sorcerer. You stay out of my way and I'll stay out of yours, deal?"

"Pretty close. But know this, if you hurt any of my people, you will answer to me. Understood?"

"Everything okay here?" a voice asked from behind the witch and her wolf. Whirling around, Mesmerala was face to face with the Rider and Pistol Ann. "Just fine sir Virgil," said Casey Mojo as the witch and the wolf skirted past him, moving swiftly east.

"Is she returning to her old shack?" asked Pistol Ann.

"Yes, shall we?" Casey asked and started for The Burnt Dog Saloon, Pistol Ann and the Rider in step with him.

"I reckon this one won't be causing any more trouble," said the Rider, gazing down at the result of the Black Devil's ferocity. Picking up the Billy Goat Kid's head, he tossed it over the bar to Pedro, who caught the grotesque and bloodied object with surprising deftness.

"Get rid of that ugly thing, will you?"

Then, bending at the knees, he turned Jesse James Jackson over onto his back, hooked his arms under the cadaver's and dragged it behind the bar out of everyone's sight but Pedro's, who was holding on to the grisly head of the Kid. "Come on, let's drag this trash out back," said the Rider.

"Peter O'Malley, drag that headless corpse out back, will ya?" asked Pedro. The Irish Mexican threw back a shot of whiskey and nodded once.

"I'll help," offered Casey Mojo, getting up from the table where he sat with Pistol Ann. Dragging the corpse out the back, they propped them up next to the bodies of the baby eating couple. Pedro tossed the Billy Goat Kid's fang marked head into a snow bank next to the body.

"We'll let the sheriff decide what to do with you," said the Rider, releasing Jesse James Jackson to gravity. "Or maybe I'll . . ." he drew his Bowie, hefted it, tested its weight and balance, the blade in a backhand position aimed at the outlaw's neck ready to lop off his head. "Naw, I'm feeling generous," he lowered the knife, and turned from the rapidly freezing body. Spinning back like a whirlwind, he hollered "Not!" and sliced Jesse's head off with a single stroke. It rolled slowly off the man's neck to his shoulder and then flopped into the snow bank next to the Kid's.

He couldn't say with absolute certainty the Yankees had raped his young wife before they killed her. He assumed it to be so, it was the renegade soldier's modus operandi and he'd seen enough of war's brutality to know it was the way they were.

War always turns men's ideals and their supporting morality into savagery, the unrelenting nature of the beast, always.

And the beast in Virgil Jones was fully alive.

Wiping the blade clean in the snow next to Jesse James Jackson's blankly staring eyes, he never questioned the red rage that rose up in him when he saw a woman being abused and thought of the horrible end his beloved Janice Louise had almost assuredly met.

Punish the bastards as he saw fit.

Sheathing the heavy blade he moved lithe and calm back into the saloon, Pedro and Peter O'Malley following a respectable distance behind him.

Seating himself at Casey and Pistol Ann's table, he noticed whatever conversation they were having abruptly stopped. Maybe it was about him. He didn't press the issue. He didn't care.

"Well Casey Mojo, what brings you down here?" he asked.

"I thought I heard a cannon boom, sir."

"Just a little gun play, my friend." Looking at Pistol Ann he added, "And now I know how you got your name."

"And 'twas a sight to behold, it was!" exclaimed Peter O'Malley from his usual place at the bar. "Two guns a blazin' hell fire. Four shots fired so fast it sounded like one, and was as loud as . . . well . . . a cannon booming . . . beggin' your pardon Casey." Casey nodded in O'Malley's direction, raising his glass off the table a short ways. Pardon granted.

"One shot in each man's privates, one in each man's heart. I've never in all me born days seen such lightning! Pistol Ann, boom kaboom, 'twas a glorious sight to behold!"

"Where is the bloke's bloody head?" asked Casey Mojo.

"Oh," the old geezer broke in, "a stray bullet from the other fellow's gun put another hole in the carcass of El Diablo Negro and it turns out the bruja witch was trapped inside of that mangy critter, just as we suspected. Once released, it took her no time to find a willing host in Jean Loise. Then, the big wolf come alive, leapt over the bar and tore the head right off the Billy Goat Kid's body!" he cackled and then tossed back another shot of whiskey. It went down the wrong pipe and he doubled over coughing. His face beginning to turn a bright shade of red.

"What's done is done and what's done is over with," said Pistol Ann.

"As-Is," echoed the Rider. Then, turning to Casey he asked, "How'd Gabriel's escapade with the little chestnut mare go?"

"I'd say Gabriel and ReeBa hit it off famously," he chuckled, "I'll be expecting a foal in the late spring."

"If spring comes," said the Rider. "It ain't even broke daylight here yet."

"Be patient, it will," said Pistol Ann, her demeanor calm and serene. Considering the evening's events, an unusual state. Did she know something he did not?

"As a matter of fact, sir, I was returning Gabriel to his stall when I heard the gunshots go off." Having finished that statement, he pulled the short-barreled shotgun out from under his cloak and laid it on the table.

The Rider let out a low whistle. "You came loaded for bear, didn't you?" he said.

"Yes, sir Virgil, the sound of gunfire usually means trouble."

"Why didn't you fill the witch and that black devil full of lead?" asked Pistol Ann, raising her glass to her lips.

"It would have had no effect on the witch, he answered.

If she survives one shooting, then she is no longer vulnerable to bullets, or buckshot, and, like anyone born in Right Here and Now, she will stay dead only by decapitation," he answered.

"No wonder my bullet passed through her as if she were smoke," Pistol Ann mused aloud.

"What about the wolf? Would a belly full of lead kill the beast?" asked the Rider.

"The wolf . . . yes . . . he can be stopped with bullets, but if I were the one to shoot him, I'd lop off the bugger's head, just to be certain," replied Casey Mojo.

"Here, here," quipped the Rider, smiling and raising his glass. "Here, here," agreed Ann and Casey raising and clinking their glasses with the Rider's. "To beheading the witch and the wolf!" he exclaimed, and they drained their glasses of the El Casa Blanco.

Casey set his glass down and turned his attention to the Rider. "I took the liberty of interrogating your steed, sir, concerning passing through The Other. Like my own ReeBa, the only recollection he has is simply plodding along in the midst of the blizzard until he stopped."

The Rider gave Pistol Ann a quick nod then turned to Casey Mojo. "You're one step ahead of me my friend. Ann suggested a while ago that I ask Gabriel, but I hadn't gotten around to it yet. More pressing business came up," he said with a wry smile as he waved a hand out toward the barroom floor. "Thank you," he said to Casey.

Old Charlie moved damn fast for an old geezer as he burst into the room through the door set behind the bar. "Seems that Jesse James Jackson somehow lost his head, it's settin' smack dab in the middle of a snow bank starin' stupid like up at stars what ain't even thar! The rest of him is propped up agin' the shed, freezing like he was a side of beef." Ambling up to the bar as he spoke, he stood at his usual place.

The last the Rider remembered, the old geezer was caught up in a coughing fit like he was close to choking.

Right Here and Now, such a strange place, but for now, the only place.

"Here you are, you old patron," said Pedro, pouring old Charlie a double shot of the Good Stuff. "Eess on thee house," the barkeep chortled.

Pistol Ann sat silent, thinking she should be feeling drained from the tornado of events that just struck the Burnt Dog. Instead, her fingers drummed with nervous energy on the wooden tabletop, keeping time with the wheels spinning in her head.

"A storm!" she suddenly blurted with the force that comes up without warning and captures the attention of all within earshot.

"Wha-a-a-t?" the Rider and Casey Mojo asked in unison.

"You said your mare just plodded along through the storm, didn't you?", the intensity of her question pinning Casey Mojo to his chair. "Yes, madame, so I did," he replied. The Rider leaned forward; his attention rising to the place where it buzzes loud enough inside your head it's almost audible, while your focus becomes razor sharp.

"Mr. Forlornly here," she smiled sweet and affectionate at the Rider, "said he came through in the middle of a fearsome blizzard . . . a storm."

"And . . . ?" he said.

Ignoring him for the moment she asked Casey, "And what kind of storm were you caught in?"

"Well, like I mentioned before-if I recall precisely-it was summer, I was meandering toward the south, headed I thought, to Taxes."

GET TO THE STORM! Pistol Ann wanted to scream, but she held her patience.

"Well," he continued, "on about the fourth day out-the day was very hot-near sundown, and a glorious sunset it was, I dare say, with great billowing thunderheads gathered on the southern horizon, in the direction I was headed. Then I got caught up in a frightening, yet magnificent, electrical storm. And there were consequences, mind you. It dumped buckets of water on me and my mare, soaking us to the bone. And when the rain, blinding it was, finally stopped, we found ourselves in the livery stable of the Notre Dame Cathedral. A remarkable event it was."

Long winded old coot, thought Pistol Ann.

"And how did you get back?" asked the Rider.

"The only possibility I could think of, sir, was to try back tracking, taking the route in reverse that brought us to Paris. So one day I left the city, heading north upon my steed. When the terrain looked somewhat familiar, like the plains of America, I turned ReeBa around to the south and retraced my route the best I could. To my good fortune I saw another storm developing on the horizon, only this time, it by-passed us, having shifted to the east."

"And then?" asked the Rider.

"I made it to Taxes, spent some time there, and then came back to Witchita without further incident. But, I learned I could love again, and even though it was painful, it was well worth it."

"Esmeralda," said the Rider.

"Yes, of course."

"What the Sam Hell are you two talking about?" asked Pistol Ann, her brows furrowed together in puzzlement.

"Oh . . . while Casey Mojo was in Paris, Over There, at the Notre Dame Cathedral, you were the bell ringer, weren't you?" he asked Casey.

"Yes, sir Virgil."

"He fell in love with a woman by the name of Esmeralda," the Rider continued.

"Oh . . ." said Pistol Ann as Casey Mojo nodded his head in assent, a little color rising in his natural pale cheeks.

CHAPTER TWENTY-ONE

Ma Belle placed the CLOSED sign on the door of the hotel. Turning, she looked into the crowd of shocked faces. Working women and their clients alike stood dead still, questioning looks one by one replacing the looks of shock.

Locating Lily Francine, she said, "Find Camille and take her to the main bath. I'll be along in a short while." Lily nodded and turned to do as she was bid.

Ma Belle addressed the small gathering. "Ladies and gentlemen, we have had an incident and will close this hotel until further notice. Four men are lying upstairs, dead, in room five. And in my opinion, they got what they deserved, for they had heaped abuse upon abuse on our dear Camille and I have no doubt the bastards would have killed her had she not been rescued. Her rescuer, who shall remain anonymous, has left town, headed west. I have not seen the room, but understand it is one god-awful mess and will take time to clean and perhaps be put out of use altogether."

Faces with eyes wide and mouths agape stared at her.

"That's all I can say for now. I must see to Camille and then wait for Sheriff Keller."

Finishing her speech, she hurried across the parlor, her silken gown whispering as she went, the crowd murmuring around her as they parted to make way.

A hallway, its entrance obscured by red velvet curtains, branched off to the right of the main parlor. Lit by oil filled wall mounted sconces, the lamps cast pale yellow parabolas down the walls that became bridal veils when they hit the floor creating an inviting feeling in a seductive, yet tentative, way. Two doors were on the right side of the softly lit hallway, one door was on the left. The two doors on the right led to rooms containing liquor, foodstuffs, extra linen and towels, and cleaning and medical supplies.

Ma Belle unlocked the unmarked door on the left side. It opened to reveal one single room that ran the full length of the hallway. The center part, to which the door opened, was the powder room area. Three vanities, each with mirrored backs and a soft upholstered stool, were in a line. The counters held several fragrances, face paints for shadowing the eyes and enhancing the complexions, combs and hair brushes, powders, nail polish in red and peach, lip gloss in all shades and colors, including black.

To the left of the vanities was the wardrobe area, where gowns, undergarments, hair ribbons and a few wigs hung on free standing wheeled oak valets. To the far right of the huge space were three oversized bathtubs with hot water supplied by a large copper vat fitted over a brick lined fire pit. Pipes ran from the vat to the front of each of the bath tubs with a spigot within easy reach. Another pipe ran from the main copper vat in the opposite direction to a large laundry tub. The water was kept between one hundred and one hundred twelve degrees, the fire precisely fueled by an automatic feeder dropping small chunks of wood into the fire pit.

Ma Belle insisted on cleanliness.

The powder room, the wardrobe area, the bathing area, and the laundry were tended by Sarah Jane, an elderly, rather large black woman, who took great care and pride in her duties.

Camille was soaking in the center bathtub with Sarah Jane hovering over her like a mother hen. "Feeling better darlin'" she asked the young woman in the softest of her soft voice. Camille didn't speak, but nodded her head. By now, Sarah Jane had gotten the blood washed off Camille's body and out of her hair, turning the water red in the first bathtub.

"Sarah Jane, will you please drain that tub of its bloody water," said Ma Belle, pointing at the first bathtub.

"Yes ma'am. She be doin' betta miss Belle. She going to be fine I'm thinking."

"Thank you, Sarah Jane."

"Yes'm."

Camille had settled up to her neck in the soothing bath water. She stared straight ahead, not blinking, not noticing anything around her, including Ma Belle's presence.

"Camille," Ma spoke with all of the gentleness within her. The young woman turned her head so slow it was almost imperceptible to see it move. Her dazed eyes took a moment to focus and another moment to recognize the Madame. Ma could see she was still frightened to the point of shock.

"Ma? They're not gonna hurt me anymore are they? They're gone aren't they? They won't hurt me anymore will they? They can't hurt me, can they?"

"They're dead honey . . . no, they won't hurt you anymore."

She turned her head to resume her blank stare, showing no emotion, no sign of relief. "I can't," she whispered.

"You can't what, honey?"

"I can't stay here, can't work here anymore."

"Of course you can't, I understand, but we're closed for a while now anyway. Give yourself a few days to get feeling better, then we'll talk, alright sweetie?"

"Alright . . . sure, Ma."

"Did Sarah Jane look at your cut?"

"Yes . . . she put some salve on it. It was only a scratch."

She burst into sobs. "Oh Ma, you should have seen that man's face! It was there, then it wasn't . . . it was . . . splattered all over the wall!" Sobbing now with enough force to make her shoulders shake, the tears running like rivers from her glazed eyes, she covered her face with her hands as if it might black out the grisly scene.

"There, there dear," said Ma Belle, patting Camille's shaking shoulders, "Sarah Jane is right here and she'll take good care of you. I'll be back in a short while, okay?"

"Ma?"

"Yes."

"I need to thank the man who saved me. Is he around?"

"No hon, he left town, he was worried there'd be trouble with the sheriff and he didn't want to get caught up in it."

"I'd like to thank him," said Camille.

"Just get yourself well, that would be thanks enough for him."

Camille remained silent, her dark circled and sunken eyes closed, but she nodded her head in understanding.

Ma stood up from where she had been kneeling by the tub and motioned for Sarah Jane to come over. The big woman ambled over to the tub and taking a soft sponge began washing Camille's back. Her sobbing slowed and her shoulders stopped shaking and only twitched and then relaxed under Sarah Jane's soothing hand.

Ma Belle left the huge three-in-one room wondering just how deep Camille had gone into herself, hoping she wasn't so far gone that she would never come back. She'd seen it happen before and the idea of sweet Camille going there infuriated her. It made her want to kill. The feeling surprised her, but everyone is capable of murder if pushed far enough.

No matter what manner of death the Rider had meted out to those men, it hadn't been close to enough punishment. She wished they'd have had to suffer the ordeal of torture first, maybe even twice, before they were killed.

Nothing like that would ever happen again, not in her house, she vowed to herself.

Chapter Twenty-Two

Henry James left the Longhorn Saloon with the sheriff in tow, crossed the street, and burst through the door of the Oasis Hotel, their faces taut with anxiety.

"Upstairs," Ma Belle said, pointing up at door number five. "That one."

Striding with cautious purpose to the stairway, both men ascended with care. A minute later, they disappeared into the room, closing the door behind them. "Mother of God!" exclaimed Henry James, his voice carrying through the door into the parlor below.

Must be one gory mess, he was nowhere near a religious man, thought Ma Belle. "Where's Lily?" she suddenly asked herself.

"Lily," she called out. "Over here Ma," came a soft reply from out of the shadows by the far wall. Moving through the hushed crowd toward the sound of Lily's voice, she found her seated on a sofa pushed up against the wall. A bottle of Chateaux Le Blanc sat on a low table in front of her. She had a glassful raised to her lips and drained it down in one gulp.

"Mind if I join you dear," Ma asked. Lily scooted to the side of the sofa, allowing the Madame room to sit. Seating herself, Ma Belle grabbed the bottle of whiskey and took a long satisfying pull from it.

"I needed that," said Lily, indicating her empty glass and then setting it down on the table. "I might just continue until I'm good and drunk."

"Me too," replied her companion as she poured Lily's glass full. They both took another long drink. Setting her glass down on the table, Lily asked, "How is Camille?"

"She's retreated deep into herself, to some secret place where she feels safe. It will take time before she emerges . . . if she ever does," Ma answered with sadness heavy in her voice.

"My God," said Lily.

"I know dear . . . it is so very tragic."

"Due to the nature of the business it was inevitable that a tragedy come around at some time, and it finally struck; Camille the random victim," said Lily. She then decided to broach the next subject hoping to make a transition from the pangs of sorrow felt in the heart to the detachment of calculations made in the mind.

"How will this affect business in general?" she asked.

Ma Belle hesitated, moving from her heart to her head. "I'm not sure. A lot of it will depend on what Henry and the sheriff have to say," she answered from far away, the heart to head transition not close to complete.

As if on cue, the two men stepped off the stairway and into the parlor. Standing still, they searched the room.

"Henry! Sheriff! Over here," called Ma Belle, standing and waving her arm. Having their attention caught, the two men moved slowly through the stunned and murmuring crowd toward the waving Madame.

Lily pushed two upholstered parlor chairs up to the low table, then headed down the hallway to the liquor supply room. She returned carrying three glasses and another bottle of Chateaux Le Blanc on a silver tray and set it on the table.

"You gentlemen look as though you could use a drink. Pull up a chair and help yourselves," Lily said and seated herself on the sofa. "I didn't bring anything to eat. There's crackers and jerky I can get if you want," she said, looking first at Henry and then at the sheriff.

"No thanks, Lily," replied Henry, "we don't have much of an appetite right now."

"I figured so," she replied.

Henry threw down a shot, the sheriff did likewise, and they wasted no time refilling their glasses.

"Well . . . ?" queried Ma Belle.

"It's bad," said Sheriff Keller.

"Bad! It's a god-awful, gut wrenching, gory mess. The worst I've ever seen . . . anywhere or anytime," and Henry had been a Texas Ranger for twenty years before he owned the Longhorn saloon for the next ten.

"That bad? Damn," quipped Lily.

"Double that," said Ma Belle as she stood up and then placed a hand on Lily's shoulder. "I'm going to clear the place out, but I'd like you to stay, not to help clean up, but to help me lay some groundwork plans for the immediate future. Will you please?"

"Sure Ma, anything I can do. I'm just glad Vir . . ." she caught herself, "that man was here to rescue Camille."

"It's all right Lily. Sheriff Keller knows it was the Rider's doing," said Henry. The sheriff kept silent, whiskey glass in hand.

Ma excused herself, saying she'd be right back, and moved to the center of the parlor.

"May I have your attention please!" She had it and it was undivided. "This hotel is officially closed until I don't know when, so you gentlemen can call it a night," she said with a wan smile. A few moans and groans and damns came from the crowd, but they understood the situation and no one raised a ruckus.

Michelle stood at the exit door, ready with their coats and hats, as the remaining unserved clientele shuffled toward the door.

"The Longhorn is open gents. You can hear all the gory details over there!" called Henry after them.

Ma turned to the six girls remaining in the parlor. Some were seated, some were standing, and all were downcast. Altogether she kept ten on the payroll, plus Sarah Jane.

"Are we ready to call it a night ladies?" Most nodded, a couple managed to mumble an affirmative answer. "All right, you may retire to your rooms. If you need to change rooms, please let me know and we'll see what we can do. Although Sarah Jane is real busy right now, tending to Camille." They nodded in understanding and headed up the stairs.

"I'll bring a couple of deputies over right away and we'll remove the bodies," said Sheriff Keller who had moved over to stand beside Ma. "The clean-up will have to be done by you folks."

"We can manage," she replied.

"You'll most likely have to toss the rug, the curtains, strip and re-paper the walls on the south and west and replace the window, and that's just for starters. I can get Old Blue, my swamper, to help also," said Henry.

"Sarah Jane can help. She's seen a lot and has a strong stomach," said Ma. "And I'll help too, of course," she added.

"Alright, sounds like we'll have plenty of people," said Henry.

"We'll take care of the bodies, like I said. He got two of them with his knife," the sheriff added.

Ma Belle's stomach churned.

"I know the Rider done the killing," he continued, "and as far as I'm concerned, he done the world a favor, ridding it of them four boys. The Fremont's and the Holter's, as always, brought nothing but trouble. So, if you run across him, tell him for me I ain't a looking for him."

Ma and Lily kept silent but nodded.

"He left enough money with me to cover the cost of clean-up and damages," added Henry. Tipping his hat, the sheriff said, "Be back shortly," and headed for the door.

"Thank you Sheriff Keller . . . for everything," said Ma Belle, calling out before he could shut the door. Stopping, his hand on the doorknob, he gave her a weak but knowing smile. He never made it to the outside.

Sarah Jane burst into the parlor. "Ma! Ma Belle," she was screaming at the top of her lungs.

"Over here," Ma yelled, waving her arm in the hushed air.

"It . . . it's Camille, Ma, I . . . I think she be daid!"

"Let's go see to her," Ma responded as she grabbed Sarah Jane's shoulder, turning her back around the way she had come, and then moved into the hallway with Sarah Jane, Lily Francine, Henry and Sheriff Keller hurrying behind her.

Sarah Jane continued rambling, the panic in her voice rising with each syllable spoken. "I was addin' water to de big vat—I swear I wasn't gone more'n thirty seconds—I look over and Camille had put herse'f under de water. It wasn't more'n a minute, Miss Belle, I swear."

"It's alright, Sarah Jane, it's none of your fault," assured Ma as she sped through the single door on the left side of the hallway.

Sarah Jane had propped Camille's head up on the back rim of the middle tub, tilted back with eyes closed and her face otherworldly serene. A slight bluish tint colored her lips, the same tint touched her cheeks.

Henry pulled her limp right wrist out of the tepid bathwater.

"No pulse!" he shouted and then he bent down and kissed Camille full on the mouth.

The sheriff's stomach churned in sync with Ma Belle's and Lily's. Sarah Jane covered her eyes with her large pudgy hands, sobbing at the grotesque sight. "Oh Lawd, oh Lawd," she moaned.

No one suspected Henry James to be such a man and wondered what else would he, could he, did he do?

Ma Belle's head spun, along with her stomach. Stunned, repulsed, paralyzed, she stood frozen in place.

By reflex, Sheriff Keller drew his pistol and aimed it at the back of Henry's head. His head popping up, Henry turned to see the pistol in his face. He ignored it. Moving so he could stand behind Camille's limp and unmoving body, he hooked his arms under hers and pulled her from the bathtub. He laid her face up on the floor, her nakedness exposed to the world. Then he knelt down and kissed her again. Then he put his hands between her breasts, one over the other and pushed down once, twice, three times. Then, by goddam, he bent over and kissed her on the mouth again!

Sheriff Keller turned his pistol around and raised it over his head, about to club Henry with the butt end of the wooden handled grip.

Camille gasped, and then coughed, making choking sounds. Henry quickly turned her head to the side, then, slipping a hand between her shoulder blades, he tilted her up at a slight angle.

Camille almost choked on a violent cough, and then coughed again, spewing water from her mouth onto the floor. She gasped, took in a deep breath through her mouth, and opened her eyes.

Her bluish tint disappeared.

Working her mouth up and down without any sound, Camille finally spoke to her hushed audience. "Why ain't I dead? I want to be dead," she said like a child awakened from a deep and dreamy sleep.

"We all want you alive sweetie," said Ma Belle, "because you didn't do anything wrong, don't you know that?"

"I was so frightened! You're my best friend and I was afraid I'd lost you!" broke in Lily Francine, placing a gentle hand on Camille's shoulder. Camille smiled, the corners of her mouth turning upward very slightly, but it was a definite smile and it reflected in her eyes.

"Well . . . I'll be a . . ." mused the sheriff, looking down at Henry who still supported the shaken woman.

"How'd you . . . ?

"Little trick I learned in the Rangers, sheriff," grinned Henry in reply.

"Come on, honey, Lily and I will get you upstairs and into bed okay?"

"Okay Ma," she mumbled.

Henry said, "I'll go fetch Doc Malladay, he can see her, then give her something to calm her nerves for a few days."

"I'll go Henry," said the sheriff. "It's right on the way to get my deputies anyhow." He headed for the door leading out of the powder room shaking his head and mumbling, "In all my born days I ain't never seen the like."

"Sarah Jane, will you get some clean linens, some night clothes and a robe for Camille, please?"

"Yes'm," she scurried off and was back in a minute with the items and quickly spread the white cotton robe over the girl. Henry gently hooked her under her arms and helped her to her feet, then Ma Belle, Lily, and Henry helped the still shocked Camille to the open powder room door.

"The Lawd be thanked," muttered Sarah Jane to no one there, well, except maybe the Lawd.

CHAPTER TWENTY-THREE

Three days after the slaughter in room five of the Oasis Hotel, Henry James stood behind the bar, looking out the window of the Longhorn Saloon. The day presented itself just this side of stunning in its beauty, not unusual for Abilene. A deep blue cloudless sky with the temperature just above freezing, was unfolding as one of those days that seems to invigorate everything living under its canopy and helps ease some people's problems, from small to large.

Mid-afternoon, the only patrons, more like fixtures, sat by the stove playing a game of checkers that went up into the thousands if they'd been counted. Never any trouble, they kept their tabs current and at times could even be helpful, like now.

"Sam, Clem, could you guys keep an eye on the bar for a minute or two?"

"Shore Henry, be glad to," replied Clem while Sam rubbed his whiskers, trying to figure out his next move.

Removing his apron, Henry hung it on a peg and stepped around the bar onto the main floor. Taking his overcoat off the wall hook by the door, he slung it on as he pulled open the door and then closed it behind him.

The stagecoach, painted bright red and pulled by a matched set of four bays, showed the professionalism of Wells Fargo. The company was moving up in the world as the world increased its pace to who knew where and for what unknown reason.

The teamster and his shotgun rider were unloading baggage in front of the Oasis Hotel. Henry stepped up on the porch as Camille and Lily Francine came out of the of the hotel door. Camille looked thin and lifeless, her face pale and expressionless under her wide brimmed hat. It was clear Lily was taking care of the girl and they were dressed for travel in broad hats, heavy dungarees, flannel blouses and heavy canvas overcoats. It was also clear they were going on a long trip.

"Afternoon ladies," said Henry, touching the brim of his derby hat with his right forefinger.

"Henry, I'm glad you remembered to stop by," chirped Lily.

"Yes, Henry, thank you," mimicked Camille, her voice near to inaudible. She hadn't begun to overcome the ordeal those four cowboys had put her through.

"I never would have quit kicking myself if I had forgot," said Henry.

In a way he felt responsible for what had happened, the Oasis was his business, so he financed their trip and provided enough money for them to live on for quite some time. Part of it was to assuage his conscience, yes, but he also cared for his girls and his care for them outweighed the pangs of guilt in his conscience.

Camille couldn't take care of herself and Lily volunteered to take her under her wing. Everyone agreed the first step was getting out of Abilene.

Ma Belle stepped out the door of the hotel. "Have you girls remembered everything?"

"Yes ma," answered Camille. Lily smiled like a mother would at her child starting to grow up. Ma hugged Camille long and tight. "I wish you the best my dear one," she said. "You two will always be welcome here, you know that don't you?" Camille gave a slight nod. Lily shot Ma a puzzled glance. "Oh no, not as working girls, but if either of you should need a place to stay, or a good meal, my door is always open."

"Thanks ma, I'll remember that," said Camille, her voice soft like a birds.

Turning to Lily, Ma gave her a motherly hug. "Thank you dear for everything you've done and everything you're going to do. I wish you the very, very best and have no doubt you'll succeed in whatever you do. Are you all set?"

"Yes Ma, and thank you." She turned to Henry. "Any word on Virgil Jones?"

"Not word one Lily. It's as if he disappeared off the face of the earth."

She dropped her eyes, the heaviness on her heart evident for all to see.

"Don't worry Lil, if he does come through, I'll let him know you've gone to . . . ?"

"St. Louis, Henry, then on to Philadelphia. We're going to become proper ladies . . . no offense Ma."

"None taken dear. Some just aren't cut out for this kind of work."

"Anyway Henry," continued Lily, "you can tell him if you see him, but I doubt Virgil would follow me to a big city. Even Abilene is getting too tame for that man."

"It's getting that way for me too," replied Henry. "But if I do see him I'll be sure to tell him. I know he'll ask about you if he does come back around."

Lily put up a smiling brave front, but deep down she felt she would never see the Rider again, causing a constant dull ache to take root.

"Oh, wait my dears," said Ma Belle as she pulled a bottle of Chateaux Le Blanc from under her shawl and handed it to Lily.

"It might get a little chilly on the way to St. Louis. You can get more there if you've a mind to."

Lily put the bottle into the bag she held.

"Aboard!" hollered the driver, as he climbed up and seated himself on the buckboard. After brief kisses on each other's cheeks, Lily and Camille said good-bye to Ma Belle and settled into the coach.

"Giddap!" hollered the teamster, slapping the reins down on the backs of the four bays. The stage lurched forward, then smoothed out on its journey east.

And they say whores have hearts as cold as ice, thought Henry as he watched a single tear trickle down Ma Belle's cheek.

Chapter Twenty-Four

"The passing back and forth across The Other seems a matter of hit and miss," said the Rider across the table from Casey Mojo. "I have not yet figured it out meself, sir Virgil, other than it is rather whimsical."

"I think there must be a key, some common thread of circumstance . . ." added Pistol Ann from the other side of the table.

"Maybe it's the type of problem that's best to sleep on. Let it stew and simmer around for a while," suggested the Rider.

"You're right sir Virgil. I'll take my leave then, if you don't mind."

"No, not at all Casey, and thank you . . . again."

Saying goodnight to Pistol Ann the hunchback stood up and glided over to the doorway, without a hitch in his gait, he then went through and closed it behind him without making a sound.

"Did you notice that?" he asked Pistol Ann.

"Notice what?"

"Casey . . . he just floated on out of here, like he was walking on air!"

"I saw him," she replied, the tone of her voice flat and factual.

"Whew . . . thought I was seeing things. But, what the hell, this is Right Here and Now after all, where strange happenings become normal occurrences."

"Normal is what a person is used to," replied Pistol Ann, the always mysterious amusement alight in her eyes.

Pedro ambled over with a fresh bottle. Setting it down in the center of the table he said, "She did it to him."

"What in the hell are you talking about Pedro?" asked the Rider.

"The bruja witch, she made Casey Mojo into the hunchback that he is."

"When did this happen?"

"Long ago, before you were born, senor."

He gave Pistol Ann a quizzical look. She shrugged her shoulders as if to say, "Time has no meaning here."

Turning to Pedro, he asked, "Why did she do that?" accepting the strange as normal.

"He is a sorcerer senor, and got in her way, trying to stop the evil she was doing. They had a long battle that he finally lost. But I don't theen he lost the war!" He winked at Pistol Ann.

"If you say so Pedro," said the Rider.

"Si, senor, I do. Can I bring you anything else senor . . . senorita?"

"No thanks Pedro, I think this will be all," answered Pistol Ann.

"Wait, Pedro! Do you have any rooms left to rent for the night?"

"Si, senor."

"UM-m-m-m, I don't think that will be necessary. Thank you, Pedro," said Pistol Ann, placing her hand softly on the Rider's forearm.

"Si, senorita," he said, ambling off, a lopsided grin on his comical face.

The Rider turned to Pistol Ann. "What's this all about?"

"I have a room already. You can stay with me if you like."

He swallowed a good gulp of his drink as he stared into her hard-to-fathom deep eyes, which spoke of serious intent. The whiskey didn't calm the butterflies in his stomach.

Butterflies? This army captain and war hero, this slayer of men, this roving executioner . . . nervous? Pistol Ann was getting to places inside of him he swore no one would ever get to again . . . especially that one place in his heart where he had enshrined Janice Louise in a tomb of his own making.

"Free for the asking," she reminded him.

In her eyes he now saw the familiar amusement, but not the type that preceded a friendly game. He saw a deep sincerity, an open invitation, a promise beyond daybreak.

Managing to get his tongue untied and in spite of the butterflies he blurted out, "May I share your room with you this night, Pistol Ann?""

"Why certainly, Mr. Virgil Jones Rider, and please call me Ann," she added, close to bursting out in laughter at this suddenly shy man, but she restrained, knowing the reason for his hesitancy.

Share your room weren't exactly the words she wanted to hear, but close enough. Oh well, he's swallowed some of his pride and had opened up just a little, and that was a step in the right direction.

Holding out her hand, Pistol Ann smiled, lighting up her face, and the rest of the room.

The Rider didn't notice the room, only her, his own smile traveling to his eyes, then downward toward his heart for the first time since he'd heard the news during the Goddam War that his wife and son had been slaughtered.

Her shack was spooky. Old, rundown, weather beaten, the tiny clapboard structure was beyond repair. It needed burning to the ground. Sitting at the western edge of town, smoke billowed from its chimney but only cleared the top opening before the north wind curled it eastward, taking the rancid cloud down the middle of Main Street.

Inside, Mesmerala burned from the fire of the rage inside of her. Hate and rage were easy for the witch to feel, since they were the only emotions she had or that ever emerged out of her black heart. She hated that little bitch Pistol Ann.

She possessed patience, usually thought of as virtue, but her's was predatory, silent as it stalked its prey. She covered The Orb—a crystal sphere passed down from eternity and destined to continue to forever—with a specially anointed Black Sabbath velvet cloth. Then she lifted it from the table and returned it to its cradle on the mantle above the fireplace.

Mesmerala hated love, for against it she had no power. But she knew the Rider's heart, and although not completely black it was full of anger and anger's brother bitterness, and with a little work she could turn it to complete blackness, like her own.

She hungered for the man, wanting to feel his warm flesh and to feed the fire of his passion and then quench it with her own. She wanted to harness his raging anger and use it for her own purposes.

Oh yes, Mesmerala hated Pistol Ann, for she was getting to the Rider's heart. She knew, The Orb had shown her, and she could not allow it to happen.

Returning to her cushioned stool, she resettled herself at the low wooden table. Reaching down with her right hand, she patted the black wolf lying at her feet, and then scratched him behind the ears.

"Come see Mama, my pet," she cooed. He stood up and then braced himself against her thin but powerful body. Reaching into a leather pouch lying on the table, she pulled out a small handful of dust made from dried butterfly and bat's wings and sprinkled it along the wolf's back. She slowly worked it into his hide all the while whispering in the Blood Spiller's ear, causing saliva to drool from his massive jaws.

Giggling like young lovers, Pistol Ann and the Rider walked arm in arm up the stairway, the Winchester in her free hand, the bottle of Chateaux Le Blanc in his. Arriving at the top landing they proceeded straight ahead down the dim hallway to the last door on the right. Unhooking her arm and then taking a key from out of her shirt pocket, she unlocked the door and swung it open. The cream colored walls were accented by a surround of pine wainscoting. A huge four poster canopy bed, centered at the far wall, with a wine colored rug on either side, appeared to float an inch or two above the wooden floor.

The bed and both pillows were encased in red satin. On each side of the luxuriant bed set an intricately carved nightstand. On the top of each one sat an oil lamp, a porcelain pitcher of water and a washbasin both painted with a swirling of roses. The lamp on the right side of the bed was lit, its light shimmering along the red satin covering. A frieze of wallpaper surrounded the room where the wall met the ceiling, with roses of the same color and pattern as the pitcher and washbasin painted on it.

Wooden pegs extended out from the back of the closed door with a coat rack of carved teakwood on its left. To the right of the door were two embroidered arm chairs angled toward each other with a small low teakwood table between them.

"The honeymoon suite," said Pistol Ann grinning up at the Rider.

"Honeymoon, now wait a minute," he protested, holding up his hand with the palm out.

"Easy Mr. Virgil Jones Rider, I never planned this night. I only wanted to enjoy a little luxury. That doesn't hurt anything once in a while, does it?"

"No, of course not," he said glancing around the room, noticing the absence of a brass spittoon.

"Then take your boots off and stay a while." She paused to look at him with her mysterious deep eyes that seemed to hold some secret knowledge of him or of the future, and they were enchanting. She smiled a seductive smile. "I'm taking off mine," she added. Seating herself like a wraith of mist in one of the parlor chairs, she bent down and began removing her boots.

He sat in the other chair and watched her for a while, then tugged and pulled and grunted as he struggled with his own tight fitting footwear.

She watched him with unmasked amusement.

"Think you could give me a hand here?" he asked, his face flushed red.

"Sure."

She removed her gun belt and hung it over the back of the chair. Straddling his right leg with her back to him, she pulled outward as he pulled his leg inward toward himself. The boot was stubborn and didn't move. She strained harder, leaning forward more. The boot suddenly pulled loose and she pitched ahead from the unbridled momentum. He reached out and caught her belt, stopping her from sprawling headlong onto the floor. She turned around, flashed him a smile and asked, "Did you like the view?" her eyes twinkling like those of a mischievous imp.

He grinned . . . big.

The other boot came off much easier.

"I've never seen this much rug in one room," he idly remarked.

"Take a walk on it. It's so-o-o soft." Accepting her invitation, he stood up and strolled over to the left side of the bed, shuffling his feet across the thick rug as he went. Taking off his gun belt, he laid it on the nightstand, the butt of the big bore Colt within easy reach, a force of habit.

Pistol Ann grabbed her gun belt from off the chair, and massaging her feet on the rug as she walked, laid it on the nightstand by her side of the bed, as a precaution. Moving languorously back to the parlor chair, she poured the glasses set on the table between them full of Chateaux Le Blanc, her Winchester leaning securely against the wall on the other side of the night stand by the bed.

The Rider pulled back the red lace curtain and gazed out the room's single window at the contrast of the white snow against the black night. The four cadavers were where he'd last seen them, propped up against the shed at the far end of the back of the saloon. The heads of the two outlaws were snow-covered lumps atop the snow bank.

Strolling from the window to the unoccupied parlor chair, he sat down and took the drink Pistol Ann offered. She raised her glass, he his. "A toast," she said.

"To what?"

"How about to us?"

"Yes, to us," he replied.

Clinking the crystal glasses together, they drank to each other with the whiskey, and drank of each other with their eyes, each one's longing reflected by the other one's promise.

"Do you like me Virgil?" she asked.

"Of course I like you. What kind of a ques . . ."

"I don't mean just as a woman who can give you pleasure, someone you'd lay money down for, but, do you like . . . me?"

"I could spend hours with you Ann and not once think about that bed."

"I like you too Virgil Jones Rider," she said, setting her glass down on the low table. Then, like an ethereal nymph, she was sitting on his lap, her arms wrapped around his neck, gazing into his gun metal gray eyes, eyes she could see were softening.

"I want to kiss you," he said.

Her lips parted as she turned her face up to his. He wrapped his arms around her waist and bent down, his mouth meeting hers.

Ah-h-h, the sweetness! He had forgotten how rapturous a kiss could be, how much could be said and felt without speaking a word. And he was amazed how she was making him forget everything but her, and it was her world he wanted more than anything right now. He was being carried away and he didn't mind, although he wasn't sure of all he was feeling, he was sure it was a cresting passion, but different. It didn't start in his loins and spread outward from there, but had started somewhere within his chest and had spread out and down to the butterflies in his belly, stopped momentarily by their fluttering, and descended from there. He let her carry him in this pleasant unfamiliar way because she had given him what no other woman had since the Goddam War, a sense of trust. Breaking apart from the sweet, sweet kiss, they held each other tight, heart to heart, ready to savor the rest of the night.

A strange scratching, click-clacking noise pulled their attention away from each other and toward the sound, their puzzled looks mirroring each other. It came again, soft.

"Do you hear that sound over by the window?" he asked.

She cocked her head in that direction.

Click. Clack. Scratch. Scrape.

"Probably the storm kicking up, tossing ice pellets around in the wind," she said.

"I'd think so too except for the scraping sound. I'm going to have a look."

She reluctantly got off his lap, allowing him to stand, then sat back down, watching the big man move with the smoothness of a cat over to the room's only window and pull the red lace curtain aside.

The Blood Spiller crashed through the window before the Rider could twitch a muscle or yell out a warning to Pistol Ann. The beast's forepaws hit him in the chest, sending him sprawling backwards, falling amidst spears of glass and splinters of wood from the window. He landed on his back with a loud grunt. The big wolf stood on the man's chest, red eyes glowering, ears flattened, lips peeled back in a hideous snarl, saliva flowing from its massive jaws and dripping on the Rider's chest.

Frozen in place by the sudden and explosive violence of the scene, Pistol Ann couldn't scream, couldn't move, and couldn't get to her guns.

Still snarling and snapping, the big lobo leapt off the Rider's chest and on to the bed, its red eyes glowing with the light of darkness. The beast lifted its hind leg and shot a stream of vile, rancid smelling piss all over the red satin spread.

Finished, the Blood Spiller lifted his dripping muzzle high in the air and howled with the fury of a thousand damned souls without hope of salvation.

It curdled the blood.

The Black Devil then turned and flew out the window by which he'd come in.

The Rider struggled up off the floor, staggered over to the window and stuck his head out. No wind, the swirling snow had abated, leaving only stillness and silence. He could see no prints, no marks of any kind on the fresh fallen snow below. Off in the western darkness, toward the livery stable, an otherworldly howl befouled the stillness of the night.

"Gabriel!" He shouted.

He spun, grabbed his gun belt off the nightstand, buckled it on, slipped the big Colt out and then eased it back into its holster. Not able to sit on the piss soaked bed, in two long strides he made it to the parlor chair next to Ann, where only seconds ago held the promise of immense delight, but now held the Rider's panic as he pulled on his boots.

"I'm going with you," said Pistol Ann, who had freed herself from the initial shock and was now pulling on her own boots, grabbing her Winchester when done.

No point trying to argue and no time to do it, he thought.

Pedro burst through the door, double barreled sawed off shotgun at the ready in spite of the fear etched across his face.

"The Black Devil, better strip the bed right away," said the Rider. Pedro sniffed, wrinkled his nose, and said, "Si senor."

"The bruja bitch sent him," added Pistol Ann.

Pedro crossed himself like Catholics do Over There, only he started at his stomach instead of his forehead and ended at his left shoulder instead of his right.

Pistol Ann and the Rider bolted out the door, down the dim hallway, and then down the stairs, taking them two at a time. Reaching the coat rack first, he grabbed her white buffalo robe coat, tossed it to her, and then slung his own over his shoulders. She levered a shell into the chamber of her Winchester as they went out the door, forgetting to close it behind them.

Reaching the frozen street they walked down the middle of it, hoping to see the Black Wolf, wanting in the worst way to kill the beast for its intrusion on what may have been the best night of both their lives. But they saw nothing, no tracks, no movement in the corner of the eye, no sound of something swishing through the snow. They stopped at the stables, no sound of commotion within. Virgil knocked on the man door.

"Come in please." Casey stood like a sentinel by the fire pit, the sawed off shotgun cradled in his arm. Gabriel and ReeBa whinnied, but were unharmed.

"El Diablo Negro," said Casey, "did he pay you a visit?"

"Quite an unusual visit," said Ann.

"He wasn't out for blood, he just pissed all over our bed, making it unfit to use," said the Rider.

"Ah, Mesmerala, she hates love. She has no power over it, you see," said Casey. "The big wolf stopped at the door and howled just to stir us up. I guess you heard the unholy wailing that comes out of that beast?"

"We did and so headed this way to make sure everything was alright. I tell you Casey, I've never wanted to kill anything so bad as I do that wolf," said the Rider.

"Well, we needn't worry for the rest of this night, the witch accomplished her purpose."

"How can you know that?" asked Pistol Ann.

"The wolf could have killed at least one and maybe both of you, is that not so?"

Ann nodded her head. "Yes, he had Virgil pinned and defenseless on the floor and for a moment I was frozen in shock."

"He just wanted to, as instructed by Mesmerala, ruin your night. Motive? Who knows what goes on in the black heart of that witch," said Casey.

"One more thing, we saw no tracks, no sign of anything moving or that had moved in the snow. Plus we were on the second floor of the hotel," said Virgil.

"The witch, she can empower the wolf to fly for a short time and for short distances."

"Great, now we gotta watch the sky and the rooftops for that Black Sonofabitch," said Pistol Ann.

Chapter Twenty-Five

Mesmerala put the The Orb to rest after watching the Blood Spiller piss on the bed. Love thwarted, nothing was more satisfying to her black and soulless heart. Well, maybe taking the Rider from Pistol Ann would come close. Why she wanted Virgil Jones was clear enough to her, it was pure lust, but this particular lust burned and could only be put out one way. And what did it matter what consequences may bring? She walked on the Shadowside, and there wouldn't be any, at least not for her.

She reached down and patted the head of the big lobo resting easy at her feet. "Good pet," she said in her most soothing voice. "You did very well tonight. Would you like a reward?" He rumbled, a low growl coming from deep within his cavernous chest. She cackled, reached into the sleeve of her black robe and pulled out an alive and kicking snow white rabbit, holding it by the ears, dangling it over the upturned and salivating jaws of the wolf.

"You like?" she asked.

He growled again but with more urgency, almost a whine.

"Take it!" she commanded.

Snapping his massive jaws, he crunched the rabbit in half, and in two gulps made it disappear . . . just like magic.

"Good pet," said the witch, scratching him behind the ears. Lying back down at her feet he closed his blood red eyes in contentment and fell asleep.

Mesmerala floated up and over to the fireplace mantle, removed The Orb, drifted back to hover over her stool and then settled onto it. Setting The Orb on the table in front of her, she removed its black silk cover, then pressed her left hand to her left eye and then touched the glass with her left hand. After doing the same thing with her right eye and right hand, she uttered one word, "See." The interior of the crystal ball cleared like mist blown away by a sea breeze to reveal . . . nothing.

"By the Blackest Night," she screeched, "they're with that cretin Casey Mojo!"

* * *

"I've been considering the problem of passing through The Other," said Casey Mojo.

"And?" queried the Rider.

"And . . . nothing new, except . . . say it Gabriel."

"You were drunk right out of Abilene and stayed that way for the whole trip old boss," replied the horse.

"I remember . . . I'd gotten a bottle of Chateaux Le Blanc from Ma Belle. Damn good stuff!"

"Ma Belle?" interjected Pistol Ann.

"I'll tell you later. Anyway, it's imported all the ways from France . . . wait a minute," he turned to Casey, "you were in France!"

"Keep going," urged the Wise Won.

"And on your return trip, from Paris back to Witchita, you mentioned you were drinking . . . Chateaux Le Blanc!" Saying this, the Rider's face went devoid of color, his eyes widened, and his mouth dropped open.

"But," he exclaimed, "the Hunchback of Notre Dame was written half a century ago! You don't look anywhere near old enough to have . . ."

"Remember, Mr. Virgil Jones Rider, time has no meaning here, it is the land of possibilities, and dreams, and magic, remember?" said Pistol Ann.

"Exactly," intoned Casey Mojo, "but apparently Chateaux Le Blanc has been around a long time, in linear terms, and it may very well provide a key to unlocking our puzzle."

"Maybe, but I don't think a single bottle of the stuff can be found in Witchita," said the Rider.

* * *

Hunched over The Orb, the bruja witch watched the Rider and Pistol Ann leave the livery stable and head up the street to the Burnt Dog Saloon.

Pistol Ann carried her Winchester loose in her left hand, pausing often to glance back down the darkened artery running through the middle of town. The Rider constantly scanned the boardwalks and the shadows underneath the overhanging roofs, not forgetting to peer up into the sky now and then; the big lobo had come from there once, no reason he couldn't do it again.

Entering the saloon without incident, they hung their buffalo robe overcoats on the wall pegs and seated themselves at what was becoming their own familiar table. Pedro ambled over and set a bottle on the table. "Ees on thee house, senor e' senorita," he said.

"Why, thank you Pedro," said Ann.

"A-I-EEE . . . that Black Devil, he roon that whole bed weeth hees piss, I'm afraid thee room ees unusable tonight, senorita."

"I'll get another, in a while Pedro."

"Si senorita," he said and returned to his comfort zone behind the bar.

"I've been thinking, Pistol Ann . . ." said the Rider.

"Don't tell me . . . we need separate rooms and a night apart, lest we draw the Black Devil once again," she replied.

She amazed him with her insight, her beauty, and her lithe and alluring body.

"Yes," he replied like a reflexive response. "How did you know?"

"Just a guess. I was thinking along the same lines that, only for tonight, it would be a good idea to stay separated. I'm weary and don't think I could handle another go-around with the witchbitch or her pet."

"Nor could I," the Rider replied, his tiredness evidenced by the low volume of his voice.

Finishing their drinks, Pistol Ann picked up her Winchester, the Rider the bottle, their weariness showing as they walked up to the bar. Setting the bottle on the bar the Rider said, "Keep this for us til morning, will you Pedro?"

"Si, senor."

"And we each need a room," he added.

Pedro leaned down, reached under the bar top, pulled out two keys and flipped them on the bar, rooms four and five, right across the hall from each other. He had room four, she, room five.

"Thanks amigo," said the Rider as he and Ann scooped up their keys, walked over to and up the stairs. Stopping in front of her door, she turned to him. "Virgil . . . will you kiss me goodnight?" He had his arms around her and pulled her to him as his heart skipped a beat. His mouth found hers. They kissed long and longingly and deep. She pulled away, breathless.

"Good night my love," she whispered. He stepped back, stunned by her words. "Uh . . . good night Ann . . . sweet dreams," he stammered. She smiled with the sweetness of the sun as it opened the morning rose, then stepped inside her room and disappeared within.

The Rider stood staring at the closed door before him, not sure what to think. He wasn't quite ready to let anyone in. Not just yet, but close, too damn close for comfort. And yet . . .

Virgil Jones trembled in the knees as he closed the door to his room. Trembling! Knees weak! Head spinning! What was this woman doing to him? Up against blazing guns or flashing knives did not make him feel this way. The entire Goddam War had not made him feel this way! Rage only served to make him feel powerful. But this . . . this was something he hadn't felt since . . . Janice Louise. He had to admit it. But he had enshrined her in his heart and left no room to love another. Or was it that he would not allow himself to love another? Unsure of himself, not ready to let loose the reins of his heart or lose the comfort of his familiar anger zone, he entered his room, slumped into the chair and began pulling off his boots.

But I am desperate for her. That much he admitted to himself and deep inside knew it was for more than a night or two.

Weariness catching up to him, he undressed, turned down the covers, blew out the lamp on the nightstand and eased himself into bed. As soon as his head settled into the softness of the pillow, he was asleep and deep into a dream only he knew.

Chapter Twenty-Six

"Good night my love, gawd, I think I might vomit!" spat the bruja witch as she watched the parting of Virgil and Ann in the hallway. "Separate rooms, eh?" she quipped. "Now that opens an unexpected door."

She stood up with a flourish, causing her black robe to swirl around her, and the fire to cast a macabre shadow dancing on the wall of the dingy shack. Floating over to a covered object, about her width and height, in the dimmest corner of her abode, she stopped, suspended in front of it. She reached out and with a flick of her wrist flung the black silken cover aside, its fluttering shadow joining hers in the macabre wall dance choreographed by the firelight, until it collapsed on the floor, a shapeless heap.

Framed by ancient rosewood upon which were carved the alternating masks of tragedy and comedy, was a full length reflecting glass.

"The joke's on you Virgil Jones," she muttered as she squared her shoulders and, peering intently into the mirror incanted:

Looking glass standing free,
Change the image that is me,
Into the woman Janice Louise.
Looking glass, if you please.

The bruja witch, though free of warts on her face, or an elongated hook for a nose, or hairs on her chin, was neither young nor beautiful. She marveled as she watched the transformation of herself into the image of a young woman with beautiful luminous brown eyes, arching eyebrows—the left slightly higher than the right—a somewhat long nose with naturally flared nostrils centered over a ruby red mouth, a lithe and supple frame robed in a rose red silken gown, elegant and flowing, with tantalizing breasts accentuated by the upper thrust of the gown. She watched as her hair morphed into dark brunette and then turn into tight curls framing a strong compassionate face with a complexion like pearl.

After admiring her reflection a moment longer, she returned to her stool in front of The Orb. "See," she said after touching her eyes in the left to right order and then touching The Orb in the same manner.

Too late, the Rider was already in bed and asleep. She had hoped to see him strip down before getting underneath the covers. Oh well, soon, she thought. Staring unblinking into The Orb she whispered, "I will seem a dream." After covering it with its silk cloth, she stood and floated over to the looking glass shroud, picked it up off the floor, glided over to the mirror and draped the black cloth over it. Moving from there over to the fireplace on the opposite wall, she placed her hands over the flames into the smoke just beyond the burning zone and said one word, "Smoke." She became the word she had spoken and drifted under the door of the decrepit old shack on the western edge of Witchita. She drifted eastward, a formless black mist, caressing the roof tops along the street as she moved. Not the slightest of breezes was blowing. Pausing over the livery stable, sensing Casey Mojo's presence, she then continued her sinister journey. She did not wish a confrontation with the Wise Won.

Inside the stable, ReeBa nickered softly.

"Yes, I know, she is on the prowl. I don't know why, she already had her fun with the Black Wolf ruining Virgil and Ann's night. I cannot waste time hunting her down but will be on the alert," said Casey Mojo.

He could have intercepted her if he had wanted to, causing her to turn back from her intentions. But sometimes it is better to let your charges fight their own battles and learn their own lessons, for experience roots itself more deeply into a person's being than does instruction or intervention, so had learned the Wise Won.

He would have liked to rest, maybe even sleep, but tonight, knowing Mesmerala was on the prowl, he would forego the pleasure.

She seeped through the cracks around the second story room's single window, and after making sure he was fast asleep, she hovered at the foot of his bed. There, she materialized from black mist to the woman of the Rider's heart . . . Janice Louise.

"Sleep deep my sweet," she whispered, ensuring he would not awake until she wished him to. Passing her hand over his eyes she whispered the word, "Awake." Then, passing her hand over his eyes again, they opened. To her he would seem as if he were awake. To him she would be but a dream in the surreal world known as Dreamwake.

He looked at her with amazement and wonder. "Janice Louise," he whispered with what little breath he had after most of it had been taken away at the sight of her.

"I am here with you my darling," she whispered back, a false but convincing light in her eyes, her fingers fast at work untying the laces of her gown. That done, she let the garment slip down around her, and left it lying on the floor as she stepped clear of it.

"Let me look at you," he said as she stood at the foot of his bed; black mesh stockings, black garters, and a low cut black brassiere completed her attire.

"Let me look at you," she returned as she grasped the top of the covers and pulled them off of him, revealing his lean sinewy naked body. She shivered as her lust burned. "Help me out of these, will you darling?"

He stood up out of the bed while she turned her back toward him. He unlatched the hooks of her brassiere. She let it fall, then turned to face him. He put both hands on her shoulders and sat her on the bed. Kneeling before her, he undid the mesh stockings from the garter belt, peeling them off her creamy legs one by one. Unhooking the garter belt, he flung it aside. She wore no panties. Taking her hands in his, they stood, they kissed, the way they do Over There, in France. It was sweet, but not as sweet as . . . he wasn't allowed to finish the thought. The woman turned and pushed him onto the bed, then straddled him and eased herself down on his manifest manhood.

Did her eyes flash blood red? He was in no position to puzzle that out, he could only move with the ecstasy of it all. Janice Louise . . . it had been so long and she was so dreamlike.

CHAPTER TWENTY-SEVEN

The Rider awoke and reached to his left, expecting to find the soft warmth of Janice Louise. But she wasn't there, the bed was empty. "It must've been a dream. Had to be," he whispered to himself. Looking around the moonlit room, he couldn't discern anything unusual.

Getting out of bed and lighting the oil lamp, he again took in the room, still nothing, no evidence that it hadn't been anything other than a dream. "Only a dream," he muttered.

A knock came upon the door.

"Who is it?" he called.

"Pistol Ann."

"Ann, I just got up, give me a chance to get my clothes on."

"Well . . . if you insist," she giggled.

Hustling around, he found his shirt and pants, pulled them on, and, minus his boots, opened the door. It was indeed Pistol Ann, alive and in the flesh, and she was vibrant. This was no dream. Her hair shone copper in the dim light of the hallway. Her eyes, accepting and kind, accentuated her easy manner. Her smile, not a ploy, came from deep within her.

"Well . . ." she said.

"Oh, come in, please."

"Sleep well?" she asked, seating herself in one of the chairs. He plopped down in the other one and began pulling on his boots.

"Sleep well?" she asked again.

"Yes, sort of."

She watched with amusement as he struggled with his boots.

"Dream?"

"Yes."

"Sweet?"

"Yes."

"Of who?"

He finished pulling on the second boot, and then looked up at Pistol Ann. Her amusement evident, he hoped what he said wouldn't take away her smile.

"Janice Louise."

"You sure?"

"Of course."

"Did you enjoy it?"

"Immensely."

Her smile didn't fly away, it brightened.

"Good, I'm glad for you," she said, and then, "I wonder what the bruja witch was up to last night?"

"Why would you wonder that?"

Pistol Ann wriggled in her chair, reached under her thigh, and pulled out a piece of black fabricated cloth. Holding it up to let it dangle, she asked, "What's this?"

"A garter belt!" he exclaimed.

"So it is Mr. Virgil Jones Rider, and it sure ain't mine," she said and flipped it at him. He caught it in midair, and then turned it over and over, examining it as if it were some artifact having monetary value.

"It's only a garter belt," said Pistol Ann.

"But how, it was a dream, that's all."

Her laughter at his remark was filled with mirth. The woman was guileless. "I think you've been seduced, Mr. Jones, and not by Janice Louise."

"It was only a dream, I think," he replied.

"To you probably, but to her it was real . . . you know . . . in the flesh," she laughed again, her eyes dancing with merriment.

"Join me for breakfast?" she asked.

"It's not even daybreak."

"It won't be either until the night is done with its work. Come on, let's go eat." She offered him her hand. He took it and they stood up together.

"Ann, if I'd known, I would have never touched her."

"Sure you would have. You're a man aren't you?"

He didn't know if that was a compliment, an insult, or just a plain statement of fact.

"Come on, Virgil Jones, I'm starving," she chirped and brushed his cheek with a light kiss.

"You're not upset?"

"No. Why should I be? You really had no choice in the matter, did you?"

"I guess I didn't."

"The old bruja bitch," she said, laughing.

He couldn't explain the deep sense of relief he felt because she understood and wasn't the least bit upset. He did know he cared what she thought and felt about him. He couldn't help it, and that's what scared him, that and the fact that the bruja witch had morphed into Janice Louise, seduced him, and he didn't regret it.

* * *

Pedro brought a plate of sizzling Huevos Rancheros and two plates to their table.

"Thank you, Pedro," said Pistol Ann.

"Maybe it's morning, maybe it's not, but I'd like a drink regardless. Pedro, bring us that bottle we left with you earlier, and a couple of glasses, sil vous plait," said the Rider.

"Oui monsieur," replied Pedro as he ambled away, his lopsided grin plastered across his face.

Back at the livery stable, Casey Mojo stood looking out the man door. The wind and the snow it swirled were both at rest. He'd felt no threat to himself from the presence of the bruja witch as she had passed over. The Rider would have to deal with whatever she had in store for him. He turned, closed the man door and took a seat by the fire pit. Gazing blankly into the glowing red coals, he reached for answers to the mystery of The Other. Whatever it was, or whatever it was made of didn't matter. How one managed to cross it did. And that was the essence of the puzzle, back and forth, back and forth, and back again. How?

Two riders lost in a storm, with their only solace coming from a bottle, a storm coupled with a bottle seemed vital to finding the answer. He had a sudden notion, vague, but maybe valid.

"Gabriel, are you ready for some exercise?"

"More than ready," replied the big buckskin, stamping his hooves on the plank flooring of the stall.

With his energy flowing strong, Casey scuttled over to the man door. Yanking it open, he stuck his head out and peered down the street to his left and saw a light glowing through the small window of Mesmerala's shack.

She was home, good.

Exiting the stable, he walked one block west, in the direction of the witch's shack, and then turned north up an intersecting street to get a clear view of the horizon. The seam of white hovering just above it portended another storm. Again, that was good. Although the wind remained dead calm the chill found its way to him despite the heavy woolen cloak he had draped over his shoulders. Returning to the comfort of the livery stable he hurried over to Gabriel's stall, opening the gate for the big buckskin. Gabriel stepped out as Casey pulled the horse's tack from a bin against the stall wall. He tossed the saddle blanket and then the saddle on the horse's back and finishing cinching the saddle, he asked him, "ready?"

"For what?"

"I'm taking you up to the saloon. You and Virgil are going for a ride, what do you say about that?"

"Will you put my bridle on and slip the bit in my mouth so it won't be frozen later?"

Casey laughed. A thinking horse, he liked that.

Honoring the horse's request, he took the reins and led him out the double doors into the motionless heavy air and onto the frozen street. Turning east, they headed toward the saloon.

Upon arriving, he wrapped the reins loosely around the hitching rail that fronted the Burnt Dog.

Opening the door to the warm interior, he was greeted by the warmth of Pistol Ann's voice. "Casey Mojo, come join us for breakfast!"

Pedro was on the way to their table carrying a clean plate, forks and knives.

Pulling up a chair, the hunchback helped himself to the still heaping platter of hot food. "Another glass also," he hollered at Pedro's receding back. Without turning, Pedro lifted his hand in acknowledgment.

"Sir Virgil, I have Gabriel saddled and ready to mount right outside the door," said Casey between mouthfuls of food.

"Why?"

"Yes why?" echoed Pistol Ann, giving him a piercing and quizzical look.

Pedro set the requested glass on the table, Casey poured himself a drink.

"Another storm is coming in. It's brewing on the northern horizon at this very moment."

"So . . . ? said the Rider.

"I think if you retraced your ride here, without getting caught in the storm itself . . . you may return to Over There! That's how it happened to me at any rate."

The Rider took a slow drink from his glass, then pushed away his empty plate.

"I'm not so sure I want to go back," he stated.

"What?" asked an incredulous Casey Mojo.

"Lately I've been asking myself just what is waiting for me Over There? More killing and that is all."

He looked at Pistol Ann who met his penetrating gaze with her own equally steadfast and unfaltering one.

"There may be something here for me. But I've got to be willing to let something else go," he replied, his eyes never leaving hers.

Her eyes misted. "You have to try Virgil," she said. "And you will someday, you know that, so you might as well make it sooner rather than later."

Downing his drink, he stood up, pushing back his chair with his legs. Dropping a gold eagle on the table, he looked at Pistol Ann as the coin spun on its edge.

"You're right, I do have to try . . . might as well be now." He held her gaze. "It may be less painful that way," he added. Closing her eyes, and then nodding her head, she let loose a single tear.

"Oh, I . . . I didn't know," said Casey Mojo.

"It's alright, it was inevitable, As-Is, you know," she said.

He nodded, he knew, how well he knew.

The Rider pulled on his hat and headed over to retrieve his buffalo robe overcoat hanging on the wall peg. Before putting it on, he touched Pistol Ann's white buffalo coat hanging next to it, his hand lingering there a moment. He couldn't say why, it was just a part of her is all, but perhaps the last part of her he would ever touch.

Pistol Ann watched him remove his hand, sling his own coat over his shoulders, and disappear through the door to the outside.

Gabriel, seeing the Rider, tossed his head impatiently while snorting clouds of steam from his nostrils.

"Too bad you can't talk with that bit in your mouth old hoss," said the Rider as he swung up into the saddle. "Did Casey fill you in?" Again the big buckskin tossed his head up and down. "Okay then, let's ride." They turned about and headed south out of town.

Gabriel wanted to run, but the Rider held him to a walk, let him out to a trot, then to an easy lope, and finally to a gallop. When Gobbler's Knob was in sight, he let the horse have his head, Gabriel shot forward, and the Rider reined him in when they crested the knoll. Wheeling the big mount around to face north the view was exactly the same as it was on his fateful trip into Witchita, but maybe this time would bring a different result.

A wall of white roiled on the horizon. Between the Rider and the white wall the town lights seemed to hover above the stillness of the plains.

Gabriel quivered with excitement, his flared nostrils blowing out billows of steam. Snorting and pawing the ground, he wanted to run free, making his own wind.

"Hold steady old hoss, you need to rest a while."

The Rider surveyed the scene in front of him. It was the same as far as he remembered, and the same weather conditions were in place when he had crossed through The Other.

"Ready old hoss?"

Gabriel stomped and danced back and forth.

"Okay then. The idea is to stay ahead of the storm and get to town before it does. Are you up for it?"

"Less go," mumbled the horse around the bit in his mouth.

The Rider relaxed the reins.

Gabriel shot forward like a bullet from a gun, his ears laid back, his belly low to the ground, his tail flying back from the created wind, the big horse felt like a mountain of steel undulating under the Rider. Hunched low over the saddle, his eyes were slits seeing only a blur as the flat land flew by.

A scattering of ice pellets stung his face.

"Come on boy, run!" he urged, his adrenaline at full flow, he wanted to win this contest and beat the storm to town.

Gabriel swerved slightly to his right in order to enter the town from the south and head north up a street that intersected Main Street. From there he turned left, kicking up divots from the frozen ground as he spun and bolted ahead at a full gallop.

It wasn't necessary to rein him in. The horse knew what was at stake, but the Rider, feeling like he was in a battle and caught in the heat of it, pulled hard on the reins, more out of instinct than of necessity, putting Gabriel on his haunches. The big horse skidded to a stop in front of the saloon.

Leaping off of him, the Rider loosely wrapped the reins around the hitching rail. *Not necessary,* thought Gabriel.

The storm hit with a fury.

Blowing in from the north, it then swirled east, driving powdered snow and ice pellets, like desert sand, horizontally into the man and his horse.

"Be right back old hoss!" shouted the Rider as he hunkered down into the protection of his big furry overcoat. "I gotta know." The horse bobbed his head once.

The outside of the saloon looked the same. Dirty dim light escaped through grimy windows, casting a sickly yellow glow on the sidewalk, which was rapidly collecting the spew of the storm.

Pausing, the Rider glanced up at the weathered wooden sign hanging from the porch eaves and swaying in the wind. Snow and ice clung to the left side of it, driven by the blizzard wind. Through the continual swirling chaos all he could read was:

SALOON
TA, KANSAS

"Aw hell," he muttered and in two steps was inside the place.

To his left, Pistol Ann in her buckskins and Casey Mojo in his forest green cloak sat at the same table.

In the middle of the bar stood Peter O'Malley, his sombrero hanging down his back over a multi-colored serape. A wooden handle machete hung low on his left hip. At the far right end of the bar stood Charlie the old geezer with his left foot resting on the brass rail, just as the Rider had left him.

Pedro, orange hair and all, was behind the bar, off to Peter O'Malley's left.

Everything was the same.

The Rider turned, shed his heavy overcoat, hung it on its customary peg and then turned and approached the table where Pistol Ann and Casey were seated.

"I beat the storm," was all he said as he pulled out a chair and seated himself. "Not by much, maybe a minute, but I didn't spend any time riding in it. So I reckon that ain't the key, not by itself anyway. It may be a part of it, but not all."

He glanced over at Pistol Ann whose concern for him was written on her face.

"It's alright though. I'm sort of glad I wasn't shifted back across," he said, smiling at her. Her face lit up dispelling the concern.

Turning to Casey, he said, "The storm's hit with a fury. I gotta get Gabriel down to the livery and out of its way."

"I'll come with you," said Casey.

"Thanks amigo." The Rider had no idea how long he'd been gone. The plate that had been heaped with Huevos Rancheros when he'd left was empty and the table cleared away. The bottle remained; he poured himself a shot, then another, draining them both.

"Pedro," he hollered, "another bottle, and one of your famous burritos." He looked at Ann. "Want anything?" he asked her.

She pondered before answering. "Just you," she replied.

Her response left him stunned and unable to speak for an instant. He got rescued by Pedro bringing the bottle and burrito for the Rider. Ann poured herself a shot as the Rider, his appetite ravenous, made short work of the burrito, chasing it down with El Casa Blanco.

"I'd better get Gabriel out of this weather and into the stables," said the Rider.

"I'll come with you too," said Pistol Ann.

The Rider, Pistol Ann, and Casey Mojo stood up and headed for the door.

"What the hell is going on out here?" said the Rider. The storm had come to a halt. No wind, no driven snow or ice pellets, the air had climbed up over the freezing point and was calm and quiet. He unraveled Gabriel's reins from the hitching rail.

"Come on old hoss, we'll take you down to the stables," he said, staying on the ground and leading Gabriel by the reins.

"It's almost balmy out here," said Pistol Ann.

"In a way it's a little eerie feeling," added Casey as they headed side by side down the street toward the livery stables, Gabriel and the Rider on the right, then Ann, and Casey on the far left.

CHAPTER TWENTY-EIGHT

The red Wells Fargo stage pulled to a stop amidst its self-made dust cloud. After the northeast breeze cleared it away, Lily Francine peered out the small coach window at the weathered wooden sign hanging from the porch eave and swaying back and forth in the slight wind. Her eyes coming into focus, she read:

THE RED DOG SALOON
WICHITA, KANSAS

Camille had been dozing for the last hour or so, in large part due to the Chateaux Le Blanc. She'd been hitting the liquor hard lately. Lily knew the reason why and hoped once they got on track in Philadelphia her consumption would taper off before it became a problem. It wasn't one for now.

She gently jostled the young woman awake. The shotgun rider opened the door. "Stretch your legs ladies, we'll be here about an hour," he reported, then turned and spit a stream of tobacco juice into the street. "We'll go on down to the livery and change teams. The Red Dog's got some pretty good grub and of course plenty of good drinks," he said, pointing over at the place with his thumb.

Lily stepped out, her movements slow due to the stiffness in her legs. The shotgun rider helped steady her until she was fully on the ground. It was early afternoon; the sky was darkening, heralding a storm coming in from the north. Lily turned and offered her hand to Camille. "Come on dear, time to take a break," she said.

Camille's response was like she struggled to awake from a faraway dream, but she managed to take hold of Lily's hand. She gripped it extra tight as Lily helped her navigate the single step to the ground. Knowing she had the equivalent of a child on her hands, Lily hooked her arm around Camille's waist and guided her to the door of the saloon.

Closing the stagecoach door, the shotgun rider hollered, "We'll be back to get you when we're ready to roll out," and then clambered up onto driver's seat.

The air stopped moving as if it had been sucked into an unseen hole somewhere in the sky, the town felt dead still, and silent, except for a dog barking way down street. The sky darkened to its limit and lowered to the point of feeling suffocating. A sound like thunder boomed somewhere up the street, splitting the silence. But Lily knew the sound well and it wasn't thunder. There was no mistaking the roar of a Colt forty-five.

Standing on the porch, she turned, keeping a hold of Camille's hand. A tall man wearing a buffalo overcoat and a drover's slouched hat stood over the prone body of a huge black animal, his smoking gun hanging loose in his hand and pointed at the ground. Was it some sort of dog, or a wolf maybe? It was hard to tell from where she stood. Behind the man a big buckskin horse pawed the ground, plumes of steam rising from its flared nostrils. The man put out a spurless boot and with the toe prodded the animal lying at his feet. No movement, nothing.

The way he stood, the way he moved, the smoking forty-five in his hand, could it be? Lily wasn't sure if it was Virgil, but she was sure of her increased heartbeat.

A thin man dressed in a black frock coat with black dungarees tucked into black riding boots came running over from an intersecting street waving a black hat wildly in the air, a pearl handled revolver riding low on his hip.

"You shot my dog you low life bas . . ."

The man in black pulled up short, both with his stride and with his words, because of the Colt forty-five pressed against his forehead.

"You'll be next, you don't watch your words friend," the man said soft and easy and deadly. "Drop your piece," he continued, "just to make sure we can have a civil conversation. Real slow, two fingers."

The man let his pearl handled pistol fall to the ground. The man in the buffalo robe overcoat holstered his forty-five.

"This dog came at my horse, foam flying from its mouth. Hell, look at him! He's half the size of my horse! What the hell kinda hound you got here anyway?"

"He is . . . was, an Irish Wolfhound."

The shooter let out a low whistle. "Biggest dog I ever saw. I've heard of the breed though, somewhere or other. Sorry, mister. It looked like he was fixing to take a hunk of hide out of my horse, and maybe me. Putting a bullet in him was just a natural reaction."

"I guess," said the man. "I don't know what got into him. He'd never done anything like that before. Oh well, what's done can't be undone. As-Is I reckon."

"Say what?"

"Oh, it's just a saying where I come from. It is as it is and means there's no changing it."

"Reckon not. No hard feelings then?"

"No, no hard feelings, I'da done the same thing," the man in black replied, putting on his hat after picking up and holstering his pistol.

"I'll be spending some time at the Red Dog after I get Gideon down to the livery. Stop over, I'll buy you a drink," said the big fellow in the buffalo overcoat.

The man in black nodded, and then bent over his dead dog. "What got into you, you White Devil?"

Lily could not believe what she had just witnessed and heard. Opening the door of the saloon, she ushered Camille in ahead of her.

That man . . . everything about him was so much like the Rider . . . but still somehow not quite. But it could be, couldn't it, she wondered as she maneuvered Camille to a table near the front window so she could watch the goings on in the street.

The place wasn't busy at all, but it was early by bar time.

The barkeep, a short jovial looking Mexican fellow ambled over to their table. He would have been common in Texas, but not this far north into Kansas.

"Buenos días, senoritas. I am Pedro. Wha' can I do for you?"

"We'd like something to eat, a sandwich if you have them. And, would it be alright if we drank our own liquor?" Lily asked pulling the near empty bottle of Chateaux Le Blanc from her oversized handbag.

"Si senorita, but first allow me to pour you each a glass of our very finest, on the house. I theen you will find it a very good tonic, and you can't get it anywhere else this side of the Mississippi."

"I'd heartily recommend Pedro's burritos," piped up an old codger bellied up to the far end of the bar. "Without the hot sauce, of course," he laughed.

"Alright, Pedro, we'll each have a burrito. Is that okay with you, Camille?" She nodded, her face expressionless.

Pedro ambled off and then soon returned with two glasses full of an amber liquid. "On thee house," he said, setting them down.

"Thank you," Lily Francine replied.

Camille took a swallow of Pedro's finest, looking puzzled at Lily. "When did you pour me a drink? I didn't see you pour me a drink," she said.

"I didn' . . . you were looking out the window honey." Lily caught herself and paused in mid-sentence, taking a sip from her own glass. It tasted exactly like Chateaux Le Blanc. Not likely to be that whiskey, but not impossible either, she supposed. The women finished their drinks and Pedro brought over two piping hot burritos. They smelled so delicious Lily's mouth began to water.

"Pedro, what is the name of the whiskey you served us?" she asked.

"El Casa Blanco, señorita. Mucho bueno, no? Would you like another?"

"Si," she smiled and then took a bite of her burrito. It was as delicious as its aroma had promised.

Without warning the door slammed open, cracking against the wall. The big fellow in the buffalo overcoat strode through like he owned the place, and slammed the door closed with the same amount of force as he used opening it. He turned and shed his heavy overcoat, hanging it on a wall peg. He glanced over at Lily and Camille's table. Lily caught his eye, and then she caught her breath. No denying it, it was him!

The same face, the same gun metal gray eyes, but he made no sign of recognition. Instead he went straight to the bar, and stood at the center of the free standing mahogany behemoth, exposing a huge Bowie knife hanging on his left hip.

To Camille she said, "Be right back." Camille stared in silence out the window without responding, retreated deep into her own world and what she was seeing, only she could know.

Lily stood up and walked over to the tall man standing at the center of the bar and tapped him on the shoulder. His head snapped to look at her, assessing who accosted him.

"Don't you recognize me?" she asked.

His eyes lost their glint of danger and held a softer focus.

"No ma'am, I don't," he hesitated an instant, then continued, "but I sure would like to."

"I'm Lily . . . Lily Francine. Come on Virgil, how long have you been here in town?"

Genuine puzzlement took hold of his face.

"Ma'am . . . Lily, my name is Herschel, Herschel Johns, and I'm sorry to say you've got me mixed up with somebody else."

She dropped her eyes to the floor. "I'm sorry," she said, her voice no more than a whisper.

"I am too, but if I can be of some service to you, let me know," he added.

She walked back to her table, sat down and took another bite from the still hot burrito. Camille was staring out the window. She pointed. "Bad man," she said. It was the dead wolfhound's owner, the tails of his coat flying out behind him as he marched toward the door, pistol in hand.

"Mr. Johns! The door!" hollered Lily with all her breath.

The big man whirled just as the door burst open. The man in black held his pistol shoulder high, straight out, and aimed at Herschel Johns' chest. In a blur, Herschel dropped to his haunches, drew his Colt and fired twice, the bullets penetrating deep into the man's chest, their impact driving him off his feet and landing him on his back on the planks of the outside boardwalk.

Camille watched him land, watched him vaporize into a black mist that moved west up the street, against the wind. "Bad man," she whispered.

"Senor Johns! You have done what no other has been able to do!" exclaimed Pedro from behind the bar.

Standing, the smoking Colt held loose and pointing at the floor he asked, "What's that Pedro?"

"You have rid us of the malo brujo senor."

"Malo brujo?"

"Si . . . the warlock . . . he was an evil sorcerer!"

"Bad man," sighed Camille as the Wells Fargo stage rolled to a slow stop in front of the saloon.

"Come on honey," said Lily as she donned her heavy cloak. Walking around behind Camille, she helped her to stand. Handing her overcoat to her she helped her slip into it. "The stage is here, we have to be on it," she explained to her lost and far away friend. Holding Camille's upper arm, they turned. Mr. Johns was right there; close enough to bump into if they had been moving any faster.

"You saved my life," he said in a low voice.

"Well, it was just a warning," replied Lily, trying to be casual.

"No, you saved me."

"Well, you remind of someone I used to know. It was just a natural reaction I guess." She could not believe the heat of a blush she felt rising in her cheeks.

"Catching the stage?" he asked.

She nodded, her eyes searching his as if seeking an answer for the reason of her sudden blush. After all, she was a very experienced woman.

"Where ya headed?" he asked.

"St. Louis."

"I'll ride along and make sure you and your friend get there," he said.

"Mr. Johns, there's no need for that," she protested in a very mild tone.

"Nothing tying me down here, besides I'd be glad to even if I didn't owe you for saving my life."

Her blush deepened.

Camille slipped a bottle of El Casa Blanco into her shoulder bag.

Chapter Twenty-Nine

Ann, Casey, the Rider and Gabriel continued down the eerie and silent Main Street of Witchita. Nothing moved, making the world feel as if it had become desolate.

Maybe it was a scent so faint no one could smell it, or a whisper of sound as quiet as a breeze skimming across the top of a snow bank, but Gabriel caught the scent and heard the soft breeze blow by. The big buckskin threw his head back as far as it would go, taking the reins out of the Rider's hand. The Rider, surprised by his horse's action took a step away as Gabriel turned around to face the opposite direction. Then they all heard the loud guttural snarl and looked up at the rooftop in time to see the Blood Spiller come flying off of it, fangs bared, blood red eyes focused on the Rider.

Gabriel planted his front hooves firmly on the ground, then lifted up his rear legs and with all his strength back kicked the wolf with both hooves landing them square on his side. His breaking ribs sounded like twigs snapping as someone walked through a dry forest. The force of the kick drove him sideways yowling in pain.

Pistol Ann had her gun out when Gabriel did his turn. The wolf stopped moving from the momentum of Gabriel's kick and hung suspended in the air for a split second. Pistol Ann fired a single shot into the his wide open mouth, the bullet taking off the back of its skull and sending his brains splattering on the street. The big lobo fell to the ground to lie there in an unmoving heap, one front paw twitching as if trying to run.

After the initial shock cleared, Casey looked at the Rider and said, “I think he was sent to kill you.”

“Well, looks like he failed,” said the Rider as he rubbed Gabriel’s nose. “Thanks old hoss,” he said.

“My pleasure,” said the horse around the bit in his mouth.

“And thanks Ann for being ready so quick.”

“I’m a shooter and whenever something strange or out of the ordinary occurs, I always pull one of my pistols out. Just a natural reaction of mine,” she said.

The Rider pulled his Bowie out. “I’m taking off its head, just to make sure.”

They turned toward the wolf, but all they saw was a swirl of black mist rising until it disappeared into the night.

The Rider turned to Casey. “I thought bullets or buckshot would keep that black devil down.”

“That used to be true. Mesmerala must have come up with something new, a potion or incantation that doesn’t allow gunfire to permanently kill the wolf, it probably still holds for other animals.”

“It may last a short time or a lifetime for the wolf,” said Pistol Ann, “But at least we know now to take its head off if we ever get the chance, just to make damn sure he’ll never be a threat again.”

Mesmerala watched through The Orb as her beloved pet got its ribs crushed by the horses hooves and its brains blown out by that Pistol Ann bitch. She didn’t bother opening her door, knowing that the dark essence of the Blood Spiller would seep underneath it in due time. Even as she thought about it, black smoke drifted underneath her door, materializing into an indiscernible mass the size of a man.

“Come over here and lie down by me my pet,” she ordered. The black cloud drifted over by the stool she sat on.

She covered The Orb with its silk cloth, the blackened cloud holding still by her side.

In a blinding flash and as quick as lightning, she stood up, made three complete spins, her cloak swirling like a black tornado and wrapping around her until she became as a statue suspended in the air, her eyes red and glowing with ferocity. She spread her arms and tilted back her head, causing her raven hair to spill out and down across her back. It then stood straight out and up as if touched by electric lightning.

> "Pain begone, no longer to feel
> Skeleton of bone, be knitted and heal
> Bullet within the skull depart!
> Now heal the dead gray matter!"

The mist that was the Blood Spiller was sucked down flat against the floor, held there by a force stronger than gravity. It began to solidify into the shape of the wolf, but lay as still as death.

Floating to her stool, Mesmerala seated herself and then put her hand on the wolf's crushed side and said one single word—

"Breathe." His burnt orange and yellow flecked eyes opened and he did as commanded, he breathed.

"Lie still now my pet."

The Blood Spiller whimpered, the only sound he could make as saliva drooled from his jaws, his forepaws twitching on their own.

Mesmerala left The Orb uncovered. She knew what was going to happen now, and without the services of her familiar, she was powerless to stop it. The big wolf continued to twitch and drool, but no longer whimpered.

CHAPTER THIRTY

Pistol Ann and the Rider returned to the Burnt Dog after making sure Gabriel and Casey felt safe enough. Casey pulled out his shotgun, "This will blow that devil wolf in half," he said. Good enough.

Ann and Virgil settled at a quiet table in a corner.

Pedro brought them their usual beverage and a couple of glasses. "Would you like anything to eat?" he asked. "No thanks Pedro, don't have much of an appetite right now." "Me neither," said Ann.

"Where'd you learn to shoot like that?" the Rider asked her.

She slid the wide brimmed hat off her head, the chinstrap catching it so it hung down her back. "My dad taught me until he got so stove up he couldn't straighten himself enough to shoulder a rifle or sight down a pistol."

"I'm sorry to hear that."

She gave him a wan smile, her eyes dropping to the drink on the table. Idly running her index finger around the rim of the glass she looked up at the Rider, her eyes earnest and searching his.

"He showed me the mechanics of shooting, taught me about the selection, cleaning, and care of guns, and timing . . . all that. I never tired of practicing, sometimes sunup to sundown."

She drifted off, taking a long look out at the darkness held back by the glass window.

The Rider took a swallow of his whiskey.

"Then I started shooting at moving targets. First small game and then larger. One shot, one kill, was dad's creed. He said if I was going to be a real shootist, I'd have to learn to kill men, and approach it as if I were target shooting. I didn't think I could do that, but found out I could. But mostly he said I just had a natural talent."

"Is your dad still alive?"

"Yes, but the three hombres who tried to kill him aren't."

The Rider nodded, understanding that she had killed those three men. How long ago? What did it matter? Once the ice water got in your veins, it never left. It was just a matter of turning on the spigot when needed.

"And what about you Mr. Virgil Jones Rider, what's your story, your reputation aside?" she asked.

"A Civil War—Over There—about, guess what, political ideologies. Long story short, the North—it was North versus South—took away my wife, my newborn son, my mother and father, their plantation, my plantation, scattered the people, and took from us our way of life.

Before the Goddam War I was an attorney. I believed in justice and the impartiality of the legal system; innocent until proven guilty, and all that kind of happy horseshit. The war took that ideal from me also and so the only justice I believe in is whatever I decide to mete out to others."

"Thus the Rider and his reputation," she said.

"Yeah, something like that. And then I end up in Right Here and Now."

"You have a broken heart," she said, her words hitting the bulls-eye and striking home.

The Rider stared at her trying to fathom the depth of her perceptions, but could not. "Yeah, you could say something like that I reckon," he conceded.

"You can't heal it yourself you know. All you can do is wrap it in hard rock granite."

Bulls-eye again.

The Rider tried again to fathom her depths. She was getting too close, but what really bothered him was he didn't mind.

"Mr. Virgil Jones Rider, judge, jury, and executioner," she proclaimed.

That got his hackles up . . . almost.

"It's a rough country, Over There."

"Right Here and Now isn't? I can't remember going on any picnics lately."

Point taken.

She took a sip of her drink; he took a gulp of his. Their glassed thudded in unison on the table. Reaching over, she placed a gentle hand on his forearm. "Virgil," she whispered, "maybe there's a reason for you being here."

"What reason? To confuse me more, to take more lives, to stir up hate against me? Look Ann, I like spending time with you, but I'm afraid you'd end up hating me—seems everyone does sooner or later—and I don't want to be responsible for planting hate in your heart."

"If I should ever hate you, Virgil Jones, that would be my fault. Besides, it's a risk I'm willing to take. Are you?"

He weighed the question in silence. Risk? Nothing ventured, nothing gained, right? God, he wanted this woman! But at the same time was afraid want would turn into need, need into love, and then love would rotate into hate, it happens so often it can almost be counted on. Time is the only variable.

Risk. Was he willing to take it? Well . . . this was Right Here and Now, and maybe things worked a little different here.

"Yeah . . . I reckon I am," he said, answering her question.

She smiled the kind of smile that showed relief, gratitude, and joy all at once, the kind that could light up an entire room. And Virgil Jones could not detect any hint of triumph or guile lurking in the background of Pistol Ann's open, honest, loving face and heart.

"Will you spend some time with me, Ann? I don't think the big bad wolf will bother us for a while."

"I will, he won't, let's go," she said. Letting loose of his forearm, she took hold of his hand and led him toward the stairway.

★ ★ ★

He stood naked in front of the windowpane with the curtains drawn back exposing the night. He didn't believe the storm had ended, but instead had hidden in a subtle lull. The clouds had broken and dissipated, allowing the moon to show the fullness of its glory. The resting snow sparkled like diamonds in a jewelry store.

The Rider stepped aside, letting the moonlight grace the woman sleeping softly in the oversized bed. Her breathing was rhythmic, slow and steady, her breasts rising and falling under the sheet like gentle waves lapping at a whitened shore.

Pistol Ann's hair looked silver under the moonlight, and her face, in peaceful repose, like alabaster.

She was all woman and didn't need fancy trappings to prove it or draw a man's attention. But as looked upon her face, more beautiful than any he remembered, she did something to him other than make his toes curl. She made him feel complete, somehow, and that was the mystery. He pondered the mysterious feeling, for it remained long after the heat of passion had reached its sweet climax and then began to subside, nothing unusual there; it was the feeling of completeness they felt and shared that was new to them.

Not an introspective man, the Rider was forced to take a look at what was stirring around inside of him. She was no one-night stand, no love 'em and leave 'em wham-bam-thank-you ma'am woman. Not to him she wasn't, but why? He dug deep in the reflective moonlight, hoping it would help him to reflect on his feelings.

She made him feel complete, yes, but how? Of course it was a matter of the heart, but the heart felt many things, including hate. But he could not deny it felt as if a piece of his soul had been returned, the part torn away and missing had been locked back into place . . . a completion.

Then he knew, and he wasn't sure he was ready. But then, how does one prepare for love? It creeps up on us or blindsides us, stripping away our defenses, our hardness, our cynicism, and leaves us with the joy of just being alive and complete once again.

He wasn't sure he could let go of the reins of his heart, even though he found out what it was saying and what its desire was.

She lay in the big brass bed softly sleeping. He looked upon her with love, and Mr. Virgil Jones Rider—judge, jury, and executioner—was afraid of what he felt. But perfect love drives away fear, does it not?

Quickly dressing, strapping on his gun belt—now *that* was comforting—he slapped on his hat, was careful to close the door as quiet as he could, and headed down the stairs.

Pistol Ann opened her eyes and stretched like a contented kitten. Smiling demurely, she snuggled deeper into the covers just to feel the comforting warmth and relaxation. Sighing, she inhaled the lingering scent of her man, at the same time reveling in his vivid recent memory. Her man . . . she embraced that thought. He'd be back soon; she knew what he wanted as a man. She knew what he needed as her man.

Smiling with comfort, she drifted off to a peaceful sleep.

But Virgil Jones couldn't join her, not with the twisting and tumbling thoughts carried by the freight train roaring through the middle of his skull. He quietly opened and closed the door and headed down the stairs.

He shoved his fried potatoes around on the plate mixing them with the runny eggs Pedro had served him. The emotions swirling around inside him matched the movements he made on his plate, round and round, back and forth, a nibble here, a bite there, but nothing he could sink his teeth into. Wash it all down with gulps of whiskey, maybe it would just go away.

Did it ever turn daylight in this hell hole called Right Here and Now?

Would he ever make it back to Over There?

Leaving his breakfast unfinished, taking a half-full glass of whiskey with him, he went up to the bar and stood next to Charlie the old Geezer.

"Pedro, fill old Charlie up, will ya?" he hollered.

Old Charlie the fixture, maybe he knew or could at least offer some insight into the essence of the nature of Right Here and Now.

"Thankee sonny!" the old boy said as Pedro filled his glass.

"You're welcome Charlie. Say, does it ever turn daylight around here?" the Rider asked.

"Well, we're deep inta winter ya know. Ain't never much daylight in winter nohow anyways. Maybe not bein on a regular skedjul, maybe ya'll just been sleeping away the few daylight hours we have, eh?"

Charlie nudged his glass ahead a notch or two.

"Pedro! Bring us a bottle of your good stuff, por favor."

Pedro ambled down the bar and placed the bottle between the Rider and Old Charlie. "Help yourself, ya Old Geezer," said the Rider, motioning toward the bottle. Old Charlie cackled and did just that. "I haven't been sleeping enough to miss whole days, Charlie." "Time doesn't exist here Mr. Jones, you know that by now. But it don't mean those that's used to it don't get the idee all tied in a knot. Days and nights all wrapped and mixed up into one single day or one gol darn long night." Charlie filled his glass.

"All right Charlie, you can have the bottle, but stop pussy footing around with me. Why is it always dark? And I've already been told the night ain't finished with its work yet."

"In a way, that's true sonny. But it ain't really the night what's doing the work. It stays dark round here long as any darkness remains in the heart of a stranger." The Rider was taken aback, that hit too close to home. "What about the bruja witch? She's gotta have a black heart. With her around, it'd always be dark, wouldn't it?"

"Naw . . . cuz ya see, like me she's a fixture in these here parts. But she can only do her dirty deeds when it is dark . . . savvy?"

"This place is plumb loco, I reckon," huffed the Rider. Wanting to be alone he returned to his table and motioned for Pedro to bring him a fresh bottle of El Casa Blanco and a clean glass.

He knew the old geezer was right. What he'd said made perfect sense in the warped world—but was it really—of Right Here and Now. He knew that darkness lurked inside of him and had a good strong grip on his soul. Darkness wrapped in a heart of stone, stone chiseled and fashioined from fear, fear born from the type of pain and suffering that does not bleed.

He conjured the image of Janice Louise in his mind's eye. She was there, but faded, hazy, and was soon replaced by a crystalline image of Pistol Ann, her voice like music and carrying the same can't-help-but-listen-to-it authority.

"Your pain has been your comfort, hasn't it? Your pain has driven you and given you a dark reason to carry on, hasn't it? Your pain is married to your fear, isn't it? You need your pain to exist, don't you?"

Was it his conscience talking? Maybe, but a voice in his head nonetheless. A voice he didn't want to hear, but had to listen to, because it rang of truth.

Virgil Jones burst out the door of the saloon, throwing on his buffalo overcoat as he did so. The night was still, moonlight turning the world into a crisp contrast of light and shadow, not quite black and white, but then, was anything? Maybe, and he aimed to find out.

Casey Mojo heard a dull thud-thud-thud sound bang against the man door. A friend or a seeker of shelter, of that he was sure. Nothing with malignant intent would knock politely, would it?

Scuttling over to the door he slid back the bolt and opened it without asking who was there. Virgil Jones stepped through.

"Sir Virgil, good to see you!" he greeted him.

"Casey, we need to talk and get some things ironed out."

Taken slightly aback at the Rider's abruptness, the hunchback was slow to respond. "Alright then, pull up a chair by the fire," he said as it greedily consumed a fresh supply of fuel.

"Gabriel, ready to cover some ground tonight old hoss?" The animal snorted an indifferent response to the Rider.

The two men seated themselves at the fire pit as it burned at full strength, throwing out a deep comforting heat.

"What's on your mind?" asked Casey.

"I need to find my way back."

"Why?"

"Why! What kind of a question is that? Because that's where I'm from, that's why! Besides, this place is plumb loco and that's reason enough!"

"Why do you assume this place is plumb loco?"

"Because everything here is backasswards, that's why."

"Maybe not, maybe everything Over There is backasswards, as you say."

"Gawd!" exclaimed the Rider, his exasperation flaring bright and hot. Casey knew he had to be careful here.

"Isn't it really about the heavy stone you call your heart and is lodged in your chest?" asked the Wise Won. He didn't expect an answer, nor was one given. It was a question designed to provoke thought. The Rider continued staring into the fire until, after taking in a deep breath, he turned to Casey Mojo.

"You sound like . . ."

"Pistol Ann?" finished Casey.

Stunned, the Rider remained silent, his stare now fixed on the hunchback.

"Now, shall we get down to business?" asked the Wise Won.

"The sooner the better, I reckon."

"Alright then, you tried beating the storm and not getting caught in it and you were successful, but did not return to Over There."

"Yes, and when you came back you weren't caught in a storm as you were when you passed through The Other to Over There," said the Rider.

"Very well, so what other ingredients are in the mix?" asked Casey.

"I'd been drinking whiskey when I crossed over, quite a bit of it in fact."

"As I was also. When I returned from Over There, I was full of whiskey once again. Chateaux Le Blanc it was."

"That's what I was drinking when I passed through The Other to Right Here and Now!" exclaimed the Rider.

"So . . ." paused Casey, "one common ingredient is Chateaux Le Blanc from Over There to Right Here and now. By Jove, I think we've got it, or at least part of it!" proclaimed Casey Mojo.

"Are you thinking what I'm thinking?" they asked each other at the same time.

"I doubt there's any Chateaux Le Blanc in Witchita."

"No, there is none and I have made a thorough search," said Casey.

"So I'll try El Casa Blanco, outside the storm, to try to return to Over There!" exclaimed the Rider.

"Precisely old chap!"

"Let's go for it," interjected Gabriel, eliciting a hearty laugh from the men.

"Soon's the weather allows it, old hoss," answered the Rider. Turning back to Casey Mojo, he said, "So, I'll need to have a storm coming in from the north, and as I ride south to Gobbler's Knob, I'll guzzle El Casa Blanco, then turn right around and try to beat the storm to town."

"That sounds like a good plan, sir Virgil."

"Hold tight for a while Gabriel," he said as he left the livery stable. ReeBa's voice hovered in the background inviting the big buckskin to come over and see her sometime . . . soon.

The Rider didn't see any clouds to lighten the night-blackened sky, didn't feel a hint of wind on his face, or, stopping to inhale deeply, catch the slightest scent of snow. Taking a stroll up a north running side street to get a read on that horizon, he was rewarded with . . . nothing, just stillness and the same never-ending flatness of the pancaked prairie.

"Need a northern blizzard," he muttered as he turned and headed to the Burnt Dog Saloon, his soaring hopes brought crashing back to earth with a thudding finality.

The bruja witch caught the Rider in The Orb as he left the stables. It couldn't penetrate the interior due to the hunchback's spell. Everything else in and around town was open for viewing.

"A blizzard from the north, eh, well, anything to keep you from that buckskin wearing bitch," she cackled as the fire blazed hotter. The Blood Spiller stirred as he lay still at her feet, his breathing shallow but steady. "Not long now, my pet, not long now," she said, scratching the monstrous wolf behind his ears.

Taking a large cast iron kettle from under the table, she carried it outside and filled it with drifted snow. Once inside the shack, she dumped the snow into a cauldron suspended over the fire, then repeated the process two more times. She sat on her stool and waited for the mixture of snow and ice to come to a boil. As the steam began to rise from the cauldron, Mesmerala filled the iron kettle with the melted and boiling water. Taking it outside and setting it on the snowy ground she incanted:

"Giant of the North,
let thy winds blow.
Clouds blot the sky bringing
swift the snow.
Blizzard by the wizard told,
on the North Horizon hold."

The conjured storm clouds, crystallized by the freezing air, moved away at Mesmerala's words, disappearing into the prickly blackness of the north.

CHAPTER THIRTY-ONE

Scanning the interior of the Burnt Dog Saloon, not seeing Pistol Ann, the Rider hustled up the stairs and stopped halfway to the top.

"Pedro, if you find out a blizzard starts brewing in the north, you be sure to let me know, okay amigo?"

"Certainly senor," answered Pedro. He could be counted on.

Taking the rest of the stairs two at a time, he paused to collect himself, then entered the upstairs room as quiet as he could. Pistol Ann lay in sweet repose, the moonlight falling full upon her face. The brightness of her beauty eclipsed the memory of Janice Louise, confining it to shadow.

He slid naked into the bed beside her as her eyes opened. Wrapping her arms around his neck she whispered low and husky, "Welcome home." Disappearing into each other, the two became one, he knew it and she knew it and on the downside of their spent passion, she felt his troubled soul.

"What's bothering you?" she asked.

"I have to try to return to Over There."

"Why?"

He turned and looked into her deep and mysterious eyes, and along with the reflected moonlight, they shined with a brilliance that seemed to see into his very soul. He did not know how, but he felt comforted and his fears were quieted.

"I need to settle some things, put some issues to rest, bury some skeletons, and see some people."

"You don't absolutely need to you know. What would be so bad about staying here?"

"Nothing, in fact, I could easily live with it, but in the end I'd just have the same and maybe more ghosts haunting my memory."

"What if you get back home and can't return to Right Here and Now?"

"As-Is, I guess," he replied after a prolonged pause.

"That's a cop out Mr. Virgil Jones Rider. What does your heart say?"

"I'm not sure."

"Yes you are you just don't want to admit to it."

Bulls-Eye. Before he could reply, an urgent knocking rattled the door. "Senor! Senor! The blizzard, she come up on the northern horizon thees very minute!" said Pedro through the closed and locked door.

"Gotta go, gotta try it now," the Rider said. Before he could go Pistol Ann grabbed him and gave him a long lingering kiss of promise. Letting him go, he dressed as fast as he could, Pistol Ann following suit. He flew down the stairs with her right behind him.

"Pedro, a bottle of El Casa Blanco, por favor!" he hollered as he bolted across the room, grabbed his buffalo robe overcoat, and wrapped himself in it.

Pistol Ann took the bottle from Pedro, crossed the room and said, "I'll go with you to the livery." He nodded and helped her with her overcoat. Going through the door and entering the night in a rush, they found Casey Mojo, standing right before them, holding Gabriel's reins. No need to trudge down to the livery stable.

"How . . . ?" asked the Rider.

"I saw the storm clouds brewing sir," he answered, which may or may not have been the truth, or just a part of it. Either way, it didn't make any difference now.

Pistol Ann set her rifle against the hitching rail and threw her arms around her man. "I want you to come back," she whispered, her sincerity transparent in those few words. He smiled thinly, nothing more than a noncommittal twitch of his lips, but his eyes betrayed him. In his heart of hearts he hoped he would fail in his quest. But from a young age he was taught that a man's gotta do what a man's gotta do, or some such nonsense as that.

Pistol popped open the bottle. "One last drink together," she said and tilted back the bottle, taking a healthy gulp. She handed it to him. He took two and then tenderly kissed her on the mouth. "Better have another swallow, it's going to be bitter cold all alone out there," she said, a tear frozen half way down her cheek.

He took her suggestion and took another double shot swallow.

Nodding to her, he corked the bottle and slipped it into the leather saddlebag behind his saddle. She placed her hand on his thigh and whispered, "Good luck." He had no doubt that she wanted the best for him, whatever it may be, and that truth was harder to swallow than any whiskey, rot-gut or otherwise.

"Bring him back if you can," she whispered in Gabriel's ear. He bounced his head up and down and snorted his assent.

"Let's turn out!" said the Rider and headed the big horse up the street without a backward glance.

A man's gotta do what a man's gotta do.

* * *

Horse and rider crested Gobbler's Knob, the north wind biting as it blasted in from that direction. The oncoming blizzard hung on the horizon, a white wall against the black sky, moving without hurry towards him. He pulled out the bottle of El Casa Blanco and took another double shot, put the cork in it and slipped it into the saddlebag.

Everything was the same. The oncoming blizzard was like a long white walled sepulcher, certain of its mission. The north wind bit and stung his face. Below, the lights of the town-Witchita or Wichita—made it appear to hover above the flat white of the prairie.

Gabriel snorted clouds of steam. He was ready.

Deja-vu, twice.

The Rider fought to control his swirling emotions, every bit as violent and threatening as the oncoming storm and just as impossible to stop.

Gabriel's breathing was slow and steady.

"Ready boy?"

The buckskin snorted and stomped one front hoof on the frozen ground.

"Let's run then!" The big horse surged ahead, legs pounding out a rhythm equal to the pistons of a locomotive engine pumping with the throttle full open.

With no ice pellets stinging his face, the Rider only had to squint against the icy wind, its striking force doubled by Gabriel's untiring speed.

The wall of the blizzard, though blurred by the stinging wind and no small amount of El Casa Blanco, appeared to remain stationary as the town grew larger and brighter.

Still no sting of ice pellets.

This time he rode Gabriel at full speed past the bruja witches shack. Dirty yellow light tried to escape from a couple of its windows that he thought looked blood red as he went flying past at full speed, the wind shrieking behind him, or was it the cackling of maniacal laughter only the evil know the meaning of?

He reined Gabriel up sharp in front of the saloon and looked up at the weathered wooden sign swinging from the eaves:

THE BURNT DOG SALOON
WITCHITA, KANSAS

Relief and disappointment joined hands and twisted hard inside of him. "As-Is," he muttered, trying to find acceptance of the fact, but could not.

The blizzard struck with the fury of a chained and starving predator unleashed to seek its prey.

Climbing stiffly down from the saddle, he spoke to the horse. “Find your way to the livery boy?” The buckskin turned and trotted down the street, disappearing into the swirling white dark.

“Guess that settles that,” he said as he opened the door to the saloon. The rush of warmth was a relief, but not as great as seeing all of the fixtures in their places, except Pistol Ann.

He arrived at the bar. “A shot of your best,” he said in a voice low on the spectrum of audible. Pedro obliged.

“Pistol Ann in her room?” he asked.

“No senor. She . . . she peeked up her rifle, poot on her hat, poot on her coat, and left.”

Pedro’s eyes were rounded by the softness of compassion seen in one of those rare moments when a person realizes we’re in this world together, sharing the triumphs and the sufferings, and reaches out to comfort another.

“Sorry, senor Rider.”

“Yeah, me too amigo,” he said, and then turned and left the saloon with no warming whiskey in his belly. The one reason he didn’t care if he remained in Right Here and Now was more likely than not to be gone, but to where, and why? It had to be more than Fate or As-Is. Neither could pull such cruelty, could they, he asked himself. His mind flashed to the Goddam War. Of course, he knew they could, he knew the cruelty of whatever was out there knew no bounds and on top of that was always on the lookout for new ways to practice its art.

The storm’s fury pummeled him as he continued west on the boardwalk toward the livery stable and the bruja witch’s shack.

The bruja witch! Was she behind all this? It was her maniacal cackle he’d heard on the way in, wasn’t it? He aimed to find out. Increasing his pace, the thud of his boots resounded with purpose as they echoed off the storefronts, the wind picked up and shrieked and howled as if carried by the damned when the Rider knocked on the door of the witch's shack with the butt of his Colt.

"Come in Mr. Jones," a voice said from within. Creaking on rusted hinges, the door swung open on its own.

She stood with her back to him, silhouetted by the fire in the rock fireplace. As he approached, his senses on high alert, she turned to face him.

"You!" he exclaimed as he looked into the face of Janice Louise.

"Enjoy your last dream dearie?" she asked, a malicious grin distorting her lovely false face.

"Where's Pistol Ann?" he said, kicking the door closed with his boot heel, holding the forty-five pointed at the witch.

"What do you want with her? You can have me anytime you want, in or out of a dream."

"In or out of a dream, either way, you're not real witch-bitch, now, where is she?"

"I tell you I don't know, and must you call me names? But a name is just a name. She'll break your heart you know, whereas I will give you pleasure so exquisite, so unendurable, it will be like dying and being reborn over and over again. Would you like that, Mr. Virgil Jones Rider, would you?"

He lowered his pistol, holding it loose and pointed down at the floor.

"Speaking of names," she continued, "do you remember my pet, who those cruel men at the saloon named El Diablo Negro? That is not his real name." Making a sweeping outward arc with her right arm she said, "Say hello to El Sangre Derramar, The Blood Spiller!"

The Rider's head snapped to the left in time to see the big wolf launch himself at him, red eyes glowing, fur standing straight up on his neck, massive jaws agape and dripping and coming straight at his head.

Not having enough time to aim with his eye, he snapped his wrist up and fired the Colt across his body, aiming with his instincts, at the same time jumping back a step, all in less than the blink of an eye.

The forty-five slug slammed into the open jaws of the oncoming lycanthrope and exploded out the back of its head, splattering brains and blood and pieces of bone on the ceiling of the dim and dingy shack. The lobo landed in a bloody heap where the Rider had stood a split second ago.

Cocking his Colt, he pointed it straight out in front of him at the bruja witch, but she was no longer there! He glanced first left, then right; dropped into a crouch, spun around, with his pistol held out and ready to fire . . . at nothing.

"Enough of this," he muttered aloud. Holstering his Colt, he reached across his belly to pull the big Bowie from its sheath. Dropping to his left knee he raised the heavy knife above his head, and with his arm extended, struck with all his might into the neck of the monster wolf. Striking again and again, until the edge of the knife blade was stopped by the floor underneath, the worn wooden planks soaking up the wolf's blood as his head rolled to the side, ensuring the he would remain dead this time.

He stayed down on one knee, motionless, except for his heaving chest and the sweat that dripped from his forehead. His glazed eyes began to focus as he came out of the violence-induced trance, his emotional spike and fight with the wolf leaving him exhausted and drained of energy.

He didn't feel the bruja witch materializing behind him with an axe raised high over her right shoulder, and her eyes, like burning coals, fixed on the Rider's neck.

CHAPTER THIRTY-TWO

The outer door crashed open and slammed into the wall with a piercing crack. The Rider spun and looked with widened eyes as a flash of lightning and ear splitting thunder come pounding out of the swirling snow. On instinct, he spun back and dove to the ground, drawing his pistol while in the air. He landed behind the body of the wolf, using it for cover. He held his fire for the instant it took for the smoke to clear the doorway. A smallish figure with a round topped hat stood silhouetted in the backlight of the swirling white snow. "Don't shoot," came a voice out of the shadow.

"Pistol Ann!" he exclaimed.

"It's me Mr. Virgil Jones Rider. Take a look to your right."

He stood up, holstered his Colt and looked in the direction Pistol Ann was pointing. The body of the bruja witch lay on the floor in two pieces, the axe clutched in her hand, her face etched in a grimace of hate and sudden shock. He looked back at Ann, who stood framed in the doorway holding Casey Mojo's short-barreled scattergun.

"Both barrels?" he asked.

"At the same time," she replied, "right to the mid-section."

"I'm taking her head off," he said as he picked the Bowie up off the floor, wiping the bloody blade off on the wolf's fur. He stood to his full height. "Like I did the wolf's," he added.

"It's too late; we'd better go while we can." She raised the scattergun and pointed it at a spot behind him. He turned in time to see a vapor of smoke dissipate into the murky air of the shack. The smoke being the two halves of the witch's body seeping out around a window.

Without a word he sheathed his knife, turned, stepped over the grisly body of the Blood Spiller, grabbed Pistol Ann's arm, shepherded her out the doorway, and headed up Main Street, not closing the witch's door behind him.

Pistol Ann shoved a couple of shells into the scattergun as they walked up the street, oblivious to the blizzard twisting around them.

"Quick, to the livery stable, she can't get to us there," she urged. The Rider kept pace with her.

"Where were you?" he asked as they fought their way through the storm that seemed to never end. "I thought the witch had you for sure."

"I was right here, talking with Casey Mojo," she said as she pulled open the man door of the livery. Entering, they hurried across the shadowed distance to the fire pit and seated themselves by Casey Mojo.

"Use a drink?" he asked of no one in particular, pulling a bottle of White Castle from under his chair. Setting it on the rim of the brick fire pit, he then retrieved three glasses from under the chair and placed them next to the bottle. He opened the bottle and filled the glasses.

"How'd you know where to find . . . ?" Casey held up his hand, stopping the Rider in midsentence. "Begging your pardon, but first things first, sir Virgil. You did not return to Over There, as we had hoped."

"No, I didn't. Guess I'm stuck." He glanced over at Pistol Ann, seated on his left as he handed her a glass. "But I reckon that's alright, if it'd only get daylight around here now and then."

"Once again, begging your pardon sir, but you'd be happy here for only a short while. The ghosts of your past would eventually catch up with you and overtake you. You do . . . with all respect sir, need to go back and settle up with the ghosts that haunt you."

Those weren't the words the Rider wanted to hear, but he considered their weight as he looked deep into the hunchback's eyes. He had heard long ago of the Wisdom of Ancient of Days, and in Casey's eyes he encountered it, and was captivated by the depth of its sincerity and truth.

Shaking his head slightly, he broke away; nothing needed saying. Truth stands on its own. He looked over at Pistol Ann. She nodded once, the serenity of acceptance gracing her countenance.

"No," he said.

"Yes," she countered, placing her hand on his.

"But I . . . I," he stammered.

Stammered? The Rider? He couldn't take any more of this right now . . . no more of the struggle that raged between his heart and his head. He changed the subject.

"How did . . . ?"

"I know you were at the witch's?" Pistol Ann finished for him.

"Well, yeah, how did you know?"

"As soon as you left for Gobbler's Knob, I felt a desperate need for someone to talk to, so I came here to see Casey, and he told me."

Oh yeah, he's somewhat of a wizard his own damn self, thought the Rider.

"He told me you were in danger and to go, so there I was, Mr. Virgil Jones Rider, saving your hide once again."

He turned to her with unusual quickness. "What do you mean, once again?"

"Are you forgetting the Billy Goat Kid and Jesse James Jackson?"

"I would have taken them down by myself!"

"Uh-huh," she replied.

"By the way, why did you shoot the left handed gunslinger, who was on your right and in front of me, first?" he asked.

"I wasn't sure you'd join the party soon enough, and seeing as how he was in front of you and left handed, he wasn't going to shoot across his belly at me, but would take a pop at you for starters. So I saved your hide," she stated.

Although he could have argued with her logic, he didn't. How could he and why would he? It was trust that was developing, trust that she had no hidden agenda or malicious intentions, and that her heart was open and honest, and her charm, well, irresistible.

"And so, you're still here and you need to get back to Over There if possible, agreed?" interjected Casey.

"Agreed," said Pistol Ann.

The Rider hesitated as he stared into the depths of the fire, pondering the question.

Gabriel, expressing his impatience, snorted and stomped a hoof on the floor of his stall.

"Agreed," he said with no small amount of reluctance. Then, turning to Casey he said, "Alright, let's go over the scenario of your trip over and back one more time. To begin with, you were caught in a storm, riding to nowhere in particular."

"Right, and don't forget, I was imbibing along the way."

"Riding and liquored up in a blinding storm," quipped Pistol Ann, "you suddenly—you're not sure how—arrive in the livery stables of the Notre Dame Cathedral in Paris, France."

"Precisely!" said Casey.

"And what was your motive for riding around aimless to nowhere in particular?" asked ex-attorney Virgil Jones.

"Well . . . bitterness had gotten a hold of me and was eating me up to the point where I felt lifeless and dead inside. Haven't we been over all of this before?" he said.

"Yes," answered the Rider, "but we need to make sure the facts are in place to try to find the missing key, if there is one."

"Riding in a storm all liquored up and feeling dead inside. Sound familiar Virgil?" asked Pistol Ann.

"The exact same, in every way," he acknowledged.

"Alright then, as I left Paris I was full of liquor once again, just riding, and although there was a storm, I didn't get caught in it and somehow ended up back in Witchita," explained Casey.

"What was your motive for leaving Paris?" asked Virgil.

"Why, I had lost the woman I had loved, even though it was always from a distance, the pain was unimaginable. Her name was Esmeralda."

"In my attempts," said the Rider, "I rode, beat the storm but did not return. Then, I rode all liquored up, again beat the storm, but still didn't return to Over There. So . . . what's missing?"

He paused, and after a brief reflection, answered his own question. "I was drinking Chateaux Le Blanc when I passed from Abilene into Witchita."

"And I drank White Castle when I passed from Witchita to Paris, and Chateaux Le Blanc when I returned from Paris to Witchita," said Casey.

"And on my attempts to return to Abilene—Over There—I used White Castle and then El Casa Blanco. Both times I failed. Maybe I need to try it under the influence of Chateaux Le Blanc," the Rider said.

"Someone would have to ride clear to S'Aint Looey to get any. I'm pretty sure there ain't none in town," said Pistol Ann.

"How far?" asked Virgil.

"First to the north horizon, and then east for one or two or three hundred furlongs, more or less," said Pistol Ann.

"Before we head off to S'Aint Looey, let's check with Pedro. Maybe, just maybe, he'll have some Chateaux Le Blanc in stock and hidden somewhere," suggested the Rider.

"Alright, so assuming it is the Chateaux Le Blanc and you get some and drink it and that experiment fails, what then?" said Pistol Ann.

"Then we'll have to dig a little deeper and try something different, again and maybe again."

"Or, you'd just have to accept As-Is," said Casey.

"I don't believe in As-Is . . . old chap."

“That’s quite all right, but remember, the truth remains the truth and operates on its own, whether you believe it or not,” replied Casey.

“Or entirely understand it,” Pistol Ann added.

“Back to the Chateaux Le Blanc, suppose you can’t find any, anywhere, what then?”

“I can’t say, Casey. I don’t know. All I can do is try for as many times as it takes, or until I’m ready to give up,” said the Rider.

“And I thought only horses wore blinders,” mumbled ReeBa. Gabriel snorted from his stall.

“First things first, I’ll go see Pedro. Maybe, just maybe, he’ll happen to have some Chateaux Le Blanc,” said the Rider, tossing back his drink and pushing back his chair with his legs as he stood to leave.

“I’ll go with you,” said Pistol Ann, blasting down her drink.

* * *

Alone and staring into the fire, Casey Mojo idly commented, “I thought only horses wore blinders.”

“My sentiments exactly,” said ReeBa.

“And mine,” echoed Gabriel.

“Are you two ready for a trip to S’Aint Looey?” asked Casey.

“I’m ready,” said the big buckskin.

“Well, it’s a little cold, but I’ll get Ann there. I know the way,” replied the sorrel mare.

“I’ll keep you warm,” said Gabriel.

ReeBa gave a playful snicker as Casey hustled first to Gabriel’s stall, then to hers, loading their bins with oats and their mangers with hay.

“Better fill up for the trip,” he said as he scurried to the tack room to get their gear.

Ann and Virgil burst through the man door, first stomping their feet and then shaking the snow off their shoulders.

"Casey! Pedro didn't have any Chateaux Le Blanc. We're heading off to S'Aint Looey," hollered the Rider. "Can you . . . ?"

"Already done, sir Virgil," said Casey as the two horses pranced out of the intersecting alleyways, saddled up and ready to go, turning to face Virgil and Ann. "Nice touch," she said, laughing.

Casey walked past the couple, lifted the plank holding the double doors closed, and then swung them out and open. They mounted the horses, Ann on ReeBa and Virgil on Gabriel and then moved side by side out the opened doors. Casey watched them until they disappeared in the night and then closed and barred the double doors. He ambled over to the fire pit and seated himself, not weary but very tired. Virgil Jones was a hard case and required a lot of energy; he had no doubt about that.

Knowing Mesmerala would be watching the couple he had put an Invisible Ring around the horses while he saddled them, the same kind that surrounded the stable and kept the bruja witch from penetrating the secrets inside. The travelling couple would be invisible to her eyes and silent to her ears.

"Why would they want Chateaux Le Blanc?" Mesmerala asked herself as she gazed into the glass ball, watching Virgil and Ann as they left the Burnt Dog Saloon. Well, no matter really, she no longer lusted after Virgil, not in the usual sense. What she lusted for was his blood and the head of Pistol Ann. That double-barreled shotgun blast to the midsection had hurt like Hell-Oh.

After watching the double doors of the livery stable swing open and Casey Mojo standing there looking at nothing, himself looking stupid, she was going to cover The Orb until, at the last second, she noticed the hoof prints of two unseen horses plod-plod-plodding in the snow. Angry, she covered The Orb and stood, twirled toward the fire, inserted her hands into the flames, and uttered one word, "Smoke." She became it and sifted under the door of the shack. Drifting along at an unhurried pace, she followed the horse's hoof prints as they seemed to appear by magic, moving toward the north horizon.

Arriving at it, the prints turned right. Pistol Ann and the Rider didn't know they were invisible to the bruja witch and were unaware of the witch herself being close. Their attentions were focused on each other. And although the weather was not the most agreeable—dark, cold, and snowy—he thought it perfect, for he felt as though he and Ann were the only people in the world and the feeling exhilarated him. He hoped she felt at least a small portion of what he did, but he still wasn't ready to open his heart. Besides, he had guarded it for so long he didn't know how to.

They rode side by side, silent in the silence.

"Sure is a quiet night. I'm glad there's no blizzard," he said.

"It won't be long now," she commented.

"What, until we make S'Aint Looey?"

"No, until the night is done with its work."

The Rider remained silent, not sure of what she meant and still confused by Casey's rendition of the night and its work. Maybe she wasn't sure of what it meant either, and she was just speaking words. He aimed to find out. He reined up.

"What do you mean by that?" he asked her, his manner point blank and demanding.

She pulled ReeBa to a halt and turned in the saddle toward him. "Soon, either the darkness will be driven from your heart, or you'll return to Over There with it still in place."

"Do I have a choice in the matter?"

"Yes and no."

"What the hell kind of an answer is that?" he asked his exasperation bristling outward to near palpability.

"Because being in Right Here and Now is a matter of the heart. Some people listen and a healing comes, some don't because they'd rather wander in the dark, and sometimes our hearts just plain ambush us with the truth and there's no denying it or getting around it. So, you see, the answer is yes and no. So which is it, Mr. Virgil Jones Rider, you hold the key." She smiled so bright and warm it could make snowflakes melt.

He could feel a small crack in the granite that surrounded his heart, but wasn't ready to surrender to the reason for its making.

Pistol Ann clucked her tongue, urging ReeBa forward. Gabriel needed no urging and moved ahead on his own accord.

Lost in their own thoughts—his swirling, hers clear—they arrived at the MissSoSloppy River before weariness from the journey could set in.

Halting and dismounting, they led the horses down the low angle embankment to a ferry waiting at the river's edge, visible to everyone there, the horse's hooves clip-clopped on the deck as they boarded.

Watching the lights of the city blaze, reflected and twinkling on the wide river, Virgil felt a long ago but not forgotten excitement. He hadn't been to a city just to explore it since Richmond, sometime before the Goddam War.

"Beautiful isn't it," said Pistol Ann.

"Well, pretty enough," he responded, "but I wouldn't go so far as to call it beautiful, considering what usually festers in the underbellies of big cities."

"And what might those things be?"

"The robbers, rapers, murderers, hustlers, scammers and thieves, for starters, then there's the greed and misplaced ambition, shattered hopes and dying dreams, lost souls and broken hearts. All the diseases and desperation that is refused, yet is clearly seen despite the blindfold of denial."

Bulls-eye.

"Like I said, some like to continue to wander in the dark," said Pistol Ann.

The ferry squished into the opposite shore, spilling its cargo of vagabonds and ruffians, gamblers and drunks, prostitutes and hustlers, and the broken hearts looking to find their way home; all held in thrall by the glittering city spewing out the Bloos.

"Can you point me to a good livery stable?" the Rider asked the ferry boss as his dark skinned rope tuggers took their well-deserved rest. He pointed. "Up yonder street, 'bout three blocks, take a left, and there ye'll be. Place called Joe's. Cain't miss it."

"Obliged," the Rider said to him, flipping the wizened old geezer a gold coin.

After getting the horsed unloaded, the frontier couple began their stroll down the center of S'Aint Looey. Despite being dark and the sky spitting snow, the place was as lively as if it were broad daylight, except the nightlife was in full swing to top it off.

Horses pulling carriages moved both ways up and down the street of frozen dirt, carrying ladies and gentlemen dressed in brightly colored finery. Mules pulled open buckboards carrying fur traders and country folk clad in fringed buckskins or canvas pants. Dogs meandered here and there with an occasional bark or yap.

A wide boardwalk lined each side of the street, lit by the diffused light that spilled out from storefront windows creating a constant glow under the porches that covered them. The people milling about on the walks were indistinct, the only difference was their shade of gray skirt or pair of pants.

Underneath it all played the S'Aint Looey Bloos, the famed delta music, muffled as it drifted around and through the doors of the bars and saloons scattered along the broad street.

Not forgetting their mission was to find a bottle of Chateaux Le Blanc, they decided to try their luck at the River Boat Bar and Grill. Not fancy, but not a dive, Pistol Ann and the Rider took a table by a window overlooking the street, which against the backdrop of a black sky was well lit by gas lamps on posts, one on each corner of the intersections. In the street, out from under the covered boardwalk, the myriad of activity and color swirled and intermingled in a dazzling array.

A perky red haired waitress wearing a royal blue short skirt and a sleeveless white blouse bounced over to their table with a pad in her left hand and a pencil in her right. "What can I get for you fine folks?" she asked.

"I'll have a steak, medium rare, a couple of eggs, toast, and coffee," said Pistol Ann.

The waitress wrote the order in her own private shorthand and then turned to the Rider, "Sir?"

"I'll have the same, but before all that I'd like a double shot of whiskey. Chateaux Le Blanc if you've got it."

"Chateaux Le what, never heard of it, but I'll bring you a drink of our finest, White Castle it's called. I think you'll find it to your liking."

"Sure, and bring one for the lady too, will you?"

"Certainly sir," the red head chirped as she wiggled away toward the bar.

The River Boat was, first and foremost, a bar, a run of the mill, nondescript place with nothing that would impress upon the memory and had all the usual smells, clientele, noise and goings on, except for one thing, Janice Louise was the singer at the piano.

The Rider's jaw dropped open when he laid eyes on her. Pistol Ann, following his gaze asked him, "Your long lost love?"

"She looks like her, yes, but it can't be. What do you suppose . . ."

Quick as a lightning bolt wrapped in flesh, Pistol Ann drew her revolver and shot the woman straight through the heart.

A collective gasp hissed from the crowd, a couple of women screamed, the bartender pulled a shotgun out from under the bar top, and the Rider had his Colt drawn and cocked before the boom of Ann's gun died to silence.

"Give me your Bowie!" Ann said, holstering her pistol as she stood. Reaching with his left hand, and without question, the Rider handed her the blade.

"Somebody call the police!" a woman's voice shrieked.

Ignoring the call for the authorities, Ann was kneeling over the woman's shot and bleeding body, the Rider standing behind her. Suddenly realizing the situation he said, "Better let me do that Ann." She didn't speak, just shook her head back and forth to say no and placed the gleaming blade in front of the prone woman's eyes. "Take a look bruja," she said. The dead woman's eyes opened and sparked with fear.

"Leave us, go away, and I'll let you live."

Mesmerala nodded her consent. Pistol Ann stood up. The image of Janice Louise, shot through the heart and lying on the floor, still as death, glanced at the Rider as if to say good-bye.

Ann turned toward him. "Is she finally dead to you now?" she asked.

"Yes . . . yes, she is," he answered with no hesitation.

The bruja witch dematerialized to her essence, nothing more than a sooty mist, and drifted out the door as the police were coming through it.

"Officer," said a stately woman, "there's been a murder." She pointed at Ann. "That woman shot the piano singer in cold blood."

The officer turned to look.

"Where's the body? Where's the blood?" he asked Pistol Ann, his short stout frame calm and unmoving. "Did you shoot and kill someone miss?"

"No officer," Ann replied.

He stroked his bushy moustache, his eyebrows furrowed, and his deep-set dark eyes vacant and then semi-alert.

"Anybody seen a corpse, seen a murder?" he asked. The bartender shrugged his shoulders, the rest of the patrons followed suit.

"But, but I . . . saw . . ." stammered the stately woman.

"It's alright Misses Swein, maybe you've just had too much to drink," said the officer and without further fanfare left the silent River Boat Bar and Grill.

The piano man began playing "*Camp Town Ladies*".

Pistol Ann handed the Rider his knife.

"How'd you know?" he asked, sheathing the Bowie.

"She used the same trick before, didn't she?"

"But maybe she could have been . . ." he trailed off.

"No, because in Right Here and Now and in Over There, similar people exist, but are not exact in every detail, but the same people at all times are in each world."

"Like an evil twin or a doppleganger?"

"Yes, a very real possibility. Your former love, what was her name?"

"Janice Louise."

"There could only be an image of her in this world, and her heart would be full of hate instead of love. The one you knew is dead and gone, lost to you forever. Do you understand now?"

He nodded, an undefined sadness creeping across his rugged face.

"Soon you will see the evidence of that truth," she said.

"But how did you know it was the witch?" he asked.

"I could feel the Shadowside of Magic as we travelled to the north horizon. Casey had made us invisible you know. Anyway, it slithered past us when we turned toward S'Aint Looey. I figured it had to be Mesmerala and I expected her to be here."

"What if she had been Janice Louise's actual twin in this world?"

"Like I said, Mr. Virgil Jones Rider, I can detect magic of various types."

Red the waitress bounced back to their table, somehow balancing two platters of food, two glasses, and a bottle of White Castle whiskey. Placing it down with the exaggeration of a cartoon character at work, she said, "Enjoy!" and jiggled along her merry routine.

"White Castle, that's what Casey Mojo drinks," the Rider stated without needing to.

"M-m-m-ph," said Pistol Ann around a mouthful of steak. A smile lit his face and came real close to reaching his heart. He tossed back a velvety shot of Mojo whiskey and then dove into his meal with an appetite turned ravenous.

They ate in silence, no daintiness wasted on enjoyment, Pistol Ann matched the Rider's belch at the end of the meal.

After sharing a laugh over their unacceptable big city behavior, the Rider left a gold coin on the table, and they left the River Boat.

"Keep the change darlin'", he told red the waitress on the way out the door, and they strolled arm in arm down the boardwalk of S'Aint Looey's main street. Up ahead, underneath the glow of a gas lamp, a gilded sign announced the entrance to the Chateaux Les Bien Hotel.

"Let's try that one!"

"It may be a house of ill repute, m'lady."

"That's something you don't need. You have me, remember. But I'll go in with you . . . just in case," extending her playfulness she squeezed his arm, causing a grin to split his leathery face.

"Deal," he said, "on both counts."

The hotel lobby was opulent, replete with wall to wall carpet, light green in color, on both sides of an eight foot wide polished hardwood aisle that led up to the front desk. Scattered around the lobby were French provincial style chairs and sofas holding a few patrons. Through an open double width doorway, an elegant restaurant and bar offered sustenance and comfort to the patrons of the establishment.

A crystal chandelier, holding a hundred lighted candles, hung over the center of the room.

"Must be a full time job keeping that thing going," muttered the Rider as his and Ann's boot heels thudded on the hardwood floor making their presence known.

Not noticing any working ladies, Pistol Ann turned her head and asked, "Are we out of place?"

"Only if we think we are. I reckon they'll take my money same as anyone else's once they see it shine." He paused to look at her. "So . . . whadda ya say ma'am, a room for the night?"

"The night can last a long time in these heah parts," she replied.

"All the better."

The starchy desk clerk handed an upper room key to the Rider, pointing out with great care that hot water for a bath was included in the price of the room. "All you need to do is come here to the desk and ask," he said.

"Well, tell you what, you get the tub filled with hot water, and don't forget the towels and such. This gentleman and the lady will be in the bar over there, and when things are just right, you have someone come get us."

"Yes, certainly sir," replied the clerk, some of the starch gone out of him his pale ceramic face cracked a smile.

The couple turned and sauntered through the double wide arched doorway to the bar, seating themselves at a table in a corner.

"Monsieur, mademoiselle," said a shadow as it reached a lit match to the candle in the center of the table. The lighted candle revealed a pretty waitress, maybe the sister of River Boat red. Big as it is it can often be a small world. "What is you pleasure tonight?" she asked after blowing out the match.

Before he could respond with "She is," indicating Pistol Ann, she asked, "Do you have any Chateaux Le Blanc whiskey?" remaining on the track of their mission.

"Oui, mademoiselle."

"Will you bring us a bottle and two glasses?"

"Oui," replied Auburn and then disappeared.

"Well, maybe we're in luck," said the Rider.

"Depends on your definition of luck," she responded with a low and husky voice.

Not detecting her not too veiled hint, the Rider continued. "Chateaux Le Blanc, it might be the return ticket to Over There!"

"It has to work this time. I can't take any more of this not knowing whether you will or won't return one way or another."

He covered her hand with his. "Ann, I'll stay if you want me too."

"I've already told you that wouldn't work in the long run."

"Yeah, I remember, I just figured it was worth one more shot."

Waitress Auburn set their orders on the table, pouring them each a drink into an etched crystal glass.

"Fan-see," he exclaimed.

"No belching allowed," said Pistol Ann.

Unpretentious, guileless, God how I love this woman! Oh, oh, his heart had overcome his thick head, and the piercing sweetness of the revelation took his breath for a moment.

"Ann."

"Yes."

"I . . . uh . . . was wondering what you meant when you told me I'd soon see the truth of our dual selves in the two worlds."

She smiled, and then laughed, looking at him with an I-know-what-your-game-is-look. "Let's have a few couth and culture snorts of this here liquor Mr. Jones and then I'll show you something to make your eyes pop out. Making your toes curl comes later," she quipped. All eyes in the place turned toward her as her own danced with merriment and delight. She wished she had a chew so she could spit.

No debutante was she, but oh so real.

A couple of drinks later and out the door they headed, knowing once they entered their room, they wouldn't be leaving for a long languorous time.

"Keep the bath water hot, we'll be back before daylight," said Pistol Ann as they passed the desk clerk, his ceramic face remaining meticulous and still.

"Daylight, what was she saying?"

Arriving on the boardwalk, the crowd and noise increasing, she held his arm as they walked south to a quiet open space, not far off of Main Street. The snow had stopped and the stars glittered like diamonds sheathed in a black velvet showcase. A quarter moon hung like a single earring from the sky. Though it was dark, he could see with absolute clarity in the light nature provided.

Seating themselves on a split log bench, he gazed into the light that was Pistol Ann, and her love, the light from her eyes, penetrated deep into his soul, a soul he thought dead and lost forever.

"Ann . . ."

"Sh-h-h, no time for talk right now. Drink," she said, pointing at the bottle he had carried out of the hotel. He took a long gulp then handed her the bottle and she did likewise. Setting the container of amber liquid on the bench, she placed her hands together at arm's length out and slightly above her head. Putting her thumbs and forefingers together, she then moved them apart, upward and then outward and then down and in, inscribing the shape of a heart into the air.

"Look," she said.

The air began to shimmer and wave, like the surface of a clear mountain lake when a playful breeze skims feather light across its surface.

"What's happening?"

"Watch and see," she said, tantalizing him.

The shimmer on the air became a series of slow undulations, like a thin film of glass pulsating in and out from top to bottom. The darkness on the other side began giving way to splashes of color, illuminated by an unseen light. The sky took on a subtle shade of gray. Then, where horizon should have been but was not yet a clear view, the gray lightened further, taking on a bluish hue that spread upward until the entire sky was painted a true blue, the other colors becoming sharper and forming into streets and buildings and living moving people.

Was this the daylight Pistol Ann had spoken of? No, he thought, *we aren't back at the Chateaux Les Bien yet.* He continued watching in awe as the scene unfolded behind the shimmering wall.

A red stagecoach pulled up in front of a hotel called The Best House, an exact replica of the Chateaux Les Bien. The driver climbed down, opened the stage door, and out stepped Lily Francine! Following her was Camille, the poor girl he had saved so very long ago.

"What is this, what are you doing?" he asked.

"This is . . . The Other, and you are looking Over There."

"I'm going over!" he declared, his impetuousness out of check. "Come with me Ann, please," he said as he stood up off the split log bench.

"I can't and you can't either."

"It's right here, in front of us. All I gotta do is step through it!" he declared.

She gestured with an extended hand as if to say, "Be my guest."

He walked forward, hands out, feeling for the shimmering wall of The Other, but it moved as he moved, never nearer, never farther, The Other kept the same distance from the Rider, just beyond the reach of his outstretched hands, the scene remaining the same.

After a time, and realizing the futility of his actions, he returned to the split log bench where Pistol Ann sat in perfect serenity. "Okay you win," he said, plopping down beside her.

"I don't win anything; it's just the way things are for now. We haven't found the key yet, but we're a lot closer. Look now!" she said pointing at the shimmering Other.

He looked and saw a horseman pull up near the stage. Dismounting, he took a couple of strides to Lily Francine and then wrapped her in his arms.

It was him.

"That's me, I mean an image of me!" he exclaimed.

"Yes . . . when you passed through, a replacement for you—Over There—had to be provided, and that's who you see now. Did you love that woman?"

"I thought I could but now I understand that she only reminded me of Janice Louise . . . and I have buried her for good."

"For good, yes, for your good, Mr. Virgil Jones Rider," she said and squeezed his hand.

"Yes," he replied, drinking in her beauty underneath the quarter moon's partial yet revealing light. "I want to kiss you," he said.

"No one's going to stop you."

He wrapped his arms around her waist, she, her arms around his neck. Their lips crushed together in white-hot hunger, without hesitation, without exploration.

"Wanna go home?" she asked as their lips parted one from the others, ending their kiss.

"No."

"I mean to the hotel," she explained.

"Lead the way," he said as they stood, hand in hand, and walked back the way they had come. He glanced back just before they reached Main Street, and saw nothing but dark empty space.

Just what was the key to The Other?

Right now, he didn't give a tinker's damn.

CHAPTER THIRTY-THREE

Returning to Witchita with a full bottle of Chateaux Le Blanc, time, as the Rider perceived it, and despite the days and nights cycling at regular intervals, passed in a slow whisper. But the weather remained unchanged, it was always winter, and within the season there seemed a constant threat of a blizzard coming out of the north to rip across the plains.

Pistol Ann was a constant at his side, awake or asleep. They would spend days riding to nowhere and back again until ReeBa became too swollen with foal to ride.

Virgil didn't believe it possible, but his love for Ann deepened, and the special candle that made her light burned brighter every day.

"I will never tire of you," he told her.

"Does that mean I can keep my chewing tobacco?" she asked, her comfort level high, her playful mood higher.

God, he loved her!

But underneath it all, the fear; the fear of the time of returning to Over There without her. "Can't you go with me?" he implored her several times, but always, "No . . . we've discussed that." She was tough as leather when the need arose.

He knew he had to try. Without doing so, there would always be a blank spot in his soul, an unanswered question somewhere in his mind, sometimes at the front, sometimes at the back, and a vague uneasiness would hover in his newborn heart. An uneasiness that would spill over and touch them both, like the undercurrent of a slow moving stream increasing in intensity until it became like the recognition of death as it approached, inevitable and intimate. Despite his love for Pistol Ann and hers for him, it was a hard fact waiting for him, the kind of no escaping.

In times past, he wouldn't have cared. He would have embraced the returning, but since the renewal of how it felt to be so alive, all he wanted was to have Pistol Ann at his side forever . . . and that was one thing he knew, right well.

Mesmerala had kept her promise. Leaving S'Aint Looey after having been shot the second time by Pistol Ann, she retreated to her shack on the edge of Witchita. With no familiar to help her since the death of the Blood Spiller, she had to recuperate and then rejuvenate to restore her powers and lay plans for revenge.

This time she had to conjure a storm. Preventing them from falling in love was now out of the question, and without the Blood Spiller, her chances of killing the couple were nil.

All she could hope for now was to return the darkness to the Rider's heart and inject the bitch Pistol Ann's soul with deadly poison, and as long as she kept to herself, safe within the decrepit shack, her plans would go undetected.

Done contemplating, stiff and sore from the shotgun blast, Mesmerala stood up from the table, walked slow and with effort to a barrel of snow melt over in a dark corner of her shack, picked up a bucket next to it and dipped it into the rancid water. Hauling the bucket of water across the room, she poured it into a cauldron hanging over the fire. On her third trip, she had to stop mid-way to the barrel and also back to the fire to rest. "Goddam Pistol Ann," she cursed as she found enough strength to pour the last bucket of water into the cauldron.

She returned to her table. Before long, she heard the bubbling of the water boiling. She stood, her magic weak, and ambled over to the cauldron. Scooping out a bucketful of the hot water, she took it outside and placed the full bucket on the ground. As the steam billowed in the frozen air, forming ice granules, she opened a leather bag hanging from her waist. Pulling what looked like an ordinary piece of dried meat from out of it, she tossed it into the steaming bucket of water, saying, "Buzzard gizzard, winter blizzard." She reached into her bag again and took out another dried, leathery, twisted object, tossed it into the water and incanted, "Unborn fetus now come forth, bring the storm from the north." She reached in her bag once more, and again pulled out an object that appeared to be the twisted dry fingers of a rat's paw. "Add to this the toad's toes, to make certain the north wind blows," and then she flipped it into the near boiling hot water.

The air above the steaming bucket crackled with an eerie dirty green light as the rising steam crystallized and spread out and around until the contents of the bucket were emptied. No wind to drive it and as if having a mind of its own, the cloud of ice granules drifted off toward the north horizon, a green glowing ghost against the blackness of the night.

Satisfied as she watched it move away, the bruja witch turned and headed for her shack, the empty bucket in her hand. The door creaked open for her, she entered, set the bucket down by the barrel of rancid water, retrieved The Orb from the fireplace mantel, sat on her stool, uncovered the glass ball, and waited for the coming storm; the blizzard that would force the Rider's hand, bringing darkness to his heart and damage to that of his lover's.

Her tongue darted in and out of her cold thin lips, flicking like a viper's. She rubbed her gnarled hands together in wicked anticipation of the upcoming show, with her as the director. Like a lightning flash, her face contorted with the rage of Hell-Oh and she shrieked with a high-pitched keening, the sound of grief and rage combined into one.

"My Blood Spiller, you killed my beloved pet and you will pay! Your misery will be double what I have suffered." Her hair stood straight up and out as if electrified. She floated up off her stool, as foul spittle dribbled from the corners of her twisted mouth.

Chapter Thirty-Four

He awoke to the velvety softness lying by his side. Loving Ann throughout the night, the Rider should have felt spent in completeness and satisfaction. Instead, his energy level was up near the ceiling of the sky, and blazed a blue just as deep.

Rising quietly, not disturbing Pistol Ann, he dressed, slipped on his boots, then buckled on the thick leather belt that held his Colt on his right hip and the sheathed Bowie knife on his left.

Moving with the quietness of a cat across the rug, he paused as he placed his hand on the doorknob.

"It's time isn't it?"

How did these people always discern the heart of the matter?

"Yes," he answered.

"Will you wait for me downstairs?"

"Of course," he said with a heavy sigh. He opened the door and disappeared behind it as it closed.

Pistol Ann moved lithely out of the bed, took her robe off the post, wrapped it around herself, walked around the foot of the bed and stood looking out the window to the north.

They had until mid-morning, maybe mid-day, hard to tell, they were still in Right Here and Now.

All the practice runs, all the scenarios played out in the mind, all the lines rehearsed, never seem to quite hit the spot when the time of the real deal finally arrives.

Tears flowed freely down her cheeks making tiny red circles on the rug around her bare feet that felt like they weighed a ton a piece as she took the two steps to the wash basin. She bent to wash herself and then slowly got dressed. Liveliness is hard to muster when your heart is breaking and almost impossible when the rending is complete.

Mesmerala clapped her hands in utter and complete glee as she peered into The Orb. Oh yes, it enlivened her to see the suffering being imposed on the little bitch. Double her own, was that too much to inflict? Hell-Oh no.

* * *

The western sky blazed deep purple as the rider strode down the boardwalk. Taking a deep long breath in through his nose, he slowly exhaled out of his mouth. It was calming, sort of.

The deeply inhaled air carried the distinctive smell of snow. His energy level hadn't waned since he arose to start his day. Stopping long enough to pay attention, he realized the wind had picked up and was coming from the north, a confirmation of what Pistol Ann had known since wakeup.

Wakeup. Maybe the last time he would open his sleepy eyes to gaze upon her sweet face. He loved her. Even more strengthening, he trusted her, for her heart was true, and knowing that was now breaking his. He entered the Burnt Dog for perhaps his last breakfast with her.

* * *

She had come down the stairway as he sat at their table contemplating As-Is. Acceptance, was that the key? He could not accept acceptance. He was a man of action and the plain dressed yet radiant lady coming down the stairs was someone he would lay down his life for, because he now loved Pistol Ann more than life itself.

Pedro served them up buffalo steak and eggs with fried potatoes for breakfast. He was somber, as if he knew, as if the entire town knew, that tonight would tell a tale.

They ate in silence, occasionally looking at each other. A hard time was coming in fast and finding the right words to say was near impossible.

As soon as they finished, Pedro was there to clear away the table and set down a fresh bottle of El Casa Blanco, along with two glasses. “On thee house,” he said, and ambled off to his post behind the bar.

Something was missing. Glancing around, the Rider put his finger on it in an instant. Patrick O’Malley, Charlie, and Clem weren’t in their places. Maybe they just didn’t want to say good-bye, or in fact couldn’t.

The barroom may as well have been a funeral parlor, it was so dead and quiet.

“Virgil,” said Ann. She’d never called him by just his first name before, not that he could remember anyway.

“I’m going to go visit Casey Mojo,” she said, the sadness in her eyes betraying the cheerfulness in her voice.

“I’ll stay here for the time being. Maybe you and Casey can work some kind of magic and we can get around this.”

She smiled, but as hard as she tried, it was weak and unconvincing.

He felt his heart sink along with what little hope it had held.

Pistol Ann picked up her rifle, pushed back her chair, and walked out the door without so much as a backward glance.

Sweet and tough thought the Rider, tossing back a shot of El Casa Blanco.

The western sky deepened in its purpling as the Rider continued along the boardwalk cursing Fate, Destiny, and

As-Is all at the same time, preparing his heart once more for darkness to settle in and takeover.

Not bothering to knock, he opened the man door and walked in. Seeing Casey and Ann in conversation, he pulled up a chair and joined them without saying a word. After getting settled, he looked over at Casey. "Storm brewing," he said. Casey simply nodded.

"Want to try it sir?" the Wise Won asked.

Pistol Ann stared pensively into the fire, unable to speak. The moment of her soul piercing had come.

"Might as well," he replied.

"I'll get Gabriel's gear and saddle him up for you sir," said Casey.

"Maybe throw an extra bag of oats on him," suggested the Rider.

"Certainly sir," and the hunchback scuttled off to attend to the chore.

"Do you have the bottle?" asked Ann.

"Right here," the Rider replied, patting the bulge under his overcoat.

"Maybe you should start on it. I know I'd like a drink," said Pistol Ann.

Pulling out the bottle as Ann retrieved a couple of glasses from under the chair, he poured them full of Chateaux Le Blanc.

"Here's to failure," he said, raising his glass. Pistol Ann withheld comment and clinked her glass with his. *To failure . . . please let it be so,* she thought, but no hope was coupled with it.

He didn't cry, didn't even let out a whimper, when he'd heard the news of the rapes and murders of his family, the total destruction of all he had known, all he wanted was to weep in sorrow, but not in front of his own men and he wouldn't now. He would not show weakness.

Pistol Ann didn't hold such sentiment. He tenderly reached over and brushed a tear from her cheek with the hand that had killed so often, and now only wanted to hold her.

"Ready sir," said Casey as he led Gabriel out of his stall.

"Take my Winchester, you might need it," said Pistol Ann.

That was like offering him her right arm! He could not refuse such a precious and sacrificial gift. He simply nodded yes.

"I'll fetch the scabbard for it," said Casey and scuttled off once again. Returning within minutes, he then attached it by its leather thongs to the Rider's saddle.

"It's fully loaded," said Pistol Ann, handing him the piece. Reaching into the pocket of her britches she gave him a handful of bullets. He stuffed them into his pants pocket.

Rising they walked hand in hand over to the big buckskin. Virgil turned; she raised her mouth to his for one last kiss and lingering embrace.

"I should wish you luck but I can't," she told him.

"Goddam As-Is I reckon," he replied. She nodded as he swung atop Gabriel.

Casey slowly ambled over to the double doors and opened them, letting in the stiff north wind that seemed to have a habit of curling east up Main Street.

"Giddup," he said and the big buckskin trotted slowly out the livery stables doors. The Rider never looked back. He wouldn't.

He couldn't let Pistol Ann see the tear freezing in place before it could roll off his cheek.

Casey and Ann watched the Rider disappear down a northbound side street. The hunchback gently took her by the upper arm and led her back into the livery stable where he seated her by the fire pit. Turning tear filled eyes towards him, she implored with a voice that betrayed the agony she felt, "Is there no hope?" Shaking his head sadly he replied, "No, my child. He will return to Over There." Pistol Ann dropped her eyes to the ground in meek acceptance of his words and the tone of finality in how he said them.

She lifted her eyes to meet the hunchbacks. She had one last option.

"I'm going through The Other, to Over There," she stated.

"You cannot."

"I can and I will."

A soft knock thudded on the man door of the stable. Casey Mojo stood and before going over to answer the knock said to Pistol Ann. "Better think on it for a while." She offered no reply.

He returned to the fire pit a moment later, the bruja witch trailing behind him. Her look and demeanor had changed as if by magic and maybe that was what was used. She looked beautiful. Not young, not old, she radiated a grace and wisdom far beyond normal. She sat down next to Casey, who had returned to his chair by Ann.

"She wants to cross The Other, to be with Virgil Jones," Casey told Mesmerala.

"It's possible, but very tricky," she responded after a quick contemplation of what she'd been told.

"Tricky? How?" he asked.

"We'd have to bring her double over here at the exact same time she crossed over."

"What about the Rider's double, Herschel Johns? He's still Over There," said Pistol Ann.

"He's far away, in Philadelphia with Lily Francine. They're content and not looking, and besides, invisibility covers that situation, remember?" replied Mesmerala. "Whereas your double would be attracted to Virgil Jones, like a bee to honey and it wouldn't matter how far apart they were," she continued.

"Are you still going to insist on trying?" Casey asked Ann.

"Father, how was I to know I would truly fall in love with him? I have to try." "You do understand that if you should die Over There you will stay dead without any possibility of returning."

"I would take that risk to spend one day with Virgil."

Casey nodded, knowing there would be no denying the will of Ann in the matter. Turning to Mesmerala he asked, "Will you help?"

"Of course."

* * *

Moving with stout determination through the blizzard, Casey, Ann, and Mesmerala walked to the northern edge of town, clear of all buildings, people, and lights. Mesmerala stopped and began waving her hands in the air in a circular motion, the right hand moving clockwise, the left moving counterclockwise. Casey and Pistol Ann followed her lead.

In front of them within a circle of about ten feet in diameter, the snow stopped swirling and the wind around them became dead calm. Within the circle the air visibly shimmered beyond its usual wavy surface.

The scene cleared then focused into night Over There and then went into the interior of the Red Dog Saloon in Wichita. The Rider was sitting at a table staring out the window at nothing, his eyes and face blank, a bottle of whiskey at his hand. His face had grown long and haggard and the lines in it were now deep canyons.

"Oh Virgil!" exclaimed Pistol Ann. "Has he lost all hope father?" she asked.

"Not yet child, but he is lost in very deep sorrow."

"I must get to him! Mesmerala what can we do?"

"First, we have to locate your double to see how long until they have a chance of meeting."

She waved her arms in a figure eight pattern, crossing her hands one over the other in the middle, then continuing them out in an elliptical pattern, repeating this motion over and over she chanted:

"Glass of The Other
Scan and Pan
Show the image of
Pistol Ann."

The Red Dog Saloon blurred out of focus and darkness filled the shimmering circle as it searched for the object of the witch's command. The shimmer intensified, then lightened, showing a busy main street in a western town. After panning back and forth several times the circular eye came to stop in front of a saloon. The gilded letters on its window read:

THE LONGHORN SALOON

Mesmerala incanted:

"Glass that shimmers
Don't make me wait
Show the town
And the state."

With a quick motion the scene shifted across the street to reveal another sign:

THE OASIS HOTEL & RESTAURANT
ABILENE, TEXAS

"Alright," said Mesmerala shifting the scene back to the Longhorn Saloon and scanning the interior until it found the table where the twin image of Pistol Ann was seated.

The sight took the breath out of Pistol Ann for a moment.

She took in a gasp of air as she gazed breathlessly at her twin.

"Can we switch right now?" she asked, expending the last of her breath.

"It's too soon," replied Casey. "Mesmerala can track her with The Orb, then we will make the switch just before she arrives in Wichita. She'll be headed that way soon enough."

Pistol Ann looked at Mesmerala. "What do you think?" she asked. "I think that would be best," she replied.

* * *

Mesmerala watched diligently while secluded in her shack. The Orb at last rewarded her with the scene she had been waiting for, and the wait hadn't been too long.

Ann's image Over There was boarding a stagecoach in Abilene bound for Wichita. The teamster cracked his whip in the air and brought the reins down across the backs of the six horses. Effortlessly, the coach moved ahead and was soon beyond the boundaries of Abilene.

Having only one cycle of alternating darkness and light, Mesmerala decided to reduce the risk and immediately switch Pistol Ann while her image was in the coach.

Hurrying out of her shack, she walked rapidly to the livery stable to get Pistol Ann and Casey who were seated by the fire pit enjoying the warmth it provided against the winter chill.

The fire flickered, a tiny breeze choreographing its movements. Casey and Ann turned to see Mesmerala gliding towards them. She sat herself next to Casey with Pistol Ann on the other side of him.

"We can do this from here, but we must shed all pretenses," said Casey Mojo.

With that they stood in unison and stepped around the fire pit to stand in the exact intersection of the causeway and the alleyway of the livery.

Casey, Mesmerala, and Ann were surrounded by a shimmering light as each emanated spears of light from their bodies which were becoming absorbed in and lost to the brilliance of the glow within and without them.

Casey shed his forest green cloak, straitened to the full height of a man, his face morphing into a beautiful sea of serenity, his eyes turning golden, equal, and luminous.

Mesmerala shed her black robes, Pistol Ann her buckskins, as they followed Casey into his true state, light infusing and diffusing from their celestial like bodies.

Suspended three feet in the air, they remained still and glowed with the pulsations of a single unconditionally loving heart.

Mesmerala turned to Ann. "If you cross over Ann you know you will not be able to reduce to your true essence Over There," she explained.

"Yes, I understand. But my heart will remain as it is, and my powers, though limited, will be in place. But most important, my love for Virgil will remain unchanged."

"Yes, but who would have ever thought of it. But then I brought Esmeralda over from Notre Dame." Mesmerala smiled and squeezed Casey's hand.

"What of my image?" asked Ann.

"We will bring her here and she will be to us as you are, and she will help us to heal the brokenhearted who arrive from now on," said Casey.

"Virgil Jones was a very tough case," commented Mesmerala. "And those gun shots you put in me were hard to take, but worth it my dear for the happiness that will be yours, and well worth the small amount of pain I had to endure to bring it about."

"Sorry," said Ann. "I felt drastic measures were needed."

Mesmerala just smiled, the pulse of her heartbeat uninterrupted.

"Will I see you and Casey again?" said Ann.

"Only As-Is will tell," replied Casey.

"Yes, of course."

"Now, you must speak the words which come into your mind," said Mesmerala.

Ann closed her luminous golden eyes in concentration:

"With the blessing of Father and Mother
Cross me safely 'oer The Other
Over there I shall abide
And stand along my true love's side.
Replace me now
Inside her stage."

A powerful white light penetrated every corner of the livery stable, followed by a sound like a thunderclap, followed by a bursting nova of light. When it subsided, it revealed the hunchback, the bruja witch, and the new Pistol Ann, all staring into the fire.

The alarm signaled a tremulation in The Other. It wasn't due to the arrival of the new Pistol Ann. It was due to the arrival of the next broken heart crossing over at that precise moment.

Casey looked closely at the newly adopted Pistol Ann. "Are you ready to play Gwen Aveer?" he asked her.

She blinked a couple of times as if to clear her head, searching for a remembrance with which to answer that question. Casey Mojo put his hand around her shoulders. Mesmerala placed her right arm around her waist as they helped her to become one with them.

"Uh . . . yes, of course," she replied.

"Good," replied Casey Mojo. Turning to Mesmerala he asked, "Shall I play Merlyn?"

"I think that will work just fine, and of course, I get to play the villain again . . . perhaps a temptress."

"Excellent! I'll go up in the tower and ring the Notta Damn Bell. Sir Lancelot has arrived, tarnished armor and all."

"And I'll change Witchita into Blamelot," said Mesmerala.

Pistol Ann picked up her rifle, pushed back her chair, and walked out the door without so much as a backward glance, still not sure of what she had gotten into, she was certain it wasn't harmful.

CHAPTER THIRTY-FIVE

"Any news from Abilene?" the Rider asked Pedro.

"I have heard the sheriff . . . he say . . . good riddance to those hombres, and he no press any charges or come after you senor Rider."

"Well, I reckon that is good news Pedro, gracias. I'll be at that table over there for a spell," he said, motioning with the bottle he held in his left hand.

He seated himself by a window looking out at the street, hoping helplessly to find what, he wasn't sure. He was sure of who he missed, Pistol Ann. He never thought he would need anybody again, but maybe it's true, we all need somebody. He tossed back a drink.

Before long the night scene became a blur, his speech a slur, and he held tight to the handrail as he staggered up the stairs to his corner room where he could collapse into that old, familiar and comfortable place called oblivion.

The light of day awoke him. Out of sheer instinct he reached over for Pistol Ann, but her softness was not there, only the cool smoothness of unruffled sheets. As his mind unfuzzed from the previous night's indulgence, the stark reality of where he was and the predicament he was in crashed in on it, causing his head to damn near split from the ache.

He reached again to the other side of the bed. Still empty.

The room was a mirror image of the one in which he and Ann had slept so often, and its familiarity overwhelmed his now feeling heart with bittersweet memories, much more bitter than sweet.

He reached again to the other side of the bed. Still empty and now colder.

"The hair of the dog," he mumbled, as he threw back the covers in disgust with himself and the recent and long ago events in his life; Fate, Destiny, and all that had happened and was likely to happen yet.

"The hair of the dog," he mumbled again, getting up and dressing quickly. After pulling on his boots and buckling on his Colt and Bowie, he sat down in the soft armchair and guzzled the last quarter of the bottle of El Casa Blanco.

Braced, he headed downstairs, remembering to bring the Winchester with him. Pistol Ann's Winchester, the one thing he would never lose, unless he lost his life first.

The sun seemed stuck in the middle of the blazing blue sky, but it was deceitful, it was freezing out there on the plains.

Near noon, the Rider wasn't hungry. He strolled up to the bar. "Double shot of your good stuff," he told Pedro. Placing his left boot on the brass rail, he leaned the rifle in arm's reach against the bar.

Pedro set the glass down, the Rider tossed it back in two gulps, smacked the glass down on the bar top, grabbed the Winchester and headed out to the street, his mood not cheered by the frigid air.

A young man dressed in black from head to toe stood at the far end of the bar. He motioned Pedro over.

Pedro had noticed the kid when he came in. How could he not? His get up was near to laughable. He wore a black, flat brimmed hat without a speck of dust on it, a new black shirt made of silk and black dungarees. His black boots were polished like mirrors, with no scuffmarks, or angle of wear under the heels.

Shiny silver spurs jingled musically when he took a step. The pistol on his right hip was pearl handled, large, probably a forty-five. His holster and gun belt were a single piece of black tooled leather, new enough to squeak.

A definite dude from back east acting out a fantasy thought Pedro as he sauntered over to wait on the young man. He looked up into the kid's eyes and what he saw made his blood run cold and the hair on the back of his neck shiver. For what he saw in his eyes was the cold and unrelenting vacuum of an older man who killed for the thrill of it, and it didn't matter who; man, woman, or child.

"Wasn't that the man who just left the one they call the Rider?" asked the youthful looking dude.

"Si senor," responded Pedro.

He kid talked low, quiet, almost respectful of something, but not of life.

"Whew," he whistled, "that man is a legend."

At first Pedro thought of giving the kid a mild warning about wearing such a fancy harness, unless he knew how to use it. Wichita wasn't quite tame yet, but Pedro could tell no warning would be necessary.

"Where you from senor?"

"St. Louis," he replied, his voice as deadpan as the man himself.

"And what can I get for you senor?"

"Nothing," said the kid. "I got what I wanted." On that he turned slowly and walked toward the door. His gait was slow, smooth and measured, predatory. He would have been undetectable except for the musical jangling of his spurs.

Pedro, flooded with relief at the stranger's departure, slowly crossed himself, the way good Catholics do.

Chapter Thirty-Six

The Rider strolled easy, east to the livery stable. Except for the man door being on the other side of the double doors, it could have been the stable in Witchita—Over There. He half expected to see Casey Mojo as he stepped inside. The interior was exactly the same, and why wouldn't it be?

Gabriel snorted as the Rider passed by his stall, the last one on the left, just before the intersecting alleyways. "Morning old hoss," he said, waiting for a reply from the big buckskin. None came, oh yeah, remembered the Rider, "I'd better get a grip on my new surroundings," he told himself.

"Good morning, Mr. Jones," chirped Carson Munro. The Rider turned to where the voice came from. Rounded, with Mexican undertones, the man's eyes were large, set symmetrically apart and even in size. His mouth was as wide as his nose, and was the generous type. An honest, strong, trusting face for the most part, and all evenly proportioned.

With powerful shoulders and back centered over a narrower waist and hips, he could be mistaken for having a hump back. But his was a gentle strength, the kind that takes a lot to rile, like a man abusing a woman or a child, but once it gets there, hell itself can't stand up to it.

"Just stopped by to check on my horse," said the Rider. "We'll be staying for another day or two I reckon."

"Excellent Mr. Jones! I'll take real good care of him for you. He's about the finest hunk of horse flesh I ever did see, only I can't place his breed."

"Crossed a quarter horse with a Kentucky thoroughbred."

"Ah-h, that explains it then," said the stable keeper.

"Say . . . don't suppose you'd have a chestnut colored mare boarded here would you?" asked the Rider.

"No sir, we don't. Why?"

"Just curious is all. Nothing important."

Mr. Munro gave a rather "I don't understand" blank smile as the Rider turned to leave. Overcoat still on, he held the Winchester loosely in his right hand. Curious again the Rider asked, "Anybody live in that old shack on the western edge of town?"

"Just a harmless old woman sir, seems she's lived there forever."

"She got a name?"

"Esmeralda I believe . . . yes sir, that's what it is . . . Esmeralda."

The Rider just smiled, shook his head and closed the man door behind him. The sudden stab of bright light hurt first his eyes, then travelled along jangled nerve bundles to his head, filling it with an ache to the point of splitting it apart.

The hair of the dog he thought to himself again.

Walking eastward, intending to hold up in the Red Dog for the day, or a year, it really didn't matter to him.

A loud voice from a shadow in the street interrupted his musings and halted him in his tracks. Not quite a manly voice, the kind that hadn't survived any of the harshness of life, yet. "Hey you, the big bad Rider, I'm calling you out!"

The words had no effect, the Rider kept walking slow and easy toward the Red Dog, his boots thudding out a steady rhythm on the well-worn planks of the boardwalk.

"Rider! I'm calling you out. You murdered my brothers you yellow dog!"

Yellow Dog? No, no, he was going to the Red Dog . . . looking for oblivion and such other solace as he may find there.

Yellow Dog? The words registered. He pulled up sharp and short. That's a slander on a man's character here in the wild west, isn't it? Right now he didn't give a donkey's dong about pissant codes. They'd change sooner or later. He just wanted to be left alone.

He kept walking.

The shadow materialized from under the porch on the other side of the street. A man, dressed in black from head to foot, came into view.

"Last chance Rider, or I'll just shoot you down like the dog you are!"

He would have laughed at the man's get up except the glint of sunlight off his pearl handled revolver hurt his eyes and head even more, and that put him in a surly mood.

Very slowly using his left hand, the Rider pulled the brim of his hat down over his eyes and stepped off the boardwalk onto the street. At the same time, he placed his right thumb on the hammer of the Winchester, pulled down and cocked it. He hadn't had time to test the rifle out, but figured it would shoot straight and true, like Pistol Ann. That thought made him surlier.

Getting out of the way of the reflected sun, he asked, "Who are you?"

"Ya killed two of my brothers down at the Oasis Hotel in Abilene."

"I did, did I? You got anymore I could put in the ground for ya?"

"I do but you ain't gonna be around long enough to meet 'em." You gotta pay for what you already done."

"Well, I'm sorry mister. Sorry I didn't kill all your brothers and your ass ugly pa to boot, but I will put you in the ground if you don't tuck tail, turn around, and go the other way."

The man twitched for a split second just before his hand flashed toward the pistol on his right hip.

The Rider bent his wrist upward, aimed the Winchester from his hip, and squeezed the trigger. The man flew backwards off his feet and splatted down on his back on the boardwalk. He didn't twitch again.

The Rider levered another shell into the rifle's chamber as he walked nonchalantly up to the prostrate man. He looked down at the bullet hole in the middle of his chest.

Straight through the heart.

His pistol hadn't cleared the fancy black holster that held it. Death had been quick and painless. Too bad, thought the Rider, but instinctively he'd shot to kill and the bullet found its mark.

Holding the Winchester up for inspection he said, "Straight and true, like Pistol Ann. God, I miss her," and stepped unconcerned over the cadaver, continuing on his way to the Red Dog Saloon without a backward glance.

Most of the onlookers followed him into the saloon, many curious gawkers had witnessed the dance of death for the first time, the dances becoming fewer and fewer with more distance between them as the town aged and more rules were made by the geldings.

He sat at his now customary table, a fresh bottle and glass waiting for him there. He thanked Pedro as he walked by.

It didn't bother him to shoot that young man. He'd asked for it, but this time it was different. No matter how hard he tried denying it, no matter how much he tried numbing it, Pistol Ann was a part of him now, and he couldn't turn his heart back into stone filled with raging magma.

"As-Is" he said to no one there but himself, as he caressed the stock of the Winchester laying across his knees.

Chapter Thirty-Seven

The Rider brooded at his table, pouring down the whiskey, trying to kill any feelings, good or bad, that remained in his heart. But one small spark of hope would not die. For he knew, despite the whiskey induced fog, that he could love again and that knowledge held his heart in one piece and stopped it from returning to stone.

At loose ends, more lethargic than restless, he considered trying to return to Pistol Ann and Over There. And why not? He had nothing to lose but some time, or it might add some disappointment, or it could extinguish the last small flame of hope he had. Despite all that, he felt he needed to try.

Under the impulse of the moment he rose up, crossed the room in a few long strides, pulled on his overcoat and slammed the saloon door behind him. Clomping down the boardwalk, carrying the beloved Winchester, he covered the two blocks in no time to an intersecting side street. There, he turned north until he cleared the fringe of town.

No wind opposed him or drove ice pellets into his face.

Dark was nearing, but enough light remained to accentuate the flat and endless horizon. A storm brewed in the darkening sky.

He placed the butt of the rifle against his right shoulder, levered in a shell and fired at the far left horizon. He levered in another shell and fired at the center horizon, then another round, another shot, this one at the far right horizon. Hoping to hit what? Nothing. Everything. Anything. Something that would kill his pain and drive away his frustration, or somehow change As-Is, he believed in it now. He shifted his rifle to his left hand and drew his Colt, firing another three booming rounds; left, center, right.

Guns had always worked and solved his dilemmas before.

Standing still, the Colt hanging down loose, smoke drifting out its barrel, the Rider hung his head, turned and with no wind at his back, headed for the Red Dog. And his life, as he now knew it, he hated. Take it or leave it, it made no difference to him, Gods, Fate, Destiny and As-Is be damned.

On the other hand, perhaps by some miracle wrought, he knew not how, he had no hate in his heart for those who lived and enjoyed the gift of life. But the ice water to kill remained in his veins. Once there, it never leaves.

His longing for oblivion was gaining power and before long would become an obsession.

* * *

It must've been a weekend, or a holiday—sure as hell wasn't the Fourth of July—but something brought a band of drovers to town. The place was filling up like a bucket in a downpour, bringing out the people who loved the night. *"They oughta spend some time in the Witchita night,"* he thought wryly.

Blue smoke and blue language permeated the air inside the Red Dog, and the atmosphere was no longer genial. It had gone beyond that border and came very close to dangerous.

The Rider took a different table than the one by the window. This one was by the wall and he sat with his back against it. He leaned the Winchester against the table's edge, within easy reach of his left hand. His Colt rested loose in its holster.

"Let the blood spill, even if it's mine," he mumbled, keeping a wary eye out from under the shadow of his hat. "I give notta damn! Notta Damn!" he mumbled again, chuckling to himself but that didn't stop the pang of the memory from striking his heart. He tossed back a double shot.

The piano player, a pallid man who looked more like a mortician than a musician, wore a black derby hat, white shirt replete with black sleeve garters, a black bowtie, black dungarees and black low-heeled boots. He'd been plunking out nondescript but lively tunes since dark fell. With a little luck someone would shoot him before the night was over.

Eventually the piano man broke into a tune that not only the Rider was familiar with, but the whole damn bunch of rowdies knew. The music prompted the crowd to break into song that sounded like the symphony of a swamp at dusk, but at least it broke the mounting tension.

Raw and rowdy, they belted out:

"She'll be coming 'round the mountain
When she comes
She'll be driving six white horses
When she comes."

It was a hoarse chorus at best, but harmless fun.

It caused the Rider to get up and leave. He'd heard the song before, and the memory of the pain it brought was too severe to take.

Grabbing the Winchester, he pushed back the chair, stood, walked over to the bar and standing near the left end of it attracted Pedro's attention. "My room for another night," he hollered, tossing a gold coin in the barkeeps direction.

Pedro snatched the coin out of the air, and then scurried on his busy way.

Stepping outside and inhaling deeply of the cold night air, the Rider remained still, enjoying the quiet only nature can provide. A few snowflakes drifted down through the black night, or blew in from the north, or were stirred in any and all directions by the swirling wind. He strolled up the street until he was able to turn north and take a look at the horizon. Sure enough, a blizzard was hanging there, the wind behind it moving it south toward town.

Too late, even with Gabriel's power, to make it out to Gobbler's Knob and back to town before the storm hit. Or maybe he needed to ride in the storm itself? He wasn't sure how it had happened but he was willing to try anything to get back to Pistol Ann, if she was real. Maybe some Yankee lead had caused a long drawn out dream?

No. The change that had taken place in him was real and lasting. And that he knew . . . right well.

Feeling lonely he wanted some calm and intelligible company. He turned around and headed down Main Street to the livery stable. Arriving at the same time the snow did, he knocked on the man door.

Carson Munro answered the knock and opened the door. "Virgil Jones! Come on in out of the cold sir!" He did, shed his over coat, said hello to Gabriel, took a seat by the fire pit, leaned back and tipped his hat up.

"Gettin rowdy down there at the Red Dog," he said to Carson, who had taken a seat beside him.

"It's a bunch of drovers bringing the cattle in from the foothills down to the flat lands. Stupid animals ain't got enough sense to come down themselves."

"Hope there's no trouble," the Rider idly commented. As he spoke the thunder of shotgun blasts boomed from up the street.

"Guess it's here," answered Carson.

"Hate to cut my visit short, but I think I'll go take a look," said the Rider.

"I'll go with you," said Carson. He got up, went into an empty stall, wrapped a forest green woolen cloak around himself, grabbed a shotgun from off from the wall pegs, both barrels shortened by a saw, held it underneath his cloak and said, "I'm ready. Gotta unload the stagecoach shortly anyhow."

"Stagecoach?"

"Due in soon. I always help with the luggage, feed and water the team, give the driver and his shotgun rider a couple of free drinks."

They ventured out onto the frozen street, the blizzard in full force bit and burned their faces. As they neared the saloon door some men were dragging two bodies out of the street, their chests blown out by shotgun blasts. Pedro stood in the doorway, the barrels of his shotgun pointed at the ground with wisps of smoke coming out the ends of each one.

"There will be no more trouble thees night senor Rider."

"I reckon not," he said.

A quick glance inside the open door showed that Pedro had the place under control. It had quieted down to being in the grip of silence.

Kill one and the rest will fall in line, a principle Pedro had learned along the way.

The blizzard increased in ferocity, the wind howled in intensity. From out of the west the Rider thought he heard the neighing of horses, then the clatter of hooves, then the rattle of harness, two horses, as white as the driven snow, exploded out of the whirling mass, followed by two and then two more.

She'll be driving
Six white horses

When she comes, rang the raucous chorus from out of the open door of the Red Dog Saloon.

A dull red coach followed the six horses out of the chaotic night.

"Whoa! Whoa up thar!" hollered the teamster as he pulled back on the reins with all of his might. The stage wasn't quite stopped as the shotgun rider touched down on the ground, skirted swiftly around the back of the coach and was at the door by the time the stage came to a complete stop.

The Rider could only imagine the dust cloud it would have raised in the summer "Hang on to this for me will ya?" asked Carson Munro, holding out his short double barreled shotgun.

The Rider took it without a word as he watched Carson scramble up to the top of the coach and start handing luggage down to the diver.

The shotgun rider opened the coach's door for the passengers.

A grandmother type stepped gingerly out, refusing the man's proffered hand for assistance. Turning, she held her hand out to a small girl, her honey colored hair hanging in long curls. Her overcoat was long, to her ankles, and warm looking. She was probably the elderly woman's granddaughter.

Behind the young girl stepped a smallish figure dressed in buckskin leggings, a round topped wide brimmed hat, and a white buffalo robe coat. Her right foot didn't seem to touch the step and her other was on the ground before the shotgun rider had time to offer a helping hand.

Surveying the scene with amused, yet bold brown eyes that eventually caught the Rider's, she smiled. His heart caught in his throat as the short-barreled shotgun slipped from his grasp, clattering to the ground. He froze in place, not because of the weather but because of the shock of surprise as the woman continued to meet his stupefied gaze.

As she walked towards him he got his tongue untwisted enough to work before she got by him.

"Pistol Ann?"

She stopped, appraising him with unrelenting eyes that not long ago held the light of love.

"Beg pardon?" she returned.

"It's me! It's you . . . Pistol Ann!"

She turned and spit a stream of tobacco juice on the frozen dirt. "Sorry mister, name's Crystal Ann . . . Crystal Ann Oakley."

Her exact image, but her heart was sure to be different. He could not, would not, pursue a memory again like he had Janice Louise's.

Oh God, this was torture with the cruelest of intentions.

"Buy a lady a drink, Mr. Virgil Jones Rider?" Her question shocked him into action.

"Uh . . . yeah, sure, it'd be my pleasure."

"That your scattergun?" she asked, indicating the piece lying on the ground.

"No," he said. Bending over he picked it up, then handed it to Carson Munro who had climbed down to the ground after finishing his chores on top of the stagecoach. Carson gave him a wink, the mysterious knowing kind.

He and Crystal Ann strode friendly, arm in arm, into the Red Dog Saloon. Hanging their overcoats on the wall pegs, they walked easy over to a table up against a wall. She seated herself, her eyes as bright as a bride's on her wedding day.

He leaned the rifle against the edge of the table, the butt resting on the floor, and with no hope of calming the beating of his heart, took a chair opposite her.

"They have an excellent whiskey here, want me to order one for you?" he asked.

"Sure."

Pedro ambled over, his eyes still ablaze from having to blow a couple of young men's chests open. By nature, he was a gentle man. But, they had it coming, as the saying goes in Texas. He took their order and ambled back to their table with a bottle of El Casa Blanco and two glasses. He poured her glass full, then the Rider's, then set the bottle down and went about his business.

With nothing yet to toast, the couple drank in silence and leisure.

"Tastes like a whiskey back where I'm from, called White Castle, and like another I've sampled from time to time, Chateaux Le Blanc."

He nearly choked on his drink. Could it be?

"They not only taste as good as each other, and are smooth going down, but the names all have the same meaning; White

House. But of course you probably already knew that, being a former attorney and all."

She pealed out a laugh like the sound of ringing bells, a sound he'd heard before, and one he loved to hear.

"There's nothing quite like the White House to twist and warp reality, huh Mr. Jones?" she said.

She let go with another laugh, such exquisite torture.

"How do you know my name?"

"Why, Mr. Jones, you're pertinear famous in the west, didn't you know?"

"No."

"Why, they got pictures of your face plastered up in 'most every town in the west."

"Why? I'm not wanted as far as I know."

"Not by the law anyway, but you are somewhat of a legend, leastwise in Texas. They say keep out of the Rider's way; you don't have a chance of stayin' alive if you cross him. He deals justice with his forty-five."

"I'm not that way anymore," he replied.

"Sure you are if the time's right and some low life hombres are asking for it by whatever they're doing. You might even use that rifle there."

His memory didn't have to travel too far back to the kid all dressed in black he'd killed with it.

"Mind if I take a look at it?" she asked.

Mildly surprised, he picked the piece up near the lever and passed it across the table to her. "A friend gave it to me," he said.

"I could use a shootin' iron like this in my show," she said rotating and examining it as she did, "except I've never heard of this particular brand of rifle before."

"What? Everyone's heard of the Winchester!" the Rider exclaimed.

She handed the piece back over to him. "Check the stamp," she said.

"Windchaser! Sure enough."

"We sometimes see only what we want to see, remember?"

"Pistol Ann. It really is you!"

She winked and gave him her face-dancing smile. "I could use this rifle in my act." She repeated.

"Act?"

"Yes, as Annie Oakley, the sharpshooter."

"Well, of course Ann, I still consider it to be your rifle."

She filled his glass and then hers with El Casa Blanco. "A toast then to us," she said

"To us," replied the Rider.

"Like I said, nothing like the White House to put a warp in reality, is there Mr. Virgil Jones Rider?"

"I reckon that is true," he said.

"Wanna join up with me in my show," she asked. "As I recall you're pretty damn good with that Colt forty-five of yours. And, think of the attraction of seeing the real live Rider in action and being safe from his deadly Colt at the same time."

"I got nothing better to do. Sure I'll join up with you."

And he once again had faith in Destiny, or As-Is, or in love, finally coming down on the side of love, the most powerful force of all, as Pistol Ann had once remarked.

"Tell me the truth Ann, Right Here and Now is not really a random place people stumble into now and then, is it?"

"No."

"Let me guess, it is a place for the broken hearted to be healed, isn't it?"

"Mostly."

"What do you mean mostly?"

"Well, if I had stayed there, it would have been with a broken heart."

"And if I had stayed anywhere without you, it would have been with a broken heart."

"So we had to leave. It's not too likely the brokenhearted can help to heal the brokenhearted," said Annie. "So, how is your heart now Mr. Forlornly?"

"Full, alive, growing in its love for you, and yours?"

"The same, except I'm not sure there's any room left for it to grow in its love for you."

"Well, I reckon we can find out," said the Rider.

"We have the rest of our lives to try," she said.

THE END